Blue Heaven

Blue Heaven

A Novel

Willard Wyman

University of Oklahoma Press : Norman

Published with the assistance of the National Endowment for the Humanities, a federal agency which supports the study of such fields as history, philosophy, literature, and language.

This book is work of fiction. Names, characters, places, and incidents are either products of the author's imagination or are used for fictional purposes. Any resemblance to actual events, locales, or persons living or dead is coincidental.

Special thanks to Fiona O'Neill for use of her drawings.

Library of Congress Cataloging-in-Publication Data

Wyman, Willard, 1930–
   Blue Heaven : a novel / Willard Wyman
     p. cm.
   ISBN 978-0-8061-4218-0 (hardcover : alk. paper)
   I. Title.
   PS3623.Y645B58 2011
   813'.6—dc22

                          2011008234

The paper in this book meets the guidelines for permanence and durability of the Committee on Production Guidelines for Book Longevity of the Council on Library Resources, Inc. ∞

1 2 3 4 5 6 7 8 9 10

In Memory of

David Buschena
Hunter, Economist, Packer
who left us too soon

and

Trish Hooper
Artist, Activist, Writer
who should never have left us at all

This book is about Fenton Pardee. You won't know about him unless you've read a book called *High Country*. That book was about Ty Hardin, who shows up in this book too. What that book says is true, mostly. So are the things in this book. But some of the same things happen in both books, and they might seem a little different.

But that's nothing. Everything's a little different if you look at it one way—then take another look from someplace else.

The important thing is that both books are mostly true and that one truth was just as hard to write as the other.

It's no easy thing to write what's mostly true.

With apologies to Mark Twain

Buffalo Bill's defunct . . .
ee cummings

Fenton

1
1902

The freighter puffed on the siding, catching its breath for the long pull to the Rockies. The crewmen watched in awe as *Buffalo Bill's Wild West* sped through the switchyard in the opposite direction. The big show was heading east—cars gaudy with paintings of Indians and cowboys. There was one of Buffalo Bill himself on his horse Pap, buckskin fringes flying as he gunned down a wild-eyed buffalo.

Bill Cody's performers were stopping in Sioux Falls and Chicago—wherever an audience would gather—to polish their acts before crossing the big water and bringing *Buffalo Bill's Wild West* to the crowds waiting in Europe.

The switchman sighed as Cody's cars clicked by. More than anything he wanted to see the show himself, so brilliantly painted were these cars, so vivid the posters, so exciting the press releases. The switchman read them all, as did the yardmasters and crew members and engineers—and the passengers on their lines too. It didn't matter that the reporters were dedicated mostly to topping Ned Buntline's romances. What mattered was the spectacle, the drama. Cody thrilled people wherever his show was booked, everyone hungry for *Buffalo Bill's Wild West*.

Not a word had reached that switchman about Cody's show becoming so prosperous that it now required two trains. No one was ever sure why that news hadn't sped ahead with the first. But then no one was ever sure the message had actually been sent. But the world soon knew something had gone wrong—knew that Cody's second train had met disaster.

The first had no trouble at all. It sped through the switchyard carrying most of the people who made a living from *Buffalo Bill's Wild West*—advance men and roustabouts, barkers and mustachioed men acting as buffalo hunters and scouts and cowboys. There were trick-shooters from the

carnivals and trick ropers from the stages and trick riders from wherever
Cody could find them—many who'd become Cody's glittering stars themselves.

The second, still steaming out of the western plains, was hauling
what Cody had actually discovered in the West—and wanted the world
to celebrate: Indians and their spotted horses, the intricate crafts that
let those tribes make homes of the western prairies and in the western
mountains. And with them were the range horses and packmules and
the handlers who understood them, as well as the wagons and the coaches
people used to make their way westward. In the stockcars came the very
life of the West—buffalo and antelope, elk and bear.

Filled with the richness of it, the switchman watched Cody's first train
disappear into the East, its whistle a farewell sigh as it dropped from sight.
Only then did he signal the steaming freighter back onto the lone track
and watch its lights flicker westward, serenely unaware that Cody's second
train was still rushing out of that night, this one pulling Cody's personal
caboose, pulling Bill Cody himself. The great showman comfortable in
his mirrored parlor, playing cards and drinking drinks and improving his
stories on those lucky enough to hear him. All of them honored to help
bring Cody's *Wild West* to a waiting world.

The inevitable came too quickly to comprehend: the sudden jolt from
brakes frantically engaged, wheels reversed, sparks erupting as iron screeched
against iron. One train bearing down on the other as crews, frozen by the
terrible reality, leaped away moments before the fatal conversion.

The crash, metal giving way to metal, split the night as engines jack-
knifed, cars bent, jumped tracks, sank into clouds of prairie dust. A silence
held for only an eerie moment before being ripped apart by the screams
of animals, the angry curses of men.

A gunshot cracked. Then another. Cody's dazed actors, forced into
a reality they only pretended to in his charades, going about the grisly
business of shooting to kill, putting down animals torn beyond survival.
Then clawing through the wreckage to free Cheyenne, Sioux, Pawnee—
people too broken in body and spirit to fight free of the disaster.

A stunned engineer, one leg useless after his desperate leap, was pulled
away from the carnage, away and out of sight of an enraged Bill Cody.
The famous plainsman, half-drunk and beyond reason, storming along the
burning ruins to find someone to blame, to shoot, some victim to absolve
him from being one himself—a victim beyond his imagining.

The engineer, half-carried now, saw that his rescuer was an incon-
gruously dressed Cheyenne, the Indian's black hair spilling from under

a shiny bowler. Clad only in an open waistcoat and leather leggings, the man seemed to be watching everything as he hauled the engineer free of the confusion, the flames, the shots puncturing the night—freed of the wrath of Cody himself.

They found refuge in a shallow draw, the Indian's attention fixed on what they'd barely survived. He watched as men huddled, gestured, moved forward toward the engines, looking for some explanation for the horror, the carnage.

A tall man ranged up and down the burning cars, ignoring the others as he salvaged what he could from the wreckage. He stopped, halted the scream of a broken animal with a single bullet, then moved on, saving what was useful, discarding what was not. It was as though he was on some mission, freeing animals who'd lived out into the star-sprinkled night or tying those he might use to the wheels of crumpled wagons or the frames of broken props, to whatever was free of the flames as he ministered to their wounds, working steadily until the flames began to diminish and there was no more ministering he could do.

He singled out three sound mules, tying them to a broken wagon before moving again down the train's charred skeleton, checking the few horses he'd saved, soothing a tall mare before leading her back to the waiting mules. The Cheyenne recognized the mare, the same handsome Thoroughbred they used to carry actors playing dignitaries—presidents and people from the East too proud to acknowledge the dangers of the West.

The mules stutter-stepped aside to greet her, bobbed their heads and offered low nickers. The tall man, seeking out pads, panniers, saddles and harness among the jumbled equipment, focused on his task, paid scant attention as the mules whinnied softly, nosed at one another, looked out into the quiet night as though needing its comfort.

The engineer, awash in his pain, comprehended little, but nothing seemed lost on the bowler-hatted Cheyenne, who now saw something familiar in the movements of the tall man as well. He watched him brush the waiting animals, smoothing pads onto their backs before lifting saddles into place, adjusting each rigging carefully before turning to the next.

There were sawbucks saddles for the mules, a stock saddle for the mare—which surprised the Indian. He couldn't remember ever seeing the tall beauty under a stock saddle. But the man fit it precisely, fit each saddle precisely, altering drop straps and quarter straps, breast collars and breechings—finally turning to some panniers, making sure pairs matched before going off to collect what he'd need for whatever mission was his. He found blankets and cooking utensils for himself, brushes and grain for the animals. Cody's caboose was on its side, the galley's stores spilled out like thrown cards. The man collected boxes of food and bottles of drink, stuffing what he would need into panniers, everything snug and protected, tight in its place. He looped the ears of the panniers over the crossbucks, each mule's load balanced then top-loaded before he covered everything with a manty, tucking the canvas in closely before he threw his lash cinch over it all, tightening the cinches until the mules staggered before using the rest of the rope to secure everything with an intricate hitch.

The Cheyenne realized, from the very hitches the man was tying, who it was. Seasons earlier Cody's Rough Riders had hired this man as a roustabout, the man's natural strength and easy way with animals soon moving him into their own ranks as a packer. The Cheyenne had worked with him, had actually helped him tie these same hitches before the shows— helped, at least, until they called him away to become one of Cody's painted show Indians, dangerous at first, defeated at last, the Cheyenne always loyal to whatever role they assigned him.

The Cheyenne had learned his parts thoroughly. He knew the tall man knew his as well. What the man tied onto his animals would not come off, no matter the whooping of attacking show-Indians, the shots of rescuing cowboys and cavalrymen. No matter what happened, the man's packs held.

The man tied his mules into a string, tightened the cinch on the tall mare, and mounted, leading his mules back along the smoldering ruins. The Cheyenne followed, holding to the edgy darkness but paralleling the packer's course, wanting to know what trail the man would choose for these animals he'd packed with such care.

When the packer came to the caboose—the broken elegance of its parlor succumbing to the last licks of the flames—he found Cody himself, buckskin shirt blackened and torn. Cody's fury seemed to have diminished into sadness as he contemplated the body of Old Pap, the loyal horse who had carried him through so much, carried him even when he could scarcely carry himself.

The tall packer pulled up—his mules nosing at one another impatiently as he looked down at Cody, the old plainsman ignoring the destruction around him to focus on Old Pap. The Cheyenne stepped out of the darkness to stand with the packer now, the two of them contemplating Cody together. And looking beyond him too—at the twisted steel, the smoldering fires, the random bodies of horses, mules, buffalo.

"See you still got your bowler," the packer said, turning to the Cheyenne. "Another man might have lost it in this mess."

"Do you think Cody will still get us the money?" the Cheyenne said. "We did what he told us."

"He'll get it," the tall man said. "Just wish it would do you some good. Didn't do much for him. Not this night."

"My people say we must have the money. I must stay to get it."

"Could be they're wrong," the packer said. "Cody got it. But looks like he just pissed it away."

"Will you go without it?"

"Sort of, I guess. Leastways I'll leave all this."

"Look for me where you go. I will still have my hat. Maybe the money too."

"That old bowler may be for you what money is for Cody. You might just piss it away, like he does his money."

"My people will not let me."

"You still claim they're wise?"

"Yes."

"I sure hope so. Like you to have a chance."

The packer nodded, his farewell almost formal as he moved his mare away. His mules stepping out smartly behind the mare as they cleared the wreckage and followed her down the tracks and away from the confusion. After a bit she veered away from the tracks themselves, away and out into the night.

The Cheyenne watched the country swallow them up before moving closer to Cody and realizing the old plainsman had been weeping beside the horse who'd served him so well. One of Pap's legs was akimbo, the shattered bone exposed through the ripped flesh. In one hand Cody was holding the revolver that had ended Pap's misery. In the other he was holding his bottle, as though it might end his own.

If Cody saw the Cheyenne, he gave no sign. No more than he'd given the packer—though neither had made an effort to stay out of his sight. He did tip up the bottle and take a long pull, but that was all. He'd made no offer to the packer and now he made none to the Cheyenne.

After a bit the Indian turned and started back to find the engineer he'd abandoned. He knew the engineer's leg was broken too, but he'd heard that the white-eye medicine men could fix things like that. They would be along soon. They always came to record what happened when things went bad.

He wondered, as he made his way back along the smoldering ruin, why the white-eye medicine men had not found a way to fix an animal's leg as well.

~

Fenton Pardee was the man leading the mules out onto the prairie that night, a man not nearly as sure of where he was going as of what he wanted to leave. When he'd come to Bill Cody's show he'd been just shy of manhood, as happy to be free of his parents' rocky farm as he was to replace their Baptist ways with those of Cody's free-wheeling Congress of Rough Riders. But he soon found he learned not so much from the exotic Arab and Cuirassier and Cossack riders Cody had collected as from quieter men, riders of a West much less violent than the West Cody championed. He took to the cowboys and vaqueros and old mountain men who seemed to know the country their horses had traveled as well as they knew their horses themselves. They had a way of taking the gifts of that country deep into their hearts.

Their stories were rich in the lore of the West and rich in the life the West supported. He learned from them when they were willing to teach. He learned from them even when they weren't, understanding that sometimes they didn't want to speak at all. What lived in them most completely, he came to realize, was the country that shaped them. It never left them, a truth he soaked up as he grew into a man, learning from them in every way he could about their horses and mules and the secrets of the open country they'd traveled, learning most of all from the dangers they faced in the high mountains they'd crossed.

From that spring and into the fall he traveled the country with his mules, pointing his mare west, stopping for the knowledge ranchers had of the land even more than for the sustenance they provided. They were always glad to see him, dirt farmers and wheat ranchers and cattlemen surprised to come across the tall man with the three packed mules and admiring the handsome Thoroughbred mare who was becoming such a finicky eater.

"Off her feed," he would explain. "Damndest thing. Believe something shocked her right out of her hunger." He would say nothing about what the shock had been, nothing about where he had been or what he was leaving. Something told him that mentioning Bill Cody would be too much for these people of the earth. He didn't understand himself why it was so deeply in him to leave, and so he said nothing about what it was he was leaving.

"Wouldn't mind if I let my mare recruit a spell would you?" he would ask them. "Sure like to see how your operation works."

And they would take to him, explaining the planting and the haying and the doctoring of their cattle, comparing this country and that, this way of life with another, taken by the openness of the tall horseman, the strange odyssey he was on that he had no way of explaining.

"Looking," Fenton would say. "Just looking at all this open country. Makes a man wonder what's over the next ridge."

"Makes some men want to put up a fence and count it a blessing," they would say. "Maybe build a house to stay in snug."

And they would invite him for a dinner, offer him a place to sleep.

"I got grain for that mare," they would say. "Heat in her belly might ward off what's put a chill in her heart."

So Fenton would stay—for a few nights or a week or sometimes just a night, befriending earnest wives and winning over shy children, even hearing out the dreams of the men—or the darkness of their failures.

He drifted up into North Dakota and crossed into Montana, riding into the Judith Basin and lingering before moving on, never sure of where he wanted to be but always sure of the direction to go, liking the country more as he slanted up into it, the cooling of the nights as he rode higher.

He avoided towns, big and small, riding north of Great Falls and south of Choteau across a land breaking into folds deeper and deeper, the bottoms timbered, the ridges wind-swept and grazed. He sought out gates when the land was fenced and made friends with who'd done the fencing when he found no gates, the ranchers and wheat farmers, putting him on trails, showing him routes, helping him find water and wood and grass for his camps. Or, if it was near sunset and their curiosity was rising, grain for his animals and a bed for himself.

It wasn't hard for people to like Fenton Pardee, interested as he was in their plans and as free of worry as he seemed to be about his own. Mostly he listened, which was his way of dodging their questions. Not that people didn't have plenty to ask this free-ranging man on the handsome mare with his three packed mules. Though why he worried so about his mare they couldn't see. She might be off her feed, but it changed her little. She still stood proudly and moved smartly. And when she did Fenton's mules moved smartly too.

His mules couldn't get enough of the mare and Fenton couldn't get enough of them together. He'd lift the saddle off the mare with care when day was done, reversing the saddle-blanket across the saddle, wet-side up to dry. He'd unpack his mules just as carefully, storing the gear, coiling his lash-cinches to hang them on a peg or a limb or the root of a downed tree. Then came the packsaddles and pads, all stacked as neatly as the saddle he rode. He took his time brushing his animals, often the mules first—brushing and calming and taking as much of the itch away as he could before setting them free, the mules rolling to satisfy that last need, the mare sometimes rolling too, but often too proud.

And often too proud to eat, Fenton would worry, wondering what would break the pattern, knowing something was wrong down deep, puzzling over what to try the next day—and the next.

One morning he rode up out of a bottom, easing up along the crest of a west-running ridge and there it was: the China Wall lifting high above him—the Continental Divide itself, more impressive and impenetrable than any of the ranchers had described, all of them wary of the dangers such a wild country could hold.

All but the rancher he'd stayed with three nights earlier. He had told him something different, told him to ride south until the wall diminished, curl around it there to follow a route the Indians had opened.

"They was Salish, don't you know," the rancher said. "Call 'em Flatheads. Maybe because of how they said howdy." He put his hands palms flat to either side of his head, looking up at Fenton as he did. "Tough bastards. . . . Until them Christers took over and softened them. Used to bring their spotted horses right over that divide. Wanted buff, don't you know, for the winter. Then rode right back—with the hides and the meat and whatever they needed, rode over and went down White River."

"They winter at this White River? Must be a lot of country over that divide."

"Hell no. Winter's too rough at White River." The old rancher liked it that the tall man paid such close attention. "Went down White River to cross the big one. Call it the Southfork now. Southfork of the Flathead."

"And where'd they head after they crossed that?" Fenton wanted to know. "Might just give that Indian trail a try."

"Crossed the whole damned valley and climbed the range beyond. The Swan. Had to cross that to get to where they wintered, out in the big valley under the Missions. Out beyond." He pointed to the hulking range of the Rockies, the China Wall still indistinguishable in the distant haze.

"People tell me it can't be crossed," Fenton said, looking up to where the man pointed.

"And you'll see why in a day or so. No way to do it. But ride south, keep the wall off your right shoulder—you'll hit Indian Creek flowing down from up there. Follow its north side. You'll pick up that Indian trail. Watch it close and she'll take you over. Hunters use it—sometimes. Steep, but doable. White River Pass."

Fenton had been pleased to accept the hospitality of the wiry old rancher, enjoying a few nights' rest, some grain for his animals, warm dinners for himself; learning everything he could from the man about the country he had to cross—about the country beyond it too.

He was beginning to think he'd have to go all the way to where the land dropped into the sea to figure out what he was looking for, much less why, which is why he wanted as few complications as possible getting over the country's spine.

He'd thought about that a lot, knowing that when there was no more country to travel he'd have to stop and make do. Which wouldn't be easy. He'd grown to like the journey he was on a lot more than considering how to conclude it.

He hadn't thought about what he'd find when he reached the top of that country, what would happen when he topped White River Pass and saw the endless rise and fall of the country beyond. It seemed to him impossibly vast, so complete he felt a little dizzy. It turned out to be a serene country easing down from the rough cliffs, cliffs carved by hard winters that scooped out a beautiful land from on high—a land held in place by timbered flats and shining meadows, by moving water that pooled into glistening lakes.

It kept surprising him as he dropped into it, the Indian trace disappearing and reappearing as it wound down and down into the wide valley of the Southfork. He rode through timber and meadow, timber again and more meadow, following game trails—one leading into another until he came to a place better than any he'd known. It was on a bench where the waters of White River tumbled down into the Southfork. There was wood for his fire and grass for his animals and water for all the wildlife that made their way to this place that lured him along to discover where they rested. Where they flourished.

It was late summer, the air sharp in the shade but soft in the sunlight, the country peaceful beyond his imagining. He settled in for almost a week, eating fish and recruiting his animals and crossing the Southfork to probe the country beyond, looking for some sign of the route the Indians must have forced to make their way up the drainages to cross the Swan and reach the safety of their lodges in the valleys beyond.

He had no trouble finding crossings of the river, but could find no trace of a way beyond. To scan the country more carefully, he packed his mules and forded, the handsome mare thin now, despite the rich feed that made his mules slicker and rounder by the day. He camped again on the west side and again turned his animals free. The mules, devoted to his mare as ever, would stay with her, and she never wandered far, some ennui in her too complete.

The next morning he found her quiet as death there in the lush grass of the sunny meadow. The mules grazed nearby, still not sure, as though remaining in her thrall. He took her leaving him as he'd taken most troubles in his life: something to be digested. At least she'd chosen a beautiful spot, he thought. And she'd given this country her gift. She would provide sustenance for the wild animals passing by. They would profit even as she became a loss he must absorb.

He led his mules back to camp, no hesitation in them since he had taken over. "Maybe she just wanted to get here before she gave it up," he thought as he began packing them. "Never saw her look so peaceful."

He top-packed his riding saddle, took a last look at the river, the meadows, the fingers of the forest reaching into them, making islands of shelter against winter storms. Then he set out on foot, seeking a way up a drainage tumbling its water down from high on the Swan. If he couldn't force a way up this one, he'd come back and try the next. If the Indians had found a way, he would too. He knew all too well that nothing got done by doing nothing—and winter wasn't far away.

When he came across a game trail slanting down from high above the stream, he took it—ducking under willows to start contouring upward, the mules pushing the branches aside as they followed, slowing where the way narrowed, scrambling when it steepened. He was already wondering how long he'd be afoot before he found some way to trade for a saddle horse. He'd need one to cover the country ahead, and he'd need one who could win over his mules. That was important. They carried everything he owned.

There was a lot of country to cover before he'd find anyone who could make such a trade. And he knew it wouldn't be easy.

He was in a country few others traveled.

Lost Bird Canyon

It must have been fate that the game trail Fenton Pardee followed that day led him to the camp of Tommy Yellowtail, which meant it all started with Tommy, not with Cody Jo, as so many came to think; not even with Ty Hardin, who kept Fenton Pardee alive in so many ways until Hardin was gone himself. Cody Jo and Ty may have brought more light into Fenton's life, but it was Tommy Yellowtail who pulled up the shade. It was Tommy Yellowtail who showed him the country that would make its way into his heart. Before Tommy, Fenton was just moving on and hoping for the best, going from one ranch to another and drifting down enough trails that petered out to discourage a less optimistic man.

Where Fenton got his optimism, no one knew. Most weren't even sure where he started. All they knew was that one night he'd walked into Tommy Yellowtail's camp high in Lost Bird Canyon with three packed mules and no saddle horse.

Tommy—who traveled light, never taking to cooking—was watching his fire and chewing jerked elk. If he was startled by the big man showing up in such a remote camp, he gave no sign, offering a stick of his jerky to Fenton as he noticed the riding saddle, top-packed on the lead mule.

"Lose a horse?" he asked, watching Fenton nod a thanks as he accepted the jerky.

"Shitty luck," Fenton said. "She was having trouble with her feed. Turned up dead as corned beef this morning. So peaceful I had to root around to work up some sentiment." He took a bite of the jerky and considered. "Been doing poorly. Maybe ate something that didn't digest . . ." He went on chewing.

"This jerky of yours," Fenton added, continuing to chew, "might give whatever killed her a good run for its money."

He kept chewing as Tommy took in the height of him. There was a lot to take in.

Chewing the last of it, Fenton turned to his mules. "If I can make use of your fire, I might do us some better." He began separating the mules so he could start unpacking.

Tommy said nothing as he moved to the off-side of the mules to help. He knew packing and could see that this tall man knew it too. The ropes were taut, the manties still snug and smooth, no gear sticking out to catch on anything. And after a rough day. Tommy couldn't figure how the man had gotten up Lost Bird Canyon at all. Even the game trails were hard to follow.

They turned the mules out with the paints and pintos Tommy was planning to sell over in Choteau. Everyone knew that horses with color brought in more than they deserved over there, and Tommy intended to give it a try.

Fenton had stopped to take in those spotted horses before coming on into Tommy's camp. They weren't bad looking, though all that color gave him pause. He didn't hold anything against paints—or pintos. They were all the same to him. All he knew was that more often than not those gaudy colors gave them no edge at all—except maybe in toughness. Some Indian ponies he'd known had been remarkably tough, though hardly tractable. But it was clear he couldn't be choosy. He needed a saddle horse, and this seemed his only chance without walking himself right out of his boots.

The easy way Tommy Yellowtail moved around the mules became a worry. It wouldn't take long for an Indian so comfortable around stock to figure out that someone stuck in these mountains with three pack mules and no saddle horse was in no position to bargain. And it wouldn't take him much longer to conclude that he didn't have to go all the way over to Choteau to make a considerable profit.

Though Fenton had some money, he had other ideas about what to do with it. That was a consideration that kept him occupied as he swallowed the last of Tommy's jerky. It also added considerably to the quality of the cooking he wound up doing that night.

The truth was that Fenton didn't like to cook any more than Tommy. But he knew it was a time to put that reservation aside—along with any he had about painted horses. He figured it was a time to be inventive, not critical. Though Fenton never claimed to be a particularly inventive man, everyone in the Swan came to know he could fill that bill better than most when it got around to trading for horses and mules.

He dug out a saucepan and poured in some kidney beans he'd been hydrating in a jar deep in one of his packs. He got them simmering and sliced bacon strips from a slab, frying them in a skillet. Rummaging around in another pack, he pulled out one of his bottles, poured a little in a cup and offered it to Tommy. He was disappointed when Tommy turned him down.

"Don't have to drink it all tonight, you know," Fenton said reflectively, sipping a little from the cup and turning back to his bacon. "I believe it helps a man settle after a long day."

"What brings you here?" Tommy asked suddenly. "Into this country?" His few words were a welcome surprise to Fenton, who had a feeling he and this Indian had more than a little in common, which is why he wished the man would have a drink and talk a little. He let it ride for now, guessing the man liked the smell of frying bacon better than the taste of liquor.

"Don't look like you're a hunter," Tommy added.

"I'm not," Fenton admitted. "Unless it's required. Then I can be pretty damn good. Just done enough of it to know the country a man hunts in can please him as much as the meat he harvests." He checked to see that his beans were still simmering. "Seems to me a lot of people would just like to see this country of yours. In fact guys with fancy horses like yours might could make a buck just showing it off to them."

Fenton was a little surprised to hear himself saying what he was saying, but it made sense. He forked the bacon onto some paper he'd produced and let it drain as he diced an onion into the beans, thinking about what he'd said as he added other things—molasses, a little sugar, bits of dried peppers.

He began asking Tommy about the country—trails and passes, streams and crossings—and about horses. He wanted to know if Tommy thought horses they called paints really did have quarter horse blood. "Some of your Indian pintos seem just as quick," he observed. "To my way of thinking spotted horses are all about the same—some good, some not."

It came to Fenton that he was asking more questions than Tommy was answering, but that didn't slow him. He figured that pretending Tommy was holding up his end of the conversation might do. And he was more and more sure they did have a lot in common, which seemed verified when Tommy finally accepted a drink. Fenton poured a second for himself, pointing out that the whisky blended well with his bacon and beans, which were about ready. Most of all he wanted to hear Tommy's take on his horses, still moving around in the meadow below, though he concluded it was wise to save that for later.

He drained the beans and crumbled in the bacon before pouring sizzling bacon grease into the mix. He stirred it all together and put two big helpings into bowls so they could sit by the fire and talk. Tommy was holding up his end better now, eating the beans and drinking the whisky and watching the tall man think up questions to ask him.

Tommy Yellowtail never did talk much about that night, even when he was drinking. He might have been more understandable when he was sober, but when he was sober he hardly talked at all, meaning people had to get as much information as they could when he wasn't. It all made the information people did gather seem spotty. All they could be sure of was that the conversation concluded productively that night high in Lost Bird Canyon.

Fenton, on the other hand, would talk about that night—when the mood hit him. But when he arrived at the subject, all too often he came at it from someplace so far removed that no one could figure out how he got there in the first place. All they could piece together was that Fenton wound up with all of Tommy's spotted horses—and Tommy wound up with half a business Fenton had yet to start.

Over time Buck and Jasper—and later Ty Hardin, who would become as much a son to Fenton Pardee as anyone ever would—figured out some of the ins and outs of it. It wasn't hard to imagine Fenton suddenly getting inventive and spinning out the possibilities of what they could do with a pack station, even though that concept had barely a foothold in the country when Tommy and Fenton met.

And it wasn't hard to imagine Tommy, who called that country home as few as others did, realizing how a man who talked as richly as Fenton might help him find a way to stay in it. Tommy could see deep into things, everyone in the Swan knew that. He might be quiet, and there might be times when he drank too much, but everyone knew he thought things through—and usually came out about where he wanted to be.

What was hard to figure was whether it was Fenton or Tommy who got the better half of the bargain. Where Tommy came from—and what he wanted—they all understood: he wanted to keep using the land he knew so well, land that had supported his people for centuries. To figure where Fenton came from—and what he wanted—was another matter, though hints about those things drifted down, or maybe were just invented, as the years passed.

3

Tommy Yellowtail

Trying to sell the spotted horses wasn't all that unusual an enterprise for Tommy. It was just in a different direction—and a happier one. By the time Fenton stumbled into his camp, Tommy had tried most everything else. All of it aimed at freeing himself from the shackles the government had on his tribe, and the blanket the Christians wanted over his spirit.

He had no way of saying that. Maybe no way of knowing it. It was just in him, the same way it was in him to trust the tall Fenton Pardee when the man showed up with three packed mules at his camp high in Lost Bird Canyon.

Tommy had spoken little as a child; he spoke little more as he grew into a man. But he'd heard much from his father. Even more from his uncles. Vivid stories about the old days in the Bitterroot, about still older days when his people would migrate across the big mountains for buffalo. The Salish, good hunters but not warlike, dodging the Shoshone and the Blackfoot, sometimes the Crow and the Cheyenne—fighting them when they had to, befriending them if the moment was right. All the tribes migrating toward the buffalo because the buffalo were many and where the buffalo were was a way of life that made them rich in spirit even as it gave them food for their bellies, cover for their tipis, warmth for their winter lodges.

Through all the stories ran the truth that not long after the white men came—making promises they wouldn't keep—the buffalo were gone. It was then that Tommy's people, the ones the whites called Flathead, retreated to the Bitterroot to fish and hunt and gather roots. Even when the Black

Robes came they made little fuss, many learning from them how better to farm the land and harvest the timber. Some even took on the god of the Black Robes, foolish as that seemed to the men of Tommy's family.

The tales of the buffalo were rich with the life and the spirit of the hunts, but the tales of retreating to the Bitterroot were forever angry. Though the Salish became good at using the land in the new ways, neither the Black Robes nor the god they knelt to could keep other whites from taking the Bitterroot away too, driving the Salish north to the Flathead valley, telling them this must be their land now.

Tommy's people did as they were told as the 1850s' treaties surrendered to the new treaties of the 1870s. They had to, but they were never sure of anything after that, their spirits in disarray after that. The Black Robes were in the valley already, saying they'd teach the children letters and skill them in tools, all the while telling Tommy's people to humble themselves before the Black Robe's god. Many Salish did, too—not because they understood but because once again they saw no other choice. Their old ways, and their old gods, were gone.

It was in the Flathead valley that Tommy was born—not too many winters after the men with papers and proclamations chased his people from the Bitterroot, calling it relocation. But to Tommy's family it was betrayal and defeat. And it was betrayal that filled the stories Tommy heard, his father calming his outrage by surrendering to dreams and visions; his uncles revisiting theirs again and again with anger and bitterness.

They would mock and curse anyone who trusted the whites, anyone who humbled themselves before the Black Robes' god. It made them angrier still that they had to work the fields and harvest the wood as the Black Robes wanted. Not to do so was to be denied what the Black Robes made possible: blankets for their women and knives for themselves, the chance to trade for a rifle and creep into the mountains to hunt once again.

Tommy knew that his uncles were angry beyond repair, but he came to see that their anger solved nothing, only diminished them. Just as did their disgust at so many for calling themselves Flathead, as the whites did, instead of Salish, which is what they were. But even had Tommy the words to say what he saw, he would not have spoken. Deep inside him was a hard truth: complaining about what had been taken was a surrender, an admission that it was gone—forever.

It was a gaunt missionary, haunted but determined, who brought Tommy his trouble. She saw the boy with his uncle's team trying to plow their rocky section, the boy's slight body lifted by the plough more often than the plough could pierce the earth. She knew the boy could manage the team, but saw he was unequal to the plough.

She went to the Jesuits and they came to Tommy's father saying the boy must go to the Mission school, must learn a white man's trade and the white man's ways. All Indian boys, they made clear, must now go to the school. Some could even live at the mission. Tommy, they told him, must be one.

Tommy's father, confused and unmanned by the keening lifting from deep inside Tommy's mother, found he could say nothing at all. His face, the wave of his hand, told them enough.

They took Tommy away.

The Sisters of Providence had started the school near the Flathead Mission, establishing a system of womanly chores for Indian girls as they taught them their letters, schooled them in their numbers.

The few boys who lived at the mission made do with the Fathers, handling rougher tasks without complaint, tending animals and crops and helping as the Brothers saw fit. They told Tommy to share the blanket of Paint Boy, a Cheyenne. Paint Boy's sister, Hope Woman, was the smallest of the girls— and the most able. Before her father left the tribe the Cheyenne had called her Happy, laughter being with her always. Her laughter subsided after her father left and she settled down to women's work. When the Cheyenne saw how clever she was, she became Hope Woman, her people knowing there was nothing the girl could not do with those wonderful hands. Tommy liked watching those hands fly about their work, liked listening to that voice too, her cheerful answers as she recited her lessons.

It was the mission cook, the most gentle Black Robe, who oversaw Paint Boy and Tommy, a man skilled with his cooking but gifted beyond his own understanding as a painter. He had no choice but to bring his magic to the mission walls, inventing brilliant images of his gods doing their work, offering their blessings. Quiet and sober with the Jesuits, he was forever happy and forgiving with his boys, loving them and patting them each night as he tucked in their blanket, telling them what he would paint the next day—and the next. What they would see in this world—the more beautiful things they would find in the next.

From the first the cook had taken to Paint Boy. He would paint images on Paint Boy's thin body, laughing at how apt was the boy's name, how proud Paint Boy was of the bright designs on his body. All of them laughing until a censorious Father stepped in, stopping it. Paint Boy was relegated to cleaning brushes then, sweeping the rooms, and mixing the colors—still as happy with the cook as the cook was with him and even more awed by the cook's vivid conceptions, the life he provided the mission walls.

Paint Boy was two winters older than Tommy, though in most ways Tommy took the lead. Tommy, sure his tribe and the Cheyenne shared the same beliefs deep inside, thought it made no sense that the Cheyenne would send their young across the mountains to live with these Black Robes. His uncles had told him the earth was angry with the Salish. Why else take the buffalo and the good land and leave the Salish with the White Eyes who lied and the Black Robes whose god had no power? He thought the angry gods in the earth must have abandoned the Cheyenne too. Maybe that was the reason the father of Paint Boy and Hope Girl had sent his children to live with the Black Robes, had gone off himself to learn the ways of the White Eyes' world. Maybe that was the reason Paint Boy and Hope Girl forsook the god in the earth in favor of the one in the sky. The cook's paintings even seemed to encourage them. He drew moccasins on the feet of white-eye gods, put feathers in their hair and blankets across their shoulders.

But the paintings made no impression on Tommy. His uncles' stories were so deep in him he could pay attention only to earth, a concept so complete in his imagining that within a year he led Paint Boy away from the mission and into the mountains.

With only their blanket and some bread from the kitchen, they made their way in the night, climbing high to live for a week on fish and berries and pine nuts, and a Franklin hen they plucked and roasted. When the cook found them—coming in his sandals, his plump legs torn and bloody from the undergrowth—he grabbed Paint Boy and cried out that he could not do his painting without him. Made him promise never to leave again.

Paint Boy promised, but Tommy would not. And though Paint Boy surrendered to the mission, he would not betray Tommy, who tried to escape again and then again—saying nothing when they tracked him down, making no promises to stop trying. After his fourth try they gave up, deciding on the Indian School in Spokane. The same gaunt and earnest missionary knew of the wonders it had worked, and had faith in the determination of the young man who ran it. And she saw no other choice.

"We take the Indian out of the boy," the young principal told Tommy, "to make room for the Christian man."

He was handsome and broad-shouldered, clean-shaven and even-tempered—and committed to his task, which he saw as his special calling and life's duty. He was good at the games the Indian boys played—laughing when he outran or outjumped them, smiling when one of them turned the tables and outdid him. Which was rare. He'd won athletic awards at his Christian school in the East. He knew a disciplined day of meaningful work, vigorous play, and regular prayer would lead to virtue, Christian virtue. And he knew he had it in abundance.

He cut Tommy's hair and gave him school clothes. He showed Tommy how to brush his teeth and make his bed and sweep the floors. He saw to it that Tommy learned to harness the horses and milk the cows and work the fields. It bothered him that Tommy spoke seldom and smiled rarely, but he knew change would come, that Tommy would soon put his faith in Christ. All Indian children must. That faith was the lesson he preached, that faith was one all Indian children must have.

Tommy was good at the games, even better with the animals—talents the principal praised, believing they held the key to Tommy's heart. But being better at these things was of no importance to Tommy. His heart was far from where the principal wanted it to be. It was someplace with fast-running streams that left no confusion about the life they supported. To Tommy the confusion was in the White Eyes, all of them following the same trail in their search for another life, following it to the foot of a god he could never trust.

He was quiet about it, but his resentment deepened as they tried to change him. It was four winters before he could escape once and for all, but he kept trying. And when he wasn't trying, he was planning—even as the consequences grew. The strong young principal might take no pleasure in beating him, but he continued to, sure that he must.

"This can only be God's will," he'd said the same night Tommy escaped forever, saying it just before the sharp crack of the belt. Tommy took the burning sting as he'd taken others, accepting the pain, knowing what he must do.

He crept away a few hours later, lame from the beating and less prepared than before, but more determined. The snows had melted enough so he was able to hide for three days, eating the cambium layer under the bark of pines to blunt his hunger as he began working his way back to the Flathead. Men gave him rides in freight wagons and spring wagons and on hay-loads. One rubbed his leg and smiled, said it was all right, asked Tommy how he thought the priests got through their long winters. Tommy had never considered that, but now he did, leaving the man when they stopped to rest the horses. Tommy slept in a culvert that night, then moved on, walking and hitching to make his way to his uncle—the one who knew horses.

Tommy wanted to know them too.

The uncle had traded buffalo robes to a Nez Perce for a spotted colt, now a gritty big-barreled stud, smart and tough-footed and as easy with people as he was determined to cover his mares. And so his uncle's herd had grown, which suited Tommy. Tommy liked watching the spotted horses out in the meadows. He liked gentling them too—doing as his uncle instructed but better at it, more steady, more knowing, as comfortable with horses as he was awkward with people.

It gave him work to do. And it replaced the home he'd lost. His father, fearing that if Tommy came to him they would only take him away again, had taken to drink. And when he wasn't drinking he was indifferent, lost in his dreams and distant. Except for the drinking, it was the same with Tommy's mother—though she would come to her brother to visit Tommy, bring food to him, watch Tommy and her brother work their horses.

Tommy learned about the mountains from his uncle too, even as he was learning about his horses. They would trail them up into the Swan, seeking out trails, moving across fords, climbing into high meadows for grass lush and green. Tommy took comfort in the big backcountry, as though once in it he would be as free as his people were before the White Eyes came. To be in the mountains became his dream, his peace, his comfort.

He knew it wouldn't be easy to make that dream a reality, but he did what he could. Once he even fired a deadfall in hopes they would let him help fight the blaze, join their crew, and go on to fight other fires in other mountains. He stood there with his shovel, but the men just trotted by to do their work, hardly noticing him. A boy with a shovel. Nothing more.

"At least they didn't jail you for setting the goddamn thing," his uncle told him. "Just put it out and went."

Tommy saw he was right, but it didn't change him. He still needed the mountains. If he couldn't work in them maybe he could work somewhere out of them and buy his way back to them. The need became a constant. It seemed to him the money the whites brought into his country might be the only way to buy back some of the country they'd taken away.

He lied about his age and got a job on the Great Northern, replacing ties and driving spikes and dropping gravel. Rough work but work that paid— and work that broadened and strengthened him as he grew into it.

He learned from it too, gritty an education as it proved to be. Learned that no matter how fast he brought money in, it had a way of slipping from him. Learned the language the men used was as rough as their affections—though no rougher than the language of the women the men wanted. Where the crews went, the women followed, along with liquor and cards and quarrels. The Irishmen and the Italians and the Swedes all were a part of it. Big open men, good at their work and even better at complaining—liking the drinking and loving the women and laughing as the cards turned and their wages went with them. They liked Tommy too—amused by his silent ways, giving him liquor and sometimes a woman—getting him into fights, betting on him in fights.

They liked to bet on him, winning more often than not. He'd grown into a block of a man. Tall as most, but wider, thicker. They saw how few could knock him down and taught him how to hide behind his arms, jab and counter-punch. The school principal had taught the Indian boys some of the same things. Tommy had paid attention, and it all came back as the rough men showed him tricks the principal would never have known.

One night a talky Irishman—watching Tommy absorb the blows until the other fighter tired and could fight no more—saw something he could use. The next Saturday Tommy found himself on a fight card in the big center-pole tent the Great Northern used for events. It was boxing night and everyone knew how well the man on Tommy's card understood the sport. Bets were placed, promises made, but after five rounds the boxer realized there was no way to knock Tommy down. Realized it just before he was on his back looking up at Tommy, more startled than hurt, his legs no longer working.

It did not startle the Irishman, who'd placed most of his money on Tommy, sure there was still more to be made.

He gave Tommy some and promised him more, saying there was more to be made fighting than ever could be made on the railroad. Which was good enough for Tommy.

For two years they roamed the state, getting on fight cards when they could, betting in barrooms when they couldn't. There was always someone to fight, and Tommy took on all comers. He was young and strong and knew that after the others wore themselves out they would go down quickly from his short, blunt blows.

Strong as he was, Tommy had little of the killer in him. Most of all he wanted freedom in the mountains. It was the money to buy that freedom that he needed. If he could have got it without fighting, he would have.

But he saw no other way, saw only to keep on doing what he was doing, even though he liked it less and less.

They began calling him Chief and praising him for things he believed no more than they. The foolishness tired him. He turned to drink hoping to blunt it. But he found he was growing tired of the Irishman too—tired of his clever talk and shrewd cheer. The Irishman never seemed to tire of any of it, the drinking or the talking or of Tommy, needing Tommy's validation for his excesses. Needing Tommy's toughness for his money.

One night a deep-chested Swede wouldn't go down at all. He put Tommy down instead. Tommy was more saddened than hurt, knowing it wouldn't have happened had he not been partly drunk. But that didn't change anything. It had happened, and he was through with it. He was tired. Tired of being called Chief, tired of the Irishman, tired beyond his own understanding. He gathered what money he had and left the Irishman to go back to work for the Great Northern.

They were pleased to have him back. He could do work few others could. Some who had seen him fight tried calling him Chief, but he wouldn't respond. And they needed him to respond. He was the strongest, the most able, he complained the least.

He caused no trouble, except when he was drinking, which he did less and less. He worked for two more years, saving his money now because he found himself possessed: He couldn't get the spotted horses out of his head.

No one was sure what made him quit. Because he could do so much more than the rest they would have given him a raise—if they'd seen it coming. He could carry a tie alone, drive a spike with fewer blows, climb high on the trusses to replace a strut. When the gravel in the hoppers wouldn't flow, he would drop into the hopper himself, clinging to the rim with one arm as he stomped the ballast free. He seemed to worry about nothing, though he was never completely with the others. His mind was on the spotted horses.

It was a bitter March day after dropping miles of that gravel—under snowsheds and along windblown switchbacks and through ink-black tunnels—when he decided:

"We've done the last tunnel," he told the foreman. "And we're on the pass. That's high enough for me."

"Left us right there on Marias Pass," the foreman later explained to the yardmaster. "Colder than Canada, too. Took a handcar back for his gear and left. I believe he saw some daylight at the end of that last tunnel. Decided he wanted a shit-load more."

He sighed and handed Tommy's papers over to the yardmaster. "Doubt we could have kept him much longer anyway. He seemed to take no pleasure in our line of work."

Tommy angled his way down linking watersheds until he reached the Southfork of the Flathead River, then walked south toward the headwaters of that contrary river, crossing it to climb the watersheds to the west and contouring high to find a camp at the head of Lost Bird Canyon. He knew it by its Salish name, the whites usually calling it nothing at all—even when they remembered to put it on their maps.

Tommy liked the camp and the meadows below it, liked that the White Eyes knew little of it. He vowed to return to it, if some door opened so he could. He marked the place, covering his campfire and crossing the Swan Range to move down into the Swan Valley, going still farther to reach the Flathead valley and his uncle and the spotted horses—to reach the reservation that kept its blanket over the spirits of his people.

It took him ten days to reach his uncle, and almost the whole summer to convince his uncle to let him take ten spotted horses across the mountains to Choteau.

"You're only payin' for half their value," his uncle complained as he counted out the last of Tommy's money. "And I'm likely to get no more after you sell. You're a damn fool to take them half-broke things and try to sucker them off over there. You may be good with horses—and fightin' in the bars—but you're the shits with people. And you know it."

Tommy did know it. But after he met Fenton that night in his Lost Bird Canyon camp, it didn't seem to matter so much. Fenton turned out to be the door that opened, and it changed Tommy's life forever.

But then Tommy changed Fenton's even more. And not just by providing a saddle horse, though doing that gave Fenton a leg up toward a life he hadn't even considered.

And Fenton was sorely in need of a leg up that night in Lost Bird Canyon. He might have had a hazy idea about how much he liked his journey, but he had only the faintest idea of how much he liked the country—and no idea at all where he was. Or where he was going. Until he met Tommy.

4

A Beginning

Word spread quickly. Everyone in the Swan knew of Tommy Yellowtail—his skill with horses, his tolerance of his edgy uncles, his deep silences—but none of them knew of the tall man who came back across the pass with him.

The man stirred interest. They'd watched Tommy start out going the other way, his paints and pintos flashing their colors as they climbed the switchbacks and headed toward Choteau. Some doubted he could make it through all that rough country at all, not with so many of his horses half wild. But there was agreement that if it could be done, Tommy was the one to try.

Now he'd appeared with this tall stranger riding one of those paints and coming back over the same trail, neither of the men looking as though there'd been any trouble at all. What had transpired no one could guess, but it didn't take them long to see that something new was going on with Tommy. And it didn't take them much longer to realize something new had come to the Swan.

Fenton had followed Tommy over the pass on one of Tommy's half-gentled paints, leading his three packed mules as naturally as the rest of Tommy's mottled animals had lined themselves out behind. Tommy and Fenton didn't even tail-tie them until they hit the lake, the one Tommy called Crippled Elk, the name Fenton picked up as he was doing the tail-tying. It was the name he would use always, because it was the one Tommy's people used. After Fenton had been in the Swan for a few years, half the people there called it Crippled Elk too. Fenton had a way of changing things around, many of his ways taking hold from the very first.

People took to him. Maybe it was because he arrived with Tommy Yellow-tail, and maybe it was because he had such an easy way of dealing with mules—and with Tommy's spotted horses, with Tommy himself. Somehow it became such a natural thing to go along with him that nobody bothered to look for a reason. They just did it.

Tommy knew that only a few miles down the road from Crippled Elk Lake old man Conner had a hundred acres or so, most of it meadow. They turned their animals out when they reached it and went right to work patching the fences. Conner arrived during the patching, pleased to see such industry applied to his fences and figuring if the man doing the patching was with Tommy, there must be some logic to it.

He wasn't so pleased when Fenton walked over to him and said he thought this piece of land would be about right.

"For what?" Conner wanted to know, more startled by the statement than anything else. "Only two ways to make any money in this valley: mill timber or grow cows. You might could grow a half-dozen cows here. No more."

"You know, I worked for that man Bill Cody for a few seasons," Fenton said, just as though Conner himself might know Bill Cody. "Spent some time at that Pahaska camp on the Shoshone with him, too. Might be all those people watching them shows of his have him so convinced he has to stand around lookin' like a hero the man's forgot he's not. Fact is, I'm commencin' to believe the man missed his main chance."

Old man Conner looked a little shocked. He was a little shocked. He'd been talking about his fences and now this tall man was talking about Buffalo Bill Cody. Even in the Swan they knew that Bill Cody was one of the most marketable men in the country. Maybe the richest too.

"Don't know what your idea of his 'main chance' is, but I'd sure as hell say the man didn't miss his. Unless his aim is to be president, which may not pay near as good. . . . Why, they say that man's got kings and queens wrapped around his finger just the way he is."

"I think he does," Fenton said. "And he ain't a bad man for all that. Just sad, I believe."

"I sure as hell wouldn't be sad if I had all that money." Old man Conner still wasn't sure he was hearing right. "What in hell do you mean, by sad?"

"Just seemed that way to me." Fenton was watching the spotted horses grazing far out in the meadow, his mules as comfortable with them as though they were family. "He pisses away most of his money, don't you know. Buys everyone drinks or tries some crazy idea to make still more. Now and then he comes back to country like this just to catch his breath.

But he can't find a way to stay. Someone always talks him into leaving, tryin' to take a chunk of it back so them others can think they been here too."

"Sure as hell made him rich. Famous too. Some say as famous as Jesus."

Conner quickly crossed himself. He was surprised to hear Jesus' name come out of his own mouth in a discussion about Bill Cody. But then Bill Cody was awfully important too. "Being looked up to by all them people sure as hell can't be a bad thing."

"It is if the only way you get their attention is being nailed to some limbed trees, which is what happened to your man Jesus. But bein' nailed up is not what Cody wants—though I believe some of those people do try to make him think so."

Conner was more confused than ever. They'd started out talking about his pasture and now they were talking about Bill Cody and Jesus.

"Will you tell me what you believe that man does want?" Conner was so exasperated by the crazy logic of the whole thing, he felt his face getting red. And here was Tommy Yellowtail looking even calmer than this tall man. Tommy looked like some cat who'd finished off a canary.

"You make a good point," Fenton said. "About being looked up to, I mean. I think a part of him did want to show people this country." Fenton seemed so comfortable with that idea that Conner relaxed a little, though he couldn't remember making such a point at all. "But I think they talked him into making up so much that wasn't real he kind of lost sight of what *was*—for himself is what I mean. Now if he'd brought those people to this country—just a few at a time—he might have kept a little more of the country in his heart. Might have had a little peace, don't you know. That's what I think."

"You know damn well he could never have become as famous bringing a few people out here. And sure as hell not as rich." With such logic on his side, Conner was sure he finally had the tall man in a corner. But Fenton paid no attention.

"Or as sad, is all I'm saying." Fenton was still watching his mules out in the meadow. "Who the hell wants to be nailed to a cross?"

"I'm downright sorry I brought Jesus up," Conner crossed himself again. "He shouldn't be any part of this."

And he was sorry. He was even beginning to be sorry he'd been brought up a Catholic, though he'd long ago given up going to church. Being a Catholic made talking with this tall man confusing. He'd taken a liking to him, but somehow the tall man made everything he thought he knew become kind of hazy. He was sorry he'd gotten into the conversation in the first place.

"All I'm saying," Fenton spoke gently now, "is that maybe it's better to be a regular part of this country than it is to take it somewhere else and try to sell some of it off as a truth. Specially if you gotta wear them buckskins with all the fringes flapping around. . . . A cross can be a heavy damn thing to carry, don't you know."

Old man Conner wasn't sure whether it was because he was so confused or because he was so impressed, but before he knew it he'd leased his pasture to Fenton, with a sale price attached in case Fenton wanted to turn his lease into a buy. They shook on the deal, Tommy's handshake in it too, Tommy as pleased as Fenton but letting Conner know that only by the firmness of his grip.

And it *was* a beginning for Tommy and Fenton, though that year they took only a handful of parties back into the Southfork, people Fenton drummed up from Omaha and Chicago and St. Louis. But the next year there were more—and from farther away. And more the year after that. Tommy didn't know how Fenton came up with them, but he came to realize that Fenton was most interested in learning the country, and Fenton's wanting to know the country gave Tommy plenty of reasons to stay in it.

5

The Outfitter

With the Great War barely on the horizon, Fenton was becoming so much a part of the Swan Valley and the Southfork that he was representing that country, in his Fenton-like way, to the advantage of most of the lumberjacks and ranchers scratching out a living there. At least he was in the minds of the people in the valley—and in the minds of the merchants in Missoula too. Every few months he'd go down to Helena to visit with the legislators, who saw something promising in the big man who went at things so directly. People from the cities who wanted to fish and hunt that primitive country, or just see it, had always rented pack animals from local ranchers, digging up someone as best they could to point out what trails to take into it. Their interest gave rise to a few outfitters, who made a little money taking people across the passes—when they weren't doing something else, which all too often they were.

The difference with Fenton was that he made it his business entirely. Much as he wanted to learn about that country, as able as he was about living in it and moving through it, he was even better at convincing people to do it with him. He seemed to have a special knack for putting trips together, taking people into a country that uplifted them on the one hand and humbled them on the other.

He learned everything he could from Tommy, who said little, but talked more with Fenton than anyone else. Fenton, of course, didn't mind talking at all, meaning he found more and more ways to make what Tommy taught him useful for others. Tommy wanted to stay in his mountains; Fenton wanted to learn about them. It was a combination more fruitful than anyone could have predicted, except Fenton and Tommy. They were comfortable with each other from that first night when Fenton did everything he could to make his beans palatable for Tommy, and Tommy did everything he could to hide how amused he was at how hard Fenton was working.

Thinking about it later, Tommy supposed the liquor helped them along. Not that Fenton pushed the bottle on him, because he didn't. Tommy respected that. He respected Fenton for not lecturing him about liquor too. He'd heard enough of that from the Black Robes, who controlled his people in every way they could. And he'd liked Fenton's beans and all the flourishes Fenton went through to produce them. Most of all he'd liked sitting by the fire after they'd eaten, sipping the whisky as Fenton confessed that he didn't quite know how he'd gotten to Tommy's camp but how sure he was that a lot of people would pay for an evening such as theirs—if they could find a way to Tommy's fire. How they'd probably pay just for the privilege of traveling through this big country. They just needed someone to show them the way, keep them dry and warm—and safe at night.

A certain blurring of details that came with the liquor probably did something for them too: Fenton letting one idea slide into another as he talked about what he'd learned working with Bill Cody, Tommy coming to see that this man who'd stumbled into his camp might hold the key to how he could do what he'd tried so hard to do for so long, but couldn't.

The precise details of whatever arrangement they came to were never clear, but Tommy was not disappointed in what Fenton managed to do with the few resources they pulled together—especially the spotted horses. In no time at all Fenton traded three of them for six mules that old man Conner's sons could find no way to gentle. He sold another to a drummer who wanted something pretty for his daughter. The drummer managed to get the little mare to the railroad but the mare raised such a ruckus in the stock car the drummer gave up on the idea and traded her off to a family with six hard-nosed Irish boys. Before Fenton knew it, the boys' father came back wanting two more, claiming the spotted horses were the only things he'd found that could gentle his boys. And the spotted horses did gentle his boys, though there'd been some broken bones to repair as the gentling took hold.

Wherever Fenton looked he seemed to find opportunity. He went to Wilson's sawmill and traded some future pack trips for lodgepoles and some milled lumber, then got Tommy to convince some of his people to come over to do the building. They came with their families and some tipis to live in while they worked. When Bob Ring, the new Forest Service ranger, came and pointed out that their reservation was over in the Flathead, not right there in Fenton's meadow, Fenton sat him down in one of the tipis for a talk.

In a few hours Ring got up to leave, warmed by Fenton's liquor and with much more understanding about what Fenton was doing. "I guess there's no reason these boys can't make a good wage right here—if you got the work," he admitted as they walked past the first building, logs in place and ready for chinking.

"And I got a shit-load more too," Fenton said. "Just takes a little time to line it out."

Ring couldn't think of anything to argue about in that. "Go ahead," he said. "You sure as hell seem to know what you're doing."

That much was true. Fenton always seemed to know what he was doing, even when his grip on what it might be remained tentative. And tentative as things might have been that day he talked with Ring, he found still another opportunity when the ranger admitted that this new Forest Service they'd started back in Washington wasn't yet certain of how to proceed in Montana. That was all Fenton needed in order to make sure that wherever the Forest Service found some footing, his foot was right next to theirs. It was an idea that made the Southfork a home for him as few other things could. A home for Tommy too . . .

And Tommy would never forget it.

Only a few years earlier, the glacier country just north of the Swan had been declared a National Park. Everyone was saying it would become another Yellowstone, a matter that interested Fenton no little. It didn't take him long to go up and take a look around. It was easy to see that their Pack and Saddle outfit would become one of the biggest ever. Pack and saddle was the only way into the heart of that country anyway, and how long that would remain true was of considerable interest to Fenton.

He learned some things from their packers too, though they told him little more than what he thought they would, namely that fewer and fewer people seemed able to afford the prices such a fancy outfit had to charge. He concluded that running bigger and more elaborate trips for fewer and fewer people might be the wrong way to go, especially when more and more people were finding more and more roads that took their new automobiles deeper and deeper into the mountains. The automobile people were already claiming that a car was more a necessity than a luxury, a point hardly lost on the Park's engineers and supervisors. They were already on the lookout for a way to put a road across their new park so the cars could bring them more people.

As far as Fenton was concerned, it was a Bill Cody operation turned on end. Cody's gift was realizing how much people wanted to see the West. He'd made and lost fortunes doing everything he could to bring the West to the East by rail; now cars were bringing the East to the West by road. Fenton figured that might bring more people to the mountains, but it didn't seem to follow that most of those people would have the courage—or the money—for a fancy horse trip to get still higher into them. He concluded that for most cars would take them far enough. How to scoop up the few who had an urge to go still higher was what got his attention.

When he told Tommy about his conclusions, which were that they'd be better off fighting the roadbuilding and keeping their operation rough and simple, free of all the amenities people wanted to bring along, Tommy just grunted and agreed, saying a blind man could see as much.

"Only an asshole would have to go up to Glacier to find that out, Tommy said. "My people already joined the Kootenai to bitch about them roads. It's our land they want to cut through the middle for their damn roads."

They were looking out at Fenton's pasture, which Tommy held should have remained Indian land in the first place.

"Go easy," Fenton told him. "What's done is done. We might not be able to take these people into what was your mountains without what was your meadow to hold what is now our horses."

"And without your people, we wouldn't need any of this shit. We could all run free," Tommy said. "Not a goddamned thing we can do about it, though. They took most everything that's ours. Soon they'll take what little they left us. Or find some rule to keep our asses off it. They're good at that."

Fenton knew Tommy would cool. Though Tommy had learned much of his language from the bars and from his work on the rails, he'd learned something from his own people about living with what couldn't be changed. His voice carried hardly any inflection as he opened his thinking for Fenton—just the hard reality of what had been done to his people.

Fenton watched as Tommy took his wrangle horse into the meadow, hardly stirring the herd as he caught up a paint and brought her in and began to work her. Tommy's uncle—his own anger diminished by age and excess—still brought a few of his horses over each spring, letting Fenton and Tommy use them in their strings. He knew they'd be more valuable after a season's work, and he knew he was not much good at selling them anyway, especially if they were green. It was a plus to him that they got any work at all. And it saved on feed.

It was one of Fenton's theories that working with the horses made Tommy feel comfortable with himself. As far as Fenton could see, working with the horses and being in the mountains were the only chances Tommy had left to be at home with himself.

And he was mostly right. Nothing made Tommy bluer than thinking about all the things being carved away from his people by churches and schoolhouses, rails and roads. The best way not to think about them was to work with his horses or to disappear deep into his mountains—or to get drunk.

Before Fenton came along, getting drunk seemed the easiest thing to do.

Tommy didn't like what getting drunk did to him, but at least it was a way to stop thinking about what had been.

6

Hope

Paint Boy showed up not long after Fenton's guest lodge was complete, offering to stain the logs and do whatever other painting was needed. The gifted cook was on his deathbed at the mission. The Black Robes—concerned about how much the boy and the artist needed one another—had told Paint Boy he must be useful in other ways and for other people. And so he had sought out his old friend Tommy Yellowtail, who took him to Fenton, the boy bluer than blue because he did not want to leave the old artist helpless and alone, but had been told he must.

The Black Robes considered the cook's work done. His frescos and murals had brought fame to the mission, haunting the dreams of the Salish and fulfilling those of the whites. The Salish watched the White Eyes with awe as they came declaring their faith, worshipping under the cook's artistry, pleading for salvation.

To the Black Robes alone the cook's gift was a worry—his dazzling frescos made them wary and suspicious. He was a simple man; the gift he'd been given mystified them. They were confounded by how rich it was—how earthy.

Paint Boy himself knew that there was no one better than he to keep the cook's spectacular images clean and bright, no one who so clearly saw their magic or knew more surely what was in the cook's heart. But there was no way he could explain that to the Black Robes, no way they could accept it if he tried. He resigned himself to his work with Fenton and Tommy—and buried his sadness.

Hope Woman, a teacher now at the same mission school Tommy had struggled so to escape, would come on weekends, consoling her brother and helping Tommy and Fenton. When her teaching was light and there was time, she stayed longer, made their lives better with her sewing and cooking and intelligence, brightening the days for everyone she touched.

She brought understanding to Fenton's plans too, admiring his work with the Forest Service, his efforts to protect the Southfork from roads and ranchers, from lumbermen and the cabins of squatters.

Fenton liked her, liked talking with her, watching her, learning from the direct way she described the life she'd lived, the death of her mother, the Cheyennes' conclusion that her father try the white man's way, their decision to send her and her brother to the Black Robes the better to learn the Black Robe's ways. And Fenton knew how deeply Tommy was consumed by her. Tommy, who had a hard time saying anything at all about the life he'd lived, couldn't keep his eyes away from Hope as she revealed everything about hers.

Whether Hope realized how deeply Tommy's hunger ran, Fenton never knew. He guessed she had no way to admit it even if she knew—not to Fenton, certainly not to her brother, whose eyes knew only sadness. He doubted she could even admit it to herself. There was something in Tommy too strong for the world the Black Robes had given her, a world of boundaries and structure. The need in Tommy ran deeper than she had any way to accept. And so Fenton watched Tommy as Tommy watched her, and they both watched Hope continue about her good deeds, talking to Tommy as much and as sensibly as Tommy was unable to talk to her— sensible or not.

The Great War was at last upon them and many of the young men went off to Europe, some coming back maimed and bruised—some almost silent in their melancholy. The war brought a different world at home, too, though Fenton found himself worrying more about the country's anguish than any change in their own lives. More and more people wanted him to help them escape into the mountains. Tommy's hunger for Hope only grew. The sadness in Paint Boy remained a constant, even after the gifted cook died—leaving only his work to remind them. The war brought a new sadness to Fenton, a sadness that haunted him almost as much as the cook's paintings seemed to haunt Paint Boy, the boy awed by the images of Christ in his moccasins, of the Saints in their feathers.

"I don't mind this goddamned draft they got going," Fenton told Tommy, the two of them having the chance to talk when they were deep in the mountains that they rarely had these days when out of them. "Just wish it would do us some good—not be for some war we should have slid by in the first place."

"You mean something what would do *you* good," Tommy said. "For your people. Wouldn't help mine. Couldn't. No way to unfuck us from what's already been done."

"You are a hard man, Tommy. When the snow closes us down, I'll take you in to that Bar of Justice old Horace and Messler opened up. Might be a lot happier if you went upstairs and popped your cork with one of those good old girls."

"Rent me one? Good idea. A painted woman's about all my people are allowed these days. Better you pay than me."

"That's just what I mean. Times are hard. And I just might pay—if it would quiet you down. And you ain't the only one I'd like to quiet. If that Carry Nation and those old biddies back in Kansas don't stop swinging their axes into every bar they find, rented girls might be the only justice left for the rest of us too."

The two of them watched their fire, thinking about how vocal the Prohibition movement was getting, the newspapers claiming it was growing even stronger in all the churches—and in Washington too. It made them blue. But then they found themselves talking more about the new enterprise Horace Adams and Doc Messler had carried on about one night. They'd been sitting around a fire just like this, their talk vivid and colorful.

That subject was more pleasant.

Horace Adams owned the feed store, which meant Fenton bargained with him every which way for grain and hay and used tack, even trading for free trips into the mountains, which is why Messler was along on that trip. By then Fenton owed Horace so many trips that, as far as Horace was concerned, having Messler as a guest hardly made a dent in Fenton's debt to him.

Fenton was glad to get to know Doc Messler anyway. The man seemed to have a say in whatever went on in Missoula—maybe in the whole state. It was possible that Messler wouldn't even have to close his bar if Prohibition came along. His bar wasn't legal anyway. If you knew the right people in Missoula you might be able to start up a whorehouse, but you certainly couldn't get a license for one—or for the bar that went with it, meaning if you were running a bar that wasn't legal, there would be no reason to close it down when bars became illegal. Fenton figured, in his Fenton-like way, that starting out as a whorehouse might be the salvation for The Bar of Justice. And he got a kick out of that, always enjoying unintended consequences.

Tommy's thinking wasn't as complicated as Fenton's. He figured it would be nice to go to The Bar of Justice just to go upstairs and do what they did there. He just hoped Fenton would remember his promise, which might be hard to fulfill. It wasn't always easy for a Salish to go into places where Fenton's friends were drinking, another unhappy reality for Tommy.

But that night Tommy's mind wouldn't leave the idea of Prohibition and the war and the draft—which he thought was the craziest idea of all, even if being an Indian might free him from it. As far as he was concerned, you didn't just tell young men they had to go out and do battle. You sang about it and danced about it and had visions about it. Then you went out and did it—and soared with the pleasure of it too. It had been so long since his people had a chance to do anything in the old ways that he wondered if even dancing and singing would excite them anymore—which is what he told Fenton.

"That draft is a shitty idea," he said.

"Maybe." Fenton considered it. "But maybe not. If you get people together to do something that's worth something, it might could do us all some good. What if you got your people together to get your mountains back? Wouldn't be such a bad thing, would it?"

"And it wouldn't be a bad thing to shoot some of those fuckers over at the Indian Agency, only I might could get myself hanged. Look what they did to those Kootenai boys."

"That's a sad thing all the way around."

"Being a Kootenai?"

"Gettin' hanged. Something's not human about it."

"Gettin' nailed to a cross ain't human either," Tommy said morosely. "But they paint pictures about it and pray prayers about it and act like it's dandy to get nailed up for everyone else. It's all the shits if you ask me. . . . Got any whisky? Hope said we was supposed to have a happy time up here."

"I do and we will." Fenton pulled a bottle from a pannier, pouring a cup for each. "And you ought to listen to Hope. Her brother might be a sorry bastard, but she's a real pistol."

They sipped for a while: Fenton wondering how Tommy would ever open himself up enough to talk with Hope, even to talk about her; Tommy trying not to think about her at all.

But she filled his mind, flooding out everything else.

~

Fenton did remember to take Tommy to The Bar of Justice, scheduling a trip in to Missoula not long after they came out of the mountains. The war had ended and everyone was celebrating, which gave the lumberjacks and cowboys—always on the lookout for an excuse—a patriotic reason to go upstairs. It gave the girls a good stream of money, too—the tips generous and little time needed to earn them.

After a few drinks Tommy was happy to go upstairs himself. He was already pleased. He'd caused hardly a stir when he came into the bar, which wasn't always the case. He was there with Fenton, of course, which made a difference—Fenton being a friend of Doc Messler's, who happened to be there himself. That made a bigger difference.

"Some of you damn Indians cause a shit-load of trouble," Doc Messler had told Tommy that night around their fire as he sipped his drink. "Glad you ain't one of them."

Tommy had been opening his mouth to say something about the trouble people like Messler had caused *him*, when Fenton popped up and said they'd better go out and check the horses. He was in such a hurry Tommy didn't even have time to give him hell for denying him the opportunity to respond to Messler. And then for some reason Fenton set off in the wrong direction. It took Tommy almost an hour to straighten him out so they could pick up the right tracks. It was still another hour before they heard the bells and were satisfied. When they got back to camp the fire was low, everyone off to bed. And by the time they got everything saddled the next morning, there were other things to worry about, so Tommy lost his chance altogether.

He never was sure whether Fenton had been worried about the horses or just wanted to muzzle him, though when Fenton finally took him to The Bar of Justice he was actually glad he'd kept quiet. Messler greeted him like an old friend, and it wasn't long before he was on his way upstairs with a big-boned woman who treated him like a prize because he had Messler's blessing. Not a bad blessing to have, he figured—climbing the stairs and taken by the movement under the woman's shift—if you wanted to have a good time at The Bar of Justice.

Messler, whose knowledge of what was going on in Missoula in no way interfered with his appreciation of the Southfork, was even happier to see Fenton than he was to see Tommy. After Tommy left, the two of them sat, drinking and sharing views and feeling blue about the fact that Etta had Horace pretty much under wraps these days.

Etta Adams was a serious Methodist and since the Prohibitionist movement had taken hold she'd become more and more wary of Horace's drinking, begrudging the fact that he liked to share a sip now and then with Doc Messler in their new store off Main Street.

Messler commiserated with Fenton about it, glad that Etta didn't know what went on upstairs but seeing her disapproval as somehow connected to the gains the temperance movement was making. Those gains depressed him deeply. He saw them as a serious blow against the general well-being of the population.

"They got them teaching that crap in every goddamn church and gymnasium across the country. As though a man hasn't got a right," Messler said, his voice more resigned than understanding. "They might even get their way, if they keep at it. And it looks like they will. Too many assholes back in Washington crying in their beer and saying we ought not do what everyone knows damn well they do themselves."

"They ain't the first to be hypocritical, you know." Fenton seemed resigned himself. "All you got to do is take a look at what we did to Tommy's people."

"Jesus. Are you at that again? This is serious. It'll be the shits for freedom—though I doubt it'll slow us here."

"You got a point," Fenton said. He knew he would never get Messler to understand what they'd done to Tommy's people, much as he admired the man and how smoothly he could run things. He even asked him for a few tips about how to work with the Forest Service.

"Your mountains ain't my department," Doc said, explaining that his only magic had been to hire a bookkeeper from the old Agnes Lake Show. She'd learned so much running it that she'd known just how to manage the girls and parcel out their money—even how to get them through their rocky times.

"She finds the girls. Claims they won't steal or get drunk or turn mean," he said. "Don't know where she gets them, but she treats them good and they seem content—though you know they'll take what they can when some old cowboy gets too drunk. Can't take the hump off a buffalo, don't you know."

"Old Bill Cody took more than the hump," Fenton said, "if you want to talk about buffalo." In fact, he was wondering what kind of crazy logic had him asking advice from a man who owed his success to the Agnes

Lake Show when the Agnes Lake Show owed so much of its success to Bill Cody's *Wild West*—just what he wanted to be free of. But the subject here was buffalo. And he knew that keeping a few people who did flips and swung on bars from causing damage couldn't compare with the damage Buffalo Bill's hunters had done to the buffalo herds, though Cody couldn't have known how far that damage would go when he started shipping those hides back East.

"I guess he was an innocent man. Mostly." Fenton tried to be fair. "I don't believe he wanted all them buffalo to go any more than he wanted them guys with servants and fancy guns shootin' up everything in the Shoshone. And now they've gone and buried him in Denver. What a thing. Who the hell wants to be buried in Denver?" Fenton shook his head. "My guess is he got something goin' that made him some money and he just couldn't stop. Why the damn money did him in even after he was done in."

"You take people on hunts," Messler pointed out. "What's the difference?"

"Difference is that I want people to see what's there, not kill every damn thing that depends on what's there—or change it all around by renting some Indians to yell and run around bare-legged to make it more like what someone's gone and invented in the first place. I'd as soon not do the damn hunting, to tell the truth. I'd as soon just look. I sure don't want to be done in like poor old Bill Cody."

"I wouldn't call havin' all that money being done in," Doc Messler said. "It would sure make me content."

"I still hold that it just made him blue," Fenton said, seeing he had to say what he thought all over again. "I knew him—don't you know. Toward the end there he seemed more confused than anything else. He was tryin' too hard to be what everyone wanted him to be—fancy clothes and long hair, and showin' off. Drinkin' too much, too. Hell, I think he plumb forgot what he wanted—if ever he knew." Fenton finished his drink and looked at the girl who had joined them.

"I do believe he would have been happier right here with a pretty girl like this," Fenton said, a little undone by the way the girl was watching him.

Beth Jorgeson, slim as a reed when she started off in The Bar of Justice, was listening closely, her eyes hardly blinking as she watched Fenton.

And nothing pleased Fenton more than having her listen to him. That night was the first night he took her upstairs. He hadn't meant to, but after she'd watched him awhile he seemed to have no other choice. And anyone watching them would have known it probably wouldn't be the last night he'd do that. He was that smitten. He lay there, long after he was through, just talking—Beth listening as though every word he delivered was gospel. And she seemed in no hurry at all to get back downstairs.

"She must of learned how to do that up in Canada," he told Tommy the next day as they started the bumpy drive back to the pack station. "She just looked at me and listened to me and I went right on and blabbered all over the place."

What he didn't tell Tommy was that Tommy and Hope were one of the things he blabbered about, but by then they were one of the things most on his mind, as was the packing contract he was working out with the Forest Service. He told her about that too, much to his own surprise.

If Beth ever wanted to tell him why she came down out of Canada, he never knew it. She was too good at listening—and just watching her listen as he spelled out his worries seemed to work wonders, as though her listening opened the door onto all kinds of understanding, even solutions, for whatever was on his mind.

7

Mules

Fenton's bid for the Forest Service packing contract paid off so quickly he hardly knew what to say.

"You won that contract," Bob Ring said, finding Fenton nosing around the District Office. "If 'won' is the word. The others didn't bid." Ring said it so casually he might have been talking about the weather. But it came as a shock to Fenton.

"Well, shame on them." Fenton said the only thing he could think of to say. "Anyone can see your own packers'll be caught with their pants down come fire season. Been dry as a bone. There'll be fires. Hot ones too."

They'd given him a good contract. Fenton could see that. He and Tommy would have all the work the Forest Service couldn't manage—which would be plenty. The trouble was he didn't have nearly enough mules to handle even a normal season, a truth Tommy had pointed out but that Fenton had pretty much ignored, because he didn't think they'd get the contract in the first place.

If he regretted digging himself into a hole, he didn't let on. That wasn't his style. He hardly tipped his hat to trouble, which cheered Tommy at times and worried him at others. Fenton even dropped in that night at The Bar of Justice, thinking all the hustle and bustle might give him some ideas.

It didn't. But as seemed to be happening more and more often, he wound up going upstairs with Beth anyway. He wasn't too preoccupied with his dilemma to appreciate how generous Beth could be upstairs, though she suspected something was off. That's why, when the urgency was over, she did what Beth could do better than anyone else, at least in those days: she just watched him, and waited.

Fenton had brought some beer upstairs just in case rolling around in Beth's bed worked up a thirst. He got a bottle open and balanced it on his stomach, considering. Beth was looking up at him, her head on his chest, and before he knew it he was telling her things he hadn't expected to.

"Got a dandy contract with those Forest Service boys—signed and all—for when they got too much on their plate. And damned if I'm not about twenty mules short." His laugh was a little hollow as he explained that this contract was to be the first of many more. Meet it he had to do. And he hadn't the foggiest idea of where to turn. He'd gotten rid of most of Tommy's paints and pintos. But they didn't pack all that well anyway, even on trails. And when you were supplying fire crews there were hardly any trails at all. Mules were what he needed, and mules were what he didn't have.

"Maybe that's why no one else bid on the damn job in the first place," he told Beth. "These boys around here are just locked into packing horses. As though a mule might sneak up and steal their lunch. Crazy bastards. Of course what they don't know should be good news for me. But if I can't find some mules, good news ain't gonna help."

Beth liked being held by Fenton, listening to him tell her things as she considered how to respond. This time she had something to add that went right to what was occupying him, if he would give her a chance.

Just the past week, she told him, a scratchy-looking rancher had been in, too dispirited to go upstairs, which didn't keep him from drinking and carrying on about his troubles. The biggest seemed to be that his own father had been so undone by the big freeze of eighty-seven that he'd given up on cattle and put everything they had into raising horses and mules. Over the years it evolved into being all mules, which they couldn't seem to sell anymore. "He was low about that," Beth explained. "Said they were headed for the poor house because his dad can't market the mules."

"Dear Jesus," Fenton sighed. "And he's sure to live plum across the state. Too bad. That Chinese who cooked for Cody up at Pahaska would say, 'One bird you catchem more better than six birds you no gettem,'" Fenton laughed. "He had a point: I need mules I can get hold of, not some out there in the bush."

"I guess his dad's still somewhere up in the Bitterroot." Beth said, snuggling closer, pleased to have Fenton's attention even if she couldn't help. "Said the Army bought them at first but then they went off to Missouri for bigger ones. Left the whole family out on a limb."

Fenton sat up, spilling Beth off his chest and hardly believing what he was hearing. The Bitterroot wasn't all that far away. Usually, Beth just watched him and listened. Now she seemed as smart as the woman from the Agnes Lake Show—and she wasn't even looking at him in that know-ing way of hers.

"Well let's just find out where the hell that limb is," he said. "Those Mexican mules'll do better in my country anyway. They carry as much. I just might make that man as happy as the Army did—before he got out on his limb."

Beth couldn't help smiling. Fenton was on his way to solving a problem, and she knew it would be hard to slow him until he did. He wouldn't be needing her for much of anything now, which made her almost sorry she'd provided the help she had.

Making Fenton this happy did give her a little thrill. But the smile she gave him as he pulled on his boots was kind of bittersweet, not the happy one she'd offered when she first told him about the mules.

A stop at the Elkhorn gave Fenton the information he needed. The barkeep told him it was a man named Will Hardin who'd been singing the blues that night, saying Hardin had been at the Elkhorn before heading off for The Bar of Justice. "Sad bastard. You'd spot him if he walked in right now."

The barkeep liked it when Fenton asked him for news. Fenton had such a colorful way of interpreting it that almost everyone liked sharing news with him. "That man always looks as if he's been caught holdin' the dead-man's hand," the barkeep added.

"Not a bad hand, either," Fenton said. "Just didn't do old Hickok any good. Cody could get pretty blue telling that story." Fenton thought about that. "I do believe there were times when Cody was as blue about his own life as he was about Hickok's." He finished his beer. "Ain't that the way though?"

"Maybe. . . . For some. You know that Hickok too?" The barkeep was beginning to think Fenton knew everybody.

"Knew one and heard too much about the other. But two pair's good enough for me. Hell, he still had a card to draw."

"Can't count on a draw. Poker's not fair."

"The cards are. How a man sees 'em is what screws him up. Would this Will Hardin know a good hand if he held it?"

"Ask around in the Bitterroot. His father's out there too. With his mules. Used to come in and bend an elbow. Told a good story too. He'd know a good hand when he held it."

"That'll help," Fenton said, accepting another beer. "Hard to trade with a man who don't recognize a good hand."

Fenton took Tommy up into the Bitterroot with him, Tommy riding Pinto, which is what he called whatever was under his saddle, even a paint like this one. Fenton pointed that out, but Tommy paid no attention. He wanted to give this project his full attention, which wasn't easy. He knew how Fenton's optimism could screw things up, and the mules were too good an opportunity to miss.

"I'll just romance that man a little and we'll have our mules," Fenton had told Tommy as he climbed on Custer, the big bay gelding he used as a lead horse in those days. "Call him Custer because he's pretty in two ways," he'd tell people—even if they didn't ask. "Pretty to look at and pretty damn dumb. But he runs like the wind. I'll say that."

Fenton said it again that very morning. But then he settled back in his saddle and thought it over. "When you think about it, runnin' too damn fast *toward* your people could be just what cost old Custer his whole damn outfit."

That seemed such an obvious truth to Tommy it set off alarm bells. It was always dangerous when Fenton started reconsidering things everybody else thought had been settled. You might not even know which side of an argument he favored. He could say one thing and do another. But romancing people was a talent he had in abundance. Tommy had watched him get better and better at it ever since they'd ridden down into the Swan together. He thought it came from Fenton's growing happiness, which kept improving as Tommy showed him secret places in the big valley of the Southfork. And kept improving when he got out of the Southfork too, particularly when he had a chance to relax with Beth. But it was Fenton's ability to romance ideas that had Tommy worried as they rode into the Bitterroot. All too often Tommy had watched Fenton convince people to do what they had no intention of doing. Sometimes Fenton could even convince himself of a scheme that Tommy knew made no sense. All of which is why he was worried about Fenton being in a reconsidering mood. Things could backfire.

Tommy had brought along four of his uncle's spotted horses just in case getting these mules required more than Fenton's romancing—and the money they'd borrowed from Messler and Horace. Having the spotted horses as a trading chip made him feel better. And they did look colorful, perky and alert behind him, tail-tied and moving smartly.

Old Eban Hardin surprised them both, however, offering no amenities and hardly glancing at the spotted horses.

"Got around thirty mules out in that meadow," Eban told them after Will introduced them all around. "And that damn Army has up and deserted me." He watched Fenton, his gaze level and appraising.

Tommy—pleased it wasn't Fenton who started the talking— watched Will Hardin drift a few steps away from them, looking doleful as he did.

"Trade reasonable," Eban was saying, "and they're yours. All they need is honest work and good feed. Truth is, we're gettin' a little low on that around here." He didn't look at Will, but Tommy figured this had some-thing to do with Will, who was looking away, as though not wanting to listen. And for once Fenton seemed at a loss for anything to say at all, a rare state for him. Tommy couldn't help liking Eban for bringing it about.

They stood, watching the mules out in the meadow, who were roughly collected around a compact little Morgan mare. She was belled and seemed entirely in control. Tommy estimated there were about ten more mules than they needed, but they were sleek and sound—just what they wanted. Watching them was a treat, as it was a treat for Tommy to realize Fenton still hadn't thought of anything to say.

"Nice looking animals," Fenton finally said. "Can't see what those Army people had to complain about."

"I believe they ran into a Missouri mule man," Eban said, focusing on Fenton. "Ever swap with a Missouri mule man?"

"Not that I recollect." Fenton was glad that they weren't yet down to specifics. It gave him a chance to think.

"I went down there once to do a little business. This mule man had his mules on a high line. Had a three-legged pig too, lyin' there in the shade.

"'See you got a three-legged pig,' I says to him. Right off he goes to tellin' me about how smart that pig is. Saved his child, run off a robber, even fetched the man back from the field when his place took fire.

"'Damn smart pig,' he said. And I sure had to agree.

"'How come only three legs?' I asked. And I was curious. Pig lyin' there satisfied as a fat coon.

"'If you had a pig that smart,' he says to me, 'bet you wouldn't eat him all at once, either.'

"Well. Right then I concluded not to trade with that man. I suspect those Army traders found the same man. Bet that old pig was missin' another leg by then too."

He studied his mules out in the meadow. "I'll just bring some in so you'll see what I'm givin' you." He took a feedbag and walked out, shaking the feed and clucking to the Morgan.

"Still aimin' to romance that man?" Tommy asked Fenton as they watched Eban soothe the mare as she nosed at the feed. "You know that story wasn't just for fun."

"Hell, Tommy, we don't need thirty damn mules."

"Let's take whatever he offers and go home. Fuck it up and we might romance ourselves into no legs at all."

Three days later Tommy was riding Pinto as he led the belled Morgan toward Missoula. Thirty-two mules were lined out behind, not a one of them tied but each sure of his place in the ragged line following the Morgan. Fenton brought up the rear. He knew there was no need to ride drag behind such devoted animals, but he liked watching them anyway, learning about them as he watched. He was still digesting all the things he'd learned from Eban Hardin during the days they'd spent with him. Every time the man opened his mouth Fenton picked up something new—about how to get a mule to lead, or to pick up his feet, or to get relaxed under his packs.

Fenton had learned a thing or two about trading too. The Hardins had Tommy's spotted horses now, along with all their money. Eban also had some promises from Fenton that Fenton was hoping he'd forget. But all in all, Fenton figured it had been worth it. He might have too many mules—but he'd gotten irreplaceable training in mulemanship.

The whole transaction had certainly cheered Will Hardin. Fenton thought the man enjoyed getting rid of his father's mules even more than he enjoyed counting the money. He'd seemed almost happy drinking by the fire after they shook on the deal. Eban himself was more philosophical. He was mostly concerned about how they'd get the mules back to the Swan.

8

Higher Education

"Important thing is to keep them quiet, comfortable," Eban had instructed them—meaning stay off the main roads. Which they did, working their way down the valley on little lanes east of the Bitterroot, crossing it here and there both to shorten their route and to get the mules ready for the Clark Fork crossing. There were no problems, though Tommy was sure they would come. He worried about when as he led the belled Morgan, the mules lined out behind. Now and then he'd look back at Fenton, wondering if Fenton was worried about anything at all.

The Clark Fork bothered him the most. Wide as the river was, it was swift, its bottom ever shifting. And before they could drop down to cross, they'd have to get by the university. Getting past a campus full of students would be entirely different from moving along these quiet lanes, just cattle and a few deer watching—and occasional onlookers, curious and silent as the mules jogged past.

"It's a low-water year," Eban had told them. "And that river's spread wide right in the bottom. That's your best bet. Some of these mules ain't even been halter-broke. They'll ford. But they'll mistrust that bridge. You could have some bad wrecks on it. Draw a crowd too."

"We'll ford the damn river then," Fenton had said, reaching for the bottle they'd been passing around the fire and pouring. "Don't want a ruckus. What worries Tommy—me too, to tell the truth—is having all of our mules trailin' along loose when we slip by that campus. Some might drift off." He added more to Tommy and Eban's cups to underscore his point.

"Your people ever steal mules," he asked Tommy, "without tail-tyin' them or earin' them down—or some damn thing?"

"Heard no stories about mules," Tommy said. "Never had a mare like that Morgan to use if we did."

"They stick with her because they've lived with her," Eban declared. "They might stick with your pinto—if she'd lived with them. But she ain't. My Morgan has. Might just trade her for them spotted horses of yours. Help you out."

Fenton was taken aback. Eban already had their money. Now he wanted to trade their four horses for his one. The spotted horses were no prize, but it was hard to believe the Morgan was worth all four.

"She's your best bet," Eban concluded, draining his cup as though that settled it. "And don't carry on about my generosity. I'll just count on a few more favors when the time comes." He held out his cup and Fenton found himself pouring again. He was pretty sure Eban wasn't trying to best him, but a man should at least look apologetic for how off-balance this trade was becoming.

"Hope the favors aren't too dear," Fenton said. "Or come too soon. Half these mules don't lead. The other half don't pack. Be good to bring a little money in before you take more away."

"They'll pack. Put something on that rattles and run 'em around the corral. Then point that Morgan down the trail. They'll follow."

"You do put a lot of stock in her." Fenton seemed stopped by how little headway he was making with this man. "What's her name?"

"Morgan. She answers to that."

"And does this mule answer to Mule?" A tall roan mule had left the others and come into the ring of light. He was watching Fenton's fire as though hypnotized.

"That's my Bogus mule. Damned if I know what he's all about. Can't resist a fire. Comes in regular to contemplate it."

Which is what Bogus was doing that last night before they were to cross Clark Fork. Horace Adams had found a big holding pasture on the edge of town. They were camped there, and again Bogus seemed fascinated by their fire. But as sociable as Bogus was, the mule did little to quiet Tommy's worries. And Fenton's were growing larger.

"I'd worry too," said Horace. He was at once doubtful and intrigued by what Fenton and Tommy were undertaking. "It's not crossing the damn river so much as getting past that campus. Hang right close to Sentinel Mountain. Slip around above the football field. When they're in class. Things quiet. . . . Risky though. Lotta mules."

Cautionary as Horace was, Fenton suspected he had no idea how wrong things could go. Horace sold feed to everyone around Missoula. He'd already heard how people were turning out to watch the mules pass. It was possible the people of Missoula would be as taken by the procession as those in the Bitterroot—and as quiet. But students could be another matter, which concerned Fenton even more than Horace. The last thing he wanted was a bunch of amused students pointing and calling out and trying to befriend a jumpy mule. He'd run into some fraternity boys one night at The Bar of Justice—swearing and raising hell and wanting to go upstairs but too drunk to be allowed. Only one made any sense, a sober one some wise sheriff sent down to get the drunk ones out before the law had to do it. It didn't seem logical to that sheriff to bring the law in to rescue a place that wasn't supposed to exist. It was an unusual sheriff's decision, and Fenton admired it.

He figured most sheriffs needed a duty to perform, even if the duty was hazy. He didn't want some sheriff feeling he had any duty whatsoever concerning his mules, not until they were far enough through Missoula that all any officer could say was, "Keep going. You're in too far to turn back."

He was resigned to the fact that Morgan's bell would be ringing. Each morning that bell had worked its magic, calming the mules and luring them off behind Morgan just as Eban promised. They followed that bell as though drawn by some Pied Piper. All Fenton and Tommy could do was count on what had worked so far.

Not long after dawn they were headed for the campus, Morgan's bell musical in the still air, the mules moving comfortably in its wake, satisfied after their good night's feed on the rich grass of the big pasture.

Two hours later Morgan's bell sounded more like a fire-alarm as she sprinted out onto the broad green of the campus oval, her long lead-line bouncing and popping behind her. Students, pouring out of classrooms in response to the clanging bell, watched in disbelief as Custer, with Fenton bent low over his withers, raced onto the oval in pursuit.

They were almost past the stadium when it happened. Workmen repairing the bleachers heard the bell. Astonished to see a string of mules filing past, two of them dropped the boards they were carrying, the planks cracking onto the concrete like rifle shots. The report sent Morgan scrambling backward so fiercely she almost pulled Tommy from his saddle. Unable to hold the lead any longer, Tommy watched helplessly as Morgan staggered backward and fell, rolling back into the mules who'd crowded in behind her. They whirled back into one another as she came up, legs in motion almost before she was upright so she could sprint away toward the quiet heart of the campus. Fenton, knowing she was the key to everything, spurred Custer past the roiling mules in pursuit, making Morgan sprint even faster as the swirling mules collected themselves so they could follow, Tommy and his pinto now a part of the herd—no longer in charge of anything.

Students gathered around the oval closed ranks behind Custer and Fenton as they burst onto the green in pursuit of Morgan. A warning whoop from Tommy came just in time for them to part again and let the mules pour out onto the oval themselves. Only Bogus—veering away at the last moment—went another way, the big roan clattering up a stone stairway onto a portico and disappearing through big doors into the coolness inside.

Out on the oval, Morgan—bucking and fishtailing to free herself from the pesky rope—finally skidded to a halt, legs splayed and quivering, eyes wild as she realized the lead-line was at last still, no longer the terrifying thing that had followed her so mercilessly since she'd torn it from Tommy's hands.

Halter cockeyed, long lead-line off to one side, her body shaking, Morgan fixed her attention entirely on Fenton now. He was on foot and slowly approaching her, his voice low, his movements unhurried. As he soothed her, he realized a student was standing not ten feet from the end of Morgan's lead. The man was big, almost as tall as Fenton but broader, thicker, sporting a sweater with a fat M.

"I'm talking to this mare right here," Fenton told the man, his voice low and steady even as he gave instructions. "When I say so you just nab that lead right quick. I'll just keep her mind on me until the time's right." Fenton wished he had a nosebag, but all he could do was hold out a hand and hope she'd think something good might be in it.

"Ain't I seen you somewhere before?" Fenton asked the man, his voice still low as he watched Morgan, tempting her with his hand. "Weren't you the one who quieted those wild boys down at The Bar of Justice?" He hoped it was the same man. He needed someone sensible—and strong. He moved a little closer, Morgan still edgy but growing curious, wanting to know what was in the hand.

"I guess I am," the big man said, his voice as calm and soothing as Fenton's. "I'll edge up on the rope and be ready."

Meanwhile, Bogus was trotting down the cool corridor. It was comforting after all the confusion outside, but still he wanted a way out. He knew his place was out there with Morgan and the rest.

A lab door was open; the lone student inside so engrossed in his experiment he'd not heard all the commotion and bell-ringing. Looking up, he was startled to see a mule watching him from the doorway. Jumping to his feet he upset his Bunsen Burner, his instructions leaping into flames.

The flames lifted quickly as Bogus came farther into the room for a better look. The student scrambled backward, found a fire extinguisher and sprayed, smoke billowing up in clouds and further enthralling the big mule, who stepped still closer, hypnotized.

Not until the flames died did Bogus back out the door and trot up the corridor toward a worried instructor coming in to find the source of the smoke. The student with the fire extinguisher burst out of the room behind, and Bogus broke into a canter, knocking the instructor down as he sprinted out the wide doors and crossed the portico, clearing the stairs and a line of students in a long leap to join the others on the green oval.

Fenton was within a few feet of Morgan when she spun away to greet Bogus. As she did, the big student dove, clutched the lead, and found himself dragged until Fenton joined him, the two of them managing a dally around a sapling.

"Lucky you held on," Fenton said, working his way up the lead-line to calm the mare, who quieted quickly, even nuzzled at his hand. "Been hell to pay if this mare got away on us again. You've been a hero for me twice now. Never said your name."

"Trout." The man brushed grass from his sweater and wiped at the dirt on his face. "I've got more help here for you too." Other students had gathered around, some almost as big as Trout, the same M on their sweaters.

"We're Grizzlies," Trout said. "Tell us when and we'll wrestle down your mules. They do make a mess. Might even get you expelled—or tossed in the jailhouse."

"Expelled?" Fenton was amused. "I might should try that with *my* grizzlies. Hairier than yours—less reasonable too."

Fenton looked at the men, who seemed confused but determined. His mules were still trotting this way and that, leaving scars across the lawns as they spun away from students, farting and shooting out green dung as they did. It came to him that these men might actually try to wrestle them down.

"Let's save the wrestling," he said to Trout. "Though I do appreciate the offer." He looked at Trout's men. "You boys know this won't give any leg up at The Bar of Justice. Mule service don't quite equal female service, don't you know."

Tommy rode up then, his pinto at last under control. "If you quit jawin' at this man and let him take Morgan down to that river," he said, "we'll push the others along behind." He looked around at all the havoc they'd raised. "Didn't slip by so quiet-like, did we?"

Students were packed around the oval now, the mules held within the big circle but scooting away whenever someone got close. "We'll make it, Tommy," Fenton said, still enjoying his talk with Trout. "We caught our bell-mare—and we got Trout's boys here to direct our traffic."

He turned back to the big man. "Just lead this mare down that bank to the river. Ring her bell now and then too. It'll perk up interest." He handed him the lead. "If your boys'll step back and make a lane, we'll ease our mules right along behind."

"Damnedest thing," he added, confiding in Trout who held the lead-line now. "They'll come to this mare just like your boys'll head off for that Bar of Justice." Don't have as much fun, but they sure do like the idea."

In an hour they were all down at the river. No one hurt except one of Trout's men who managed to get his belt around Bogus's neck and got dragged for his effort. But he made no complaint, not wanting to admit it hurt because what hurt mostly was his pride. Bogus hadn't even minded, shaking the man off and joining the others happily, the belt still snug around his neck.

Tommy led Morgan into the rapids, the mules lined out behind, calm as if they were still coming down the Bitterroot. A dean and a man from the sheriff's office had shown up, both trying to look stern but neither quite sure of what to do.

They were standing there with Trout's Grizzlies when Fenton herded Bogus in, the big mule happy to be bringing up the rear, the belt still buckled around his neck.

"Well," Fenton said as he rode up to the dean, "don't you bother to have your boys send any thank-you notes. College life surely gets drear. Glad we could spice it up."

He sat there on Custer, thinking about it.

"Might even be more learnin' from my mules than from your books anyway," he added. "Ask your Grizzlies here. They might remember us long after them books head south."

Custer was belly-deep in the rapids when Fenton called back, yelling to be heard above the water. "We'll send the belt back postal," he called. "For when your boy gets his long pants."

9

Coming Through

"Never seen anything like it. That's the gospel." Horace was still a little stunned by what Fenton and Tommy had done, and done in the late spring when the Clark Fork should have been high, the campus so busy you could barely get a saddle horse through, much less thirty mules. He was standing in the sun outside Fenton's corral talking through the bars as Tommy and Fenton introduced Bogus and some of the four-year-olds to packing. They'd already sacked them out and gotten their pack-saddles fitted. Now they were tying down panniers filled with empty cans, letting the mules fight the noise until they learned the rattling wasn't going to hurt them.

"It's what Eban told us to do," Fenton explained, watching his mules move around the corral. "He was right on this one too. I been tyin' some of those yearlings to that cut burro over there too. Spend a few days being dragged around by that burro and they lead like they been tied to a bendy limb."

"Which works best?" Horace was always startled by what these packers knew. "The burro or the bendy limb?"

"Damned if I know. Use either—or both, if it gets them to lead. 'Get 'em wed to a nosebag too. Handy when it's catch-up time."

"You know they're saying that man Trout is the best linebacker those Grizzlies ever had?" Horace, who loved football, went right back to what had been on his mind in the first place. "If he hadn't spoke up for you, I believe that sheriff would have give you a ticket."

"For the fire or just for my mules' general behavior? Truth is none of it would have happened if the damn students had stayed inside with their books." Fenton stepped back to see if the packs on his mule were even. "Never had a lick of trouble after we shook free of them. Come up the Blackfoot to the Clearwater, followed it up over this little divide. Here we are on the Swan. Safe and sound. Ready to collect my Forest Service money."

"You send that belt back? One of your mules ran off with that man's belt."

"Paint Boy took a shine to it and I let it be. He's been so sorry around here I'm thankful he'll take to anything. Skinny enough so it near goes around him twice." Fenton scooted the mule off toward the center of the corral, the mule kicking at the sounds of the cans before running a few steps and skidding to a halt, startled by the sudden quiet.

Fenton watched, amused. "Paint Boy's a worry," he turned back to Horace. "Somethin' inside him won't let go. Only time his sister ever looks blue is when she sees how blue he is."

Fenton thought Hope was so capable she could do anything she wanted—if her brother weren't dragging her down. He thought it was like her to sense the darkness in someone else, to turn and turn each night, sleepless with worry about her brother.

"Come to a game and watch that Trout play," Horace said, liking things he could understand better than things he couldn't. "If a runner stays inbounds, he runs them down."

"Guess he's the chief Grizzly," Fenton said, fitting still another saddle on still another mule. "I didn't know what to make of all that grizzly talk—all them stout fellows standing there. I'm just glad we got your man Trout. He makes some sense." Fenton adjusted the breeching, moving gingerly in case the mule decided to object. "Though he might be too much the Boy Scout for my complete admiration."

"He's one tough Boy Scout. You can bet on that." Horace, a smallish man, was fascinated by the big man's sport, getting season tickets to the university games each year—going to many high school games as well. He was already convinced Trout would become famous.

"Could be he's a Mormon," Fenton speculated. "Though I doubt it. Sees too many sides to life."

"Goddamn it!" Horace was forever exasperated by how quickly Fenton could leave one subject for another. "I'm talking about what might be the greatest Grizzly ever and you're moanin' about the Mormons. At least they pay their feed bills. Support them wives they collect too."

"You got a damn good wife, Horace. Don't be telling me you want another." Fenton said. "Hell, I got you and Etta scheduled for a first-rate trip, once I get these mules lined out. It'll be another honeymoon. Just more adventurous. Etta won't have to go near the kitchen. I got Jasper Finn signed up permanent. . . . I think."

"What does 'I think' mean? I don't want Etta doin' all the cookin' like last time."

"Jasper'll be all right. He was just bending an elbow when he signed on—swearin' so much about the holy mother of this and the holy mother of that I wasn't sure he knew he was gonna be the holy mother of my kitchen. He'll be right back on earth in the mountains. Etta'll like his grub. Feel like royalty."

Jasper Finn was a wonderful cook when sober, but he could be remarkably uneven when not. Thinking about that possibility might take Horace's mind off football, but it did nothing to calm his wariness about Etta's attraction for Fenton.

Despite how church-going she was, despite her distaste for the drinking that went on in The Bar of Justice—a place she knew Fenton favored—she maintained an abiding affection for the packer. It was an affection that never sat easily with Horace, who too often found himself bested by some off-beat arrangement Fenton would dream up as he drove into town for a visit—and charm Etta into endorsing.

The last time Fenton had wound up convincing them to trade his feed store debt for being special guests on a fancy pack trip. The truth was that Fenton's trips always made Etta a little nervous—the high trails and rushing fords that Fenton crossed so casually scared her. It always irked Horace that when Fenton described them to her, she melted.

Horace liked the trips himself. He was looking forward to this one especially, knowing Fenton and Tommy would take them places few others knew. It was the spell Fenton would cast over Etta that rankled, even more than forgiving Fenton his debt, which had become considerable. He just couldn't help bristling a little when he watched Etta succumbing to the big man's off-hand ways and unpredictable stories.

None of it seemed to worry Tommy, who was too wrapped up in Hope Woman to notice much else. Paint Boy's blues worried him, of course, but mostly because they worried Hope. And by then Fenton's methods of settling his accounts in Missoula were more a spectator sport than a worry—as were Fenton's different ways of luring still more people into the mountains. None of it bothered Tommy, who was even thankful: it gave him a chance to be in his mountains still longer.

To Tommy, Fenton's bartering became the most natural thing in the world—for Fenton. As Paint Boy's state of mind seemed the most natural thing in the world—for Paint Boy. He thought anyone who surrendered so completely to the Black Robes' thinking had to become pretty blue anyway. And though he went back to the mission with Paint Boy to seek work for him, it was more because there was a chance of seeing Hope than from concern for Paint Boy. He had no doubt that they would need Paint Boy's knowledge to keep the frescos spruced up anyway, just as he had no doubt they would accept Paint Boy's devotion to the paintings— and to the gifted cook who had conceived them.

Tommy had known a man in his tribe who'd become devoted to another man, one more far-seeing and talented. He'd cooked and worked for that man just like a wife. He'd shared his tipi too. Tommy took that relationship as much in stride as had his uncles, who'd known other men who'd done the same. Paint Boy's devotion to the artist seemed no different, even though one of the Fathers took Paint Boy aside, lecturing him and scolding him and striking fear into him with warnings that the only thing that would save him would be to love the Lord. Above all else, the Father would tell Paint Boy, he must give himself to the Lord. No other.

Though the Black Robes let Paint Boy stay, giving him a place to sleep in the loft above where the cook had sketched his drawings and mixed his colors, it didn't take Tommy long to realize how heavy was the price the unsmiling Father made Paint Boy pay—in confession and penance and devotion.

After that, each time Fenton and Tommy saw Paint Boy he looked more wan and haunted. The belt seemed longer than ever as he tucked it through the loops, punching more holes with one of the cook's scalpels before going on to mix the colors needed to brighten the faded places, fill the chinks that were beginning to appear in the brilliant paintings. He would find exactly the right hues, choosing carefully with a love that calmed the gnawing unrest inside him, his confusion growing steadily from the things the unyielding Father told him.

It was on the trip with Horace and Etta that Jasper's brilliance as a cook— and his weakness for cooking sherry—established themselves most completely. When an ingredient was missing, he'd invent a substitute. When the rains came down, he'd turn his kitchen tent into a home for all. When a black bear poked its nose into the cook-tent, he chunked it so sharply with a piece of firewood the bear was gone for days.

Jasper was so proud of himself he preened. And though everyone knew he wouldn't have acted this way had he not been sipping cooking sherry, his decisiveness empowered his reputation permanently, despite his mortal fear of grizzlies—and black bears too—when sober.

The people on that trip came out of the mountains sharing a bond that would never break. Even Tommy Yellowtail—who often seemed a mystery on that trip, not blending with the country the way he usually did, distant from it in ways he didn't understand himself—became part of what made them whole.

Fenton understood what Tommy couldn't. At least he came as close to understanding it as anyone. He knew it was Hope Woman who filled Tommy's days, and Tommy's nights as well. And he understood why. He saw the life and brightness of her just as clearly as Tommy, but to him she was still a girl—the promise of the woman to come. To Tommy she was here and now and life itself: her struggles his struggles; her worries his; her needs, needs he must address.

Fenton saw it all so clearly because he could still see. Tommy couldn't. He was all feelings, which is where Fenton's understanding of him grew thin. He couldn't feel the ways Tommy did because Hope wasn't filling his world as she was Tommy's, wasn't crowding out all else and spilling across the margins of everything he did.

But what Tommy couldn't see—couldn't understand—made Hope no less real, no less consuming. It was a relief when he could free himself of what was inside him, though it was hardly a triumph. . . .

It was the only thing he could do.

They were together when they found him, Tommy and Fenton driving over from the Swan, Hope coming from the school to meet them, all of them going together to cheer Paint Boy with holiday trinkets fashioned from her busy hands. She was the first to climb into the loft, the first to see his feet as she climbed the steep mission ladder and come into the loft. His feet were level with her eyes, his body turning slowly in the still air, his face canted—engorged and bluish—his bulging eyes fixed. Fenton went by her as she crumbled, Tommy taking her into his arms at last, sheltering her against his broad chest as Fenton lifted the slip of a body, unhooking the long belt from that single nail. He pried loose the leather embedded in Paint Boy's neck, pushed back the swollen tongue, closed the mouth—tried to bring order to the wreck in his arms.

Hope could not stop shaking, no matter how closely Tommy held her. Tommy turned her face away as Fenton carried Paint Boy down the ladder, cleared the paints away on a table, rested the slender body there, covered it with a canvas. He went back to see if there was more to do, trying not to look as Tommy held the shaking Hope, Tommy's face as torn as hers. Tommy as helpless as she.

The note, held down by the heavy crucifix, offered what little explanation they would ever have. "I could not be good," those words crossed out in a single stroke and below, printed in Paint Boy's careful hand: "I am not good."

Fenton put the note in his pocket and went for the Black Robes. Someone would have to record what had happened. Someone would have to take care of the body. Someone would have to care for Hope Girl too.

None of it would be easy.

10

Moving On

Paint Boy's death was more than the Black Robes could bear. They had no heart for calling the authorities. Fenton had to take care of that himself. And when he realized how unwilling they were to deal with Paint Boy's body, he took care of that too, getting Paint Boy's uncles to come and return it to the Cheyenne.

The uncles came by rail. Fenton—still wary of what traveled the rails—met them inside the station in Missoula. They would stay just a few hours before turning around, taking the body back to the Rosebud, the reservation where the Cheyenne must now live.

"Paint Boy's mother got sick with the white man's disease," the older Cheyenne explained. "After she was gone, the father was gone too. After the money you get for doing pretend things in the white man's big show."

"Was that the Bill Cody show?" Fenton asked.

"Yes," the Cheyenne said. "He does that same work still. For the pictures that move. Sometimes he even sends money."

It was all too familiar to Fenton. "Could be I know that man," Fenton said. "Does he wear a shiny hat? A bowler?" Fenton pictured the man there by Cody's smoldering train, pictured him when he helped pack Fenton's mules, pictured him trying to look fierce in the shows they wanted them to do. Always wearing his shiny bowler; they could never get him to take off his shiny bowler.

"Yes," the older man said. "We call him Small Hat now. Wanted to be like the White Eyes. Had us send his children here to be taught by the White Eyes."

"Guess he thought money would make him happy," Fenton said. "This boy you've come for might actually have found it. Without money. . . . If they'd left him alone."

"Where is the sister?" the older Cheyenne wanted to know. "She should be with him."

"She's near become a Black Robe herself now. Though I wish she weren't. Wish she were with Tommy Yellowtail."

"Tommy Yellowtail?" the older man asked. "Who is Tommy Yellowtail?"

"Salish," Fenton explained. "He went the other way. Think he's found his happiness—the other way."

Fenton did what must be done, clearing away the debris left in Paint Boy's wake. It was no chore compared with what consumed him most: his need to understand. It was beyond him that the father could have left his children so abruptly, that Paint Boy could reject life so completely, so grotesquely. He wanted to talk with Hope, learn if there were roots in the Cheyenne that might twist people into such despair. But he found that impossible. She had gone into some other world.

Something told Fenton that no good would come of it anyway. Hope Girl wanted to leave understanding and embrace faith. He wanted to reach above faith and find understanding. She was going out a door he wanted to enter. He saw no way to frame the difference.

He tried to talk with the head Father, the man who had been so censorious with Paint Boy after Paint Boy returned to the mission. But that proved impossible as well.

"Father is in prayer," a Black Robe told Fenton, coming to the door of the mission, looking up at him with a bewilderment that seemed to run as deep as the questions nagging Fenton.

"His duty is penance," the Black Robe said, as though bordering on some dark sin himself. "For what would not stay in the boy's heart. For what he could not put into the boy's heart."

He looked at Fenton as though Fenton might offer the grounding he had lost.

"Will confession help?" he asked Fenton, "Communion?"

"No." Fenton replied, made bluer by the need coming up through the Black Robe's words. "I don't think it will," he said. "Not me . . . not any of us." But in his heart he knew he could be wrong, knew it even as he spoke to the man. Tommy and Hope did need some peace, some forgiveness—some freedom from these things they had no way to understand. So did this Black Robe.

He was the one who could not be helped. Who needed so to see. No matter how dark a picture it was."

The child was born in the fall, a boy with a grip so firm Fenton knew it must have come from a powerful fusion. Prohibition had come too, just as Doc Messler had predicted. But that changed little for Fenton, or for Missoula. Fenton took Tommy to The Bar of Justice to celebrate, amused that Tommy had no interest in going upstairs on this day. He was interested only in what he'd created—the power and perfection of the child. And in the glass of whisky before him.

"He takes hold of my hand," he told Fenton, "and I think he'll never let go."

"Maybe he won't," Fenton said, "though maybe you'll come to wish he would. Boys can play hell with fathers. It's nature's truth." He sipped the bourbon Doc Messler had provided. "Does Hope take hold of your hand too?" Happy as he was with the good bourbon, Fenton was deeply concerned about Hope Girl, who had clung to Tommy after they'd found Paint Boy in ways as much beyond his understanding as Paint Boy's despair had been.

Hope had not asked Tommy for marriage or commitment or promise— she'd just needed him, the reality of him. Fenton knew Tommy would have given her anything she wanted, had she asked. Or had Tommy known. But she did not ask. And Tommy did what he must—stayed with her through the days and nights, filled her with the power of his love, his need.

"They have taken away her school job," Tommy said, putting down his glass and considering the warm brown of the liquid. "Good as she is at it, they won't let her teach. They won't leave her be either. They are there all the time now."

"And they will be," Fenton said. "Bet they pray for her too. I'm commencin' to think that's the only way they know to work these things out."

Later that night he told Beth about it, how pleased Tommy was about the child, how baffled Tommy was by Hope Girl. Beth watched Fenton as he talked, held him as he talked, feeling a deep sadness well up in her as she did. She didn't like thinking about the mother, and child, about all the pain ahead for them in this world.

She knew it all too well.

They named him Special Hands, and as Hope grew more lost—distracted and distant—it was Tommy's mother who took him in. She seemed to sense that Special Hands would be the boy Tommy had never been. Special

Hands had the brightness of his mother, the steadiness of his father. And he grew up harboring no anger for the prayers the Black Robes made him recite, nor for the verities they tried to plant inside him. He paid no attention to them at all, learning his letters from the Sisters and the ways of the mountains from Fenton and Tommy and taking on an early independence because things came to him so easily: how to learn from tracks, how to predict the flight of game, how to separate fable from fact in the tales of the tribe and in the teachings of the Black Robes.

From the first he was clever with his hands. Tommy taught him the Kootenai way of hunting deer and wapiti, how to tan their hides as the Kootenai did. Tommy worked with him slowly, taught him carefully, explaining in his halting way why the boy's mother was going to serve in the monastery of the Sisters, why she would take vows and wed the Church, would know another life. When Tommy would try to explain the logic behind it all, Special Hands' mind would drift off even as he scraped and kneaded the hide under his fingers, his thoughts no longer on the trail his father was pointing out but on other trails leading far away. Special Hands somehow realized that Tommy's explanations could take him no place useful.

Fenton watched and found himself turning more and more to the mountains, sad to think that all the promise he'd seen in Hope Girl was gone. He took comfort in the fact that the mountains were immutable, their seasons regular, the life they supported constant. He loved the secrets of the trails and the majesty of the passes that took him from drainage to drainage. He loved to watch the fast water that grew from the ice and snow of the high cirques, water that ran down through the centuries to cut the canyons that fed the South Fork. After Paint Boy's death, he found a deeper solace in riding those trails than he could explain—only realizing that he found more comfort in the country than he found in the people waiting to be taken into it.

He knew that something had happened inside him.

Most of the people in the Swan knew something had happened to him too. In only a few years his black hair had turned into a white whiter than the snow he crossed on the passes. They would comment on it to Horace when Horace brought out supplies from Missoula, stocking Murphy's store, bringing feed and tack and canvas for Fenton.

"I do believe that packing business has run your friend ragged," Dan Murphy would say. "It's whited his hair even as it made him all that money. But I think it's mostly Doc Messler's whisky that makes him all that money. He takes plenty of his booze on them trips."

"You know damn well it's more than whisky that makes people want to follow Fenton into them mountains. You sell whisky your own self. You count on it. If it gets legal again, you just might go belly up. Fenton won't."

"Are you saying what else I sell here ain't as good as what else Fenton offers up in his mountains? Or what they rent down at The Bar of Justice? All I'm sayin' is that he's different. He'll stay in business no matter what. It's just that if he'd buy his liquor from me, I might could find a way to get rich along with him."

"Fenton's another kind of rich. No way he'll change. You should be quiet and stay thankful."

Horace wouldn't say what else was on his mind, because he didn't want to go on too long about what he knew Fenton had done—for all of them. Horace no longer bridled when Etta carried on about Fenton; he took it in stride. Since Fenton and Tommy had made the packing business so successful, people were coming from all over the country to see their mountains. It was good for Horace's business and for Dan Murphy's too. It was good for the Swan and Missoula—even good for The Bar of Justice.

Horace thought it was good for everybody, except maybe for Fenton, which was a worry that nagged him. Fenton had a way of making things work for people. His trips became a kind of home even for Jasper, who, despite all the trouble his alcohol-prone ways got him into during the winters, was put to productive use through the long summers and into the fall. And they were good for Tommy, who found a life packing for Fenton he could never have realized without him. And what the three of them did spun off to help others. The busier they were, the better. If they had two trips running, Tommy would take one and Fenton the other. Dan Murphy's wife, Rosie, could be pressed into service as a second cook. Old man Conner's son, Buck, almost a regular by then, could ferry a string with resupplies for one party and then go out and resupply the next. And if they needed another wrangler, Gus Wilson would leave his sawmill and fill in.

Gus was probably the most level-headed man in the Swan—until Cody Jo came along and turned his head so sharply a snag tore a chunk from his face. The wound taught Gus that it hurt a lot more to have a broken heart no one could see than a deep scar everyone could. The scar might be more noticeable, but it didn't compare with what was not, a lesson that stuck with him forever.

Of course, some say Cody Jo tore off a big part of the Swan as well. But almost all would go on to say she put a bigger part back. She certainly put a big part back in Fenton.

His hair might have turned white, but all that life in Cody Jo made him green again on the inside. Horace saw it, realizing that after she started running the school, he never had to worry about Fenton again.

11

The Schoolteacher

Horace Adams was the first to meet her. His job was to pick her up at the station and drive her out to the Swan, a duty he took seriously enough to clean out the cab of his truck, put on a pressed shirt, and wear his Sunday Stetson. The general consensus was that the School Board might be taking a chance, but there'd been only three candidates, and most of the people up in the Swan had been persuaded—as the board had been—by her letter.

She wanted to see the West, she'd written, in a clear hand, and had a particular interest in small western communities. She went on to say that she liked kids and kids liked her and that she didn't see why ones with dirty hands from the chores they did before school shouldn't learn to like reading and doing numbers just as much as town kids who weren't burdened with any chores at all.

They'd liked it too that her childhood in Virginia had taught her something about horses. But they liked even better the record she'd established at her college in Massachusetts — grades as good in math as in literature, with courses in art and voice and drama thrown in. They were a little nervous about her being only twenty-four and that the recommendation of her college dean had pointed out that besides being a gifted student, she was strong-willed and modern, a woman who didn't hesitate to take a stand when she saw a wrong.

They thought many of the women out in the Swan were that way anyhow, concluding it was an attitude that made life more interesting— even if occasionally troublesome—and let it pass.

Horace, who'd been spending more and more time hauling feed out to Fenton and Tommy, had been asked his opinion too. He remembered having some reservations, but they seemed to take flight when she walked up to him at the station

"I'm Cody Jo Taylor," she'd said, surprising Horace with her sure hand-shake, though he couldn't recall extending his hand at all. But there she was shaking it, and taking him in. She was taller than he expected, her manner so direct, her interest in him so complete, that all his doubts dissolved.

"And you must be Horace Adams, my designated guide," she'd continued, dropping his hand and taking his arm and letting him carry her suitcase until they reached the truck. Once there she retrieved it and tossed it into the truck-bed as though to make way for more serious things—like talk.

She was in a darkish crepe dress topped by a white collar. There was a long stride and a slenderness about her that suggested boyishness, an impression dispelled immediately by the warmth of her smile. She popped into the cab even before Horace thought to open her door. He could only walk around and climb in himself. The truck misfired a few times before it caught, and they coughed and sputtered their way through Missoula and onto the road toward Bonner.

The engine smoothed out as they went up the Blackfoot, winding through river-bottom ranches, Cody Jo peppering Horace with questions. How many students in the eighth grade? Where did they go on to high school? What did the Murphys carry in their store? What was the cabin like that would be hers? How far was it from the school? Was it lumber or ranching that kept things going up in the Swan? Was there music? A community band? A church?

Horace answered as best he could, offering hazy responses when he couldn't provide sure ones. Most of all he tried to keep up with Cody Jo, who spliced so many questions about his own life into the ones about the Swan he thought she might wind up knowing more about him than Etta did. While answering still another question about Etta it came to him that he might be learning more from figuring out how to answer her questions than she was learning from him. It was astonishing how many things interested her. And she listened closely to whatever he said, often drawing her next question from his own answer, as though to clear away any underbrush from what he meant to say.

Which is why so much emerged from her questions about Murphy's store. "People get most all their supplies in town," he told her, settling in because he really did know the answer to this one. "But one of our lumber-jacks might need a file for his saw or some guy might need wire for a chicken coop or a dab of blue gentian for his mare. And then a packer might stop in for some coffee or a glass of that beer Dan makes. I believe the Murphys carry a little bit of everything you might think up."

"Packers? Is there a lot of moving around in the Swan?"

It came to Horace why he'd found himself so off-balance at the train station. Though he was almost distracted by her prettiness, the way her dark coloring set off the deep blue of her eyes, she paid no attention to it whatsoever, not unless it was helping her gather more information. She used it now, her posture perfect as she turned toward him, her smile both accepting the silliness of packing up a household and asking why anyone would need to. She even reached out to touch him, as though they were enjoying some unspoken irony together.

Light as that touch was, it seemed to free something in Horace. He had no idea of how it happened, just knew it had. He was startled by how engaged with life this woman made him feel, how much he wanted to help her, how surely he knew he could.

"Packers, here . . . they aren't what you think." He searched for the right words, needing to make her understand. "They help the rest of us get up into those mountains, you see."

The Swan Range, just appearing to the east, looked purplish in the distance, the white of unmelted snow showing bluish in the crevices. "There's no way to get into them things," he lifted his hand, pointing. "Except with our packers. They know the trails. Know places to camp. Know how to get your bedrolls in and put you under canvas. Keep you comfortable. They know the streams. Where the game is. Know to keep the damn bears out of camp." Horace looked at the schoolteacher, her attention on him so complete he realized he'd never before felt as full of Fenton's high country as at that very moment. "They make it so a man can live up there. Show you things you never dreamed. Why, they can take you all the way to where the water starts for the Missouri," he said finally. . . . "Don't know how we'd get along without our packers."

Cody Jo, so moved by Horace's sudden eloquence, she was searching for words herself, found herself stammering, "I . . . I must learn about this," she said finally. "I must learn how they do all this."

"With their mules, you see. Their mules. And they always find those rascals in the morning. That's the trick. Findin' them in the mornin'. They can be slick bastards. They'll wander."

Horace's admiration for how Tommy and Fenton handled their mules was so complete he entirely forgot his promise to Etta to watch his language with this new schoolteacher.

"Who are these men?" she asked. "These packers? I'm not sure I have the entire picture. Maybe I'll learn when their children come to the school."

"Hell, could be that some old boy who packs has a kid in school, but Fenton and Tommy Yellowtail don't. You'd learn most from them."

"Are packers Indians?" Horace was so wrapped up in his own explanations it was hard for her to squeeze in the question.

"Flathead. Tommy is. His kid, Spec—Special Hands to the tribe—was in school. For a while. Fenton's just Fenton. God only knows what he is. Hair black as a raven a few years ago; now gone to white. He might have a kid. God's the only who'd know that too. And I guess the mama."

"Goodness." Cody Jo settled back in her seat, sorting out what Horace's explanations might mean. "Parent conferences in the Swan could be a challenge."

"Not a worry, Miss Taylor. These folks want their kids to learn just as much as anyone. They just don't have a damn bit of time to help out." He smiled at her, more and more relaxed after his outburst. "I doubt many could help much anyway."

"I think you should call me Cody Jo, Mr. Horace Adams." She smoothed the wrinkles from her skirt and looked out at the trees. "And I should think this beautiful country would make these people want to write about it. Don't you think so?" They were past Seeley Lake now, the lodgepoles thicker as they neared the Swan. The way she drank in its richness made Horace, consider more carefully just what he was saying.

"I kinda wonder if they have the time," he said quietly. "They're so busy fightin' it, don't you see—one way or the other. Lumberjacks trying to mill enough trees to get by this year—and still have some for next. Ranchers trying to put enough feed in this year's cattle—but leave enough to fat up next year's mamas. It goes on that way. Year in and year out."

He sensed her concern about the hardness of it all and shifted back to the positive. "I believe Tommy and Fenton are the ones who get along with the country best. And Tommy's boy, Spec. They get to live with it, don't you know. No need to fight it. And it puts food on their table. That ain't a bad deal . . . the way I look at it."

He pulled into a dusty lot before a square building with a sign hanging from the porch saying "Murphy's Store."

"Here we are. The rest can hang fire. You'll have answers soon enough." He opened his door and hurried around to open hers. "And you'll like it. Rosie puts out a good feed." Cody Jo stirred herself and climbed from the cab to look around, surprised by how small the store seemed to be.

"Don't you worry." Horace was glad to be rid of his philosopher role and return to being a guide. "This is only the food part. Dan keeps all the gear he sells back in his barn. There's lots."

A wiry woman came out of the store and took Cody Jo's hand in hers. "You have to be Cody Jo Taylor. And you're tall." Her smile was a tangle of wrinkles and pleasure. "We worried you might be too young. Glad we overlooked that. Tall will do just fine."

She was so warm and positive Cody Jo couldn't help taking to her. A man smoking a pipe followed. "I'm Rosie and this," the woman jabbed a thumb over her shoulder, "is the other half. We got Buck too. He's down there cleaning your cabin—with Angie. They'll have it spruced right up."

"I'm Dan Murphy," the man with the pipe said. "Rosie's talking so fast she hasn't yet told you we got your cabin plumbed. Works good. Ask Buck. He's not havin' near as much success with Angie as he is with the plumbing. I believe she's more mysterious to him than that water closet." He laughed and tapped ashes from his pipe.

"We brought Angie down from north of Whitefish," Rosie explained. Best we ever had. Works hard—keeps Buck in line too. Mostly."

"She might just go off in Buck's face if he doesn't slow to a trot," Dan said. "He's a lot more persuasive in his mind than he is in hers."

"Told you you'd get to know us pretty fast," Horace said to Cody Jo, still holding her suitcase. "Before we give you the complete history, let's get you to your cabin. Let you freshen. That's why that school board voted on the plumbing. Ain't that so, Rosie?"

"Good God yes." Rosie was all smiles and apologies. "We're just silly about havin' you here. Our schoolteacher. Bet you're tuckered — and hungry." They moved together along a lane that led behind the barn. A few cabins were scattered in the trees, one of them with scraps of lumber still stacked on the side. It was to be Cody Jo's.

"You can't say we don't care about our teachers," Dan Murphy said. "Had to borrow Buck from Fenton to get this damn thing built." They stood there, appreciating it, the stain on it seeming to dry as they watched. "Not that Buck didn't jog right on over when he heard there was a chance to sniff around Angie."

A door opened and Angie herself stood there, short and perky, her sleeves rolled up, a mop in her hand, her clothes baggy from all the bending and scrubbing she'd been doing. They heard a rush of water behind her, as though someone were draining a water trough.

Angie wiped hair from her forehead, blushing a little as everyone's attention fixed on her. "Buck's so caught up by that water tank," she explained, "he can't stop pullin' the chain."

"This is our new teacher," Rosie interrupted. "You and Buck got the cabin ready?"

"And you're Angie," Cody Jo said, extending her hand. "I'm Cody Jo Taylor. I'm certainly lucky to have you around."

"And by God everything in her works," said a young cowboy appearing in the doorway behind Angie. His shirt was partly untucked and a pant-leg had caught in his boot. "The cabin, I mean," he said, quieting as he realized they were watching him.

"You must be Buck," Cody Jo said. "I've heard about you too."

"She's the new schoolteacher," Angie said to Buck. "You should get to know her. For manners I mean. Doesn't hurt to have some."

It might have been because Angie's voice gentled a little toward the end. It might have been because Cody Jo was standing there, smiling and warm as she looked at him. But suddenly Buck was unsure of himself—tucking in his shirt and straightening his hat.

"My brother Bump, he still goes," Buck said, as if it were something Cody Jo needed to know. "To the school. I went too, a few years back. Before Fenton took me on." He gestured out across the woods where the Swan Range lifted, as though the mountains might explain things.

"Isn't Fenton the packer you told me about?" Cody Jo asked Horace. She couldn't forget that name. "In the truck?"

"He is," Horace replied, shifting her suitcase to his other hand. "He is indeed a packer. But then he's a lot of other things too. . . ."

"How many other things?" Cody Jo wanted to know.

"Well," Horace said, considering. "Some of us are still figurin' that out."

12

Teaching

The next day Rosie took Cody Jo to the schoolhouse, which served for other functions as well: bingo games and bake-sales, community meetings, and voting—even an occasional religious service, if a minister was handy. But it was most popular for the seasonal dances, organized in large part by the Murphys and advertised on the bulletin board at their store, which was why Rosie knew the building so well.

There was a large coatroom just inside the front door where various country gear could be stored—or a bar improvised, tickets collected, registration tables manned. It also acted as a buffer against winter chill for the big room. That was where the teaching was done—or the dances held or the weddings or whatever might be scheduled.

Cody Jo was comfortable with it. It seemed pretty much like the grange halls she'd found spotted around New England. There was a cupola where a bell could be hung, giving it a nice symmetry and a certain churchlike quality, which Cody Jo favored. She had little affection for formal religion but maintained a firm belief in earnest thinking, which she thought most religions tended to champion as long as the earnestness didn't stray too far from their canon.

"Doesn't look like much now," Rosie said, watching Cody Jo surveying the bare walls. "But it'll fix up. You should see what we do with it for the dances. It's even electrified. I tell 'em 'decide what you want and I'm your man,'" she laughed. "I like to say 'I'm your man.' I can be a demon with that crepe paper."

"Electrified?" Cody Jo was as astonished by how casually Rosie delivered the news as she was by the news itself.

"Same guy that showed the Wilson brothers how to throw up this building. He was coming through from Maine, of all places—and doin' every derned thing at full speed. 'You need a town hall,' he says. And he designed one. 'I'll electrify it,' he says. And he got the Conners to build a little flume by the creek, and damned if we weren't electrified."

"What happened to that man?" Cody Jo was impressed by the man's energy and resourcefulness. She thought some of it must have rubbed off on Rosie.

"When this hall was half-built he up and says, 'See you latah.'" Just that way. He says to me, 'I'm understandin' that Seattle needs electrification too.'" Rosie enjoyed imitating the accent. "'And Seattle is on the watah.' Said it just like that. . . . Then he left. Never has come back. We wish he would. Ever time there's a storm the creek picks up and the lights sputter. Which is why we got a back-up generator on order. Come winter it gets dark at four. Hell, in winter everything needs a back-up—just to back up the back-ups."

Cody Jo was amused. "I think what I need to learn, Rosie Murphy, is how to keep up with you." She couldn't help laughing. "I haven't had to absorb this much information since college. At least yours is more interesting."

She took Rosie's arm and they walked outside to sit on the schoolhouse steps under the September sun. "Why did you and Dan come here?" she wanted to know. "Why do some people come and make a home and others just keep going? Tell me about the Swan. What made that man from Maine pass right on through? Why did you and Dan stay?"

"Jesus. Now you *are* soundin' like a schoolteacher." Rosie sounded resigned. "I sometimes wonder about it myself. Some think it has something to do with that." She pointed up toward the Swan Range. "It's a wild country up there. Kind of holds your attention. Snow melting all summer, starting all this water running. Fenton and Tommy Yellowtail are comfortable as can be with it. Others get edgy, think there's too much that can go wrong."

"Wrong? From what Horace told me it's wonderful. Don't people pay those men to lead them around to look at things?"

"Horace won't tell the full story. Which is that he's one of the edgy ones himself. When there's no Fenton or Tommy to take care of things, he won't go up there."

"Take care of what? Horace claims that you just have to go where they point you."

"He was romancin' you." Rosie shook her head. "What he didn't tell you is that your mules could roll into a river. Or a black bear might nose around and steal your dinner. Or a grizzly roar through and kill a horse, or chase your stock off so far it takes days to find 'em. Or that it can snow in August or freeze hail out of the sky. Or that some moose might run down a hill and kill you. Happened to that ranger—moose killed him dead as dust."

Cody Jo, having a hard time taking it all in, was at a loss for what to say. "Then why do those men go up there?" she asked. What do they gain by putting themselves in harm's way like that?"

"Fenton says it's to understand where the waters begin. Says Tommy already knows. Has it right there inside him. Claims he had to learn it for himself. You'll have to meet Fenton. He has these theories. Makes 'em pretty believable too."

"Does he make them believable to you."

"Sometimes. His theory about that Maine man made sense. He figured that some people were just more interested in looking at water at rest—its work done. Said that Maine man left one ocean and wouldn't rest until he got to another, just so he could watch the water rest up. 'Tommy and me,' he up and admitted it when he'd had a few, 'we like to see where it starts. Watch it drip from the snow and begin washing this whole country away. When it wins, we lose,' he says to me. 'It'll all be gone. We'll have to start the whole thing over again.'"

"Goodness," Cody Jo said. "There's a dark metaphor."

"Don't know about metaphors," Rosie looked at Cody Jo warily, making sure Cody Jo was serious. "All I know is what Fenton told me, 'Tommy just has it in him to know,' he said. 'I think I watch it because the beginning seems so pure—where it all starts. Water's pure to drink and pure to see. Not yet muddied up with all our trouble.'"

"Heavens," Cody Jo said—taken by all that was unleashed in both Horace and Rosie when they talked about Fenton and Tommy, talked about the country these men helped others see. "Maybe I should have them come and talk to my classes."

"Won't do much good. Tommy won't start and Fenton won't stop. Gotta pick through all he says to pull out what's useful."

"Where are they now? These packers." Cody Jo had an idea that meeting them might be as important as meeting the mothers of her students. They seemed a critical part of the Swan's culture.

"Up there findin' an elk for some guy to shoot. We won't see hide nor hair of them 'til the snow falls."

"Where will they go when they come out," Cody Jo wanted to know. "What will they do?"

"Go to Missoula, probably," Rosie shook her head. "Wash some of their wild off—probably at The Bar of Justice."

"Bar of Justice? Sounds legal. Or literary. . . . What kind of place is that?"

Rosie put an arm around Cody Jo, her face all sun-browned wrinkles. "That's for the next lesson." She laughed and stood. "Let's us go back to the store and talk about how to improve your schoolroom. A lot of education's about to happen around here—now that we got you."

In two weeks Cody Jo had the schoolhouse ready. Buck had put up a big blackboard with a chalk tray on the front wall. There were hemispheric maps on the sidewalls and a big American map showing the states. Below the maps ran a world history time-line. Tacked below it was an American time-line showing how recently Columbus had appeared, a tiny stretch near the end showed when Lewis and Clark made their way through Montana. On the other wall were big prints of paintings of people working in the fields, haying and gleaning grain. There was a large one of men trying to control a broiling mix of horses. Another was of Indians making camp on the shore of a quiet lake, a waterfall spilling into it, impossible cliffs in the background. All of it made the room more interesting, but Cody Jo still sensed something was missing. Rosie and Buck stood with her as she looked things over, impressed by what they saw.

"Bump sure will be surprised to see how late America started out," Buck said, studying the time-lines. "He's got so he's pretty sure Granddad was the guy in that garden with Eve."

"Probably good not to mix the Bible stories in," Rosie said. "Gets everyone confused. Our kids get confused enough with the stories they hear at home: Some Indian running down a deer. A mountain man's ear chewed off by a grizzly. And some of them stories are true."

"I think I'll let those things stay at home," Cody Jo said. Just aim for what's logical here. . . . Still, something seems wrong."

"Might be not havin' the kids here in the first place," Buck said. "When I see Angie everything gets real to me. I know just what I want, even though it makes me feel kinda weak in the stomach."

"He's got a point." Rosie said. "You'll probably do fine if you lighten up on the theoretical and bear down on the practical. Learnin' don't hurt near as much as you can see what it's for. When Buck was in school what aggravated him most was tryin' to be so fancy about it. These kids can't be much different."

It came to Cody Jo how fortunate she was that Buck's brother Bump would be her eighth grader—how lucky she was to have Buck and Rosie as allies. And suddenly she understood what would make her school come alive. No matter how many time-lines she invented, it was clear she needed her students as much as they needed their teacher.

Two weeks after school opened, Cody Jo had most of her teaching organized. There were only thirty-two students, but they ranged from the first grade all the way up to Bump. Sometimes even younger ones were dropped off for the day, but she didn't count them, letting brothers and sisters handle that part and going right on directing the traffic. And there was plenty to direct. Her genius was having all the children so involved with this task or that that they thought most of all about doing their job—hardly at all about whether they were learning. At first the students thought the jobs just meant sweeping and cleaning and stoking the stove. But soon they realized that Cody Jo had much more in mind. The most important job each had was teaching some student on the next level down what had to be learned to get to the next level up, meaning each had to have a firm grip on where he was as well as a good idea of where he was going. The littlest ones carried papers to the older ones and listened to them teach numbers so they could teach numbers someday themselves. Everyone liked the teaching, even Bump, who had to scramble to stay ahead of the girls. They caught onto things much too quickly for him.

When the parents first saw what was going on, reports went out about it being more a Chinese schoolroom than a Montana one. But Rosie calmed everyone down, pointing out that if the children weren't complaining their new schoolteacher had half the battle won already.

"If the kids like going off to school, step right outside and thank your lucky star. Besides," she confided to an anxious mother, "I never knew a Chinese who was a dummy. I don't think they got any. Good things must come outta all that noise."

No one ever got around to pressing Rosie about how many Chinese she actually knew. By the time they thought to ask, Cody Jo had become so popular with the parents no one cared anymore.

And Cody Jo was good with parents, good in much the same way she was with the children. Not a parent stopped by that she didn't befriend, find an interest in, enlist for some duty. Half the men found themselves with a crush on her, though they were loath to admit it — even to themselves. And the women liked her because she could get so much done with so little fuss, and because there were times when she'd stop everything just to have a talk, telling her students it was study time and pouring tea from the pot always simmering on the woodstove.

Which is what she was doing when Gus Wilson dropped by. She and Rosie were sipping tea as they watched Bump sweat bullets trying to solve a math problem. He needed to explain it to Sue Jamison, the lean and sober-faced sixth grader with brownish-blond hair who caught on to things so fast it made Bump jumpy.

The Wilsons ran their sawmill near the foot of the Swan, just above Fenton's pastures. Gus had stopped to see if any repairs were needed to ready things for the winter—and to get a look at the new schoolteacher. His brothers had told him about her, though nothing they'd said prepared him for what he found when he slid into the classroom.

"My goodness." Cody Jo stood quickly and greeted him. As she did, Gus felt something go funny inside him. Cody Jo's eyes were so darkly blue and were focused so completely on him, he lost all sense of what he'd intended to say. Seeing something was wrong, Cody Jo reached out and touched his arm. Her touch confused him all the more.

"You arrived so quietly," she said, "you might have been one of those bears they tell me about." She turned back toward Rosie. "You must know Rosie Murphy. Everyone in the Swan seems to know Rosie."

"He sure as hell does," said Rosie, "but now he looks as lost as Bump does tryin' to do that math. This here is Gus Wilson, Cody Jo, and he's usually a whole lot more collected. Always pays his store bill—though you might as well know that his brothers don't."

"He looks completely responsible to me," Cody Jo said, still worried about the man. "Didn't you build our schoolhouse? Bet you're famous for a lot of other things as well."

"I *am* Gus Wilson," he said at last. "Though I'm sure not famous." He squinted, as though having trouble focusing.

"I stopped in," he told Cody Jo, including Rosie as though fulfilling a duty, "to see if the schoolhouse needed patching or anything."

Cody Jo poured some tea for him and made him sit with them, but he seemed so distracted that he soon made excuses and left, Rosie throwing up her hands as the door closed behind him.

"Jesus," she said. "The man's smitten. And him so responsible. First Buck gone silly over Angie. Now Gus gone scatterbrained over you. Next it'll be Bump trippin' over that Sue Jamison. . . . It's enough to make a sane woman cry." She looked at Cody Jo with such resignation it made Cody Jo stammer.

"What . . . what in the world are you talking about?" Cody Jo gathered the tea cups to keep busy. "All I know is that it's nice to have a man like

Gus Wilson around. A capable man. In case a window blows out or something else happens that Bump, or even Buck, can't fix."

"Honey, what's happened to Gus ain't fixable," Rosie said, helping Cody Jo, "with anything but time." Cody Jo ran water over the cups, saying nothing, wanting it not to be true.

But she'd seen this happen to men before, men who would look at her, listen to her, then somehow become lost.

She didn't like it, didn't like seeing men get lost that way. She wanted to be a teacher now. And whatever had gotten to Gus Wilson was not what she wanted to teach. It got in the way of what she wanted to teach.

As it turned out, though, that was how she would teach Gus Wilson his most important lesson. It was one he would carry for the rest of his life, a lesson that tore at her heart and unsettled people in the Swan.

Those who could understand.

13

Learning

They scheduled the fall dance for Halloween, mostly because of Rosie's urgings. She was more interested in dancing than in Halloween, but she had an idea that Halloween would give Cody Jo some inspiration, which it did. Cody Jo got the older students to show the younger ones how to make decorations: pumpkins and goblins, black cats and witch hats. She got Buck and Bump to haul in hay bales for people to sit on. Rosie cheered her on with black and orange crepe paper—not even complaining when Cody Jo ruled out the keg of beer Dan wanted to set up in the cloakroom.

"Daniel can just keep that keg out in his truck," Rosie said. "And there'll be plenty of the stronger. Prohibition don't count for much out here, which improves the dancing considerable."

No one seemed to pay any attention to the Halloween costume idea either, most thinking clean Levis and a pressed shirt were going far enough. Cody Jo put on a long black skirt and a dark blouse, and for a while even wore a little eye mask. But she soon put that aside in favor of the dancing, at which she was graceful and somehow understated, always perfectly in step with anyone lucky enough to dance with her. And many wanted to be so lucky. That came as no surprise to Rosie, who saw all kinds of things in the schoolteacher that Cody Jo hardly understood herself. She saw even more as she watched Cody Jo on the dance floor. There was little flair to Cody Jo, who moved modestly, but each movement was so perfectly at one with the music it seemed like magic. Rosie admired it, loving to dance herself but having none of Cody Jo's restraint.

Horace had convinced Highway Round Brown to bring along some fiddlers for the music. Round played piano at The Bar of Justice, though since he'd come to Missoula from back east he'd played at different spots all the way up to Canada—which is why they added "Highway" to his name.

He'd been just Round Brown before that, washing up one night at The Bar of Justice and sitting down at the upright to play, his face sad but his rhythms so steady that everyone became entranced by the gulf between the somber brown man and the lively music emerging from his fingers. Doc Mercer and Horace had liked him from the very first, telling him to come back the next night. The night after that they offered him a room, telling him he should stay, even telling him he could take a night off now and then and drive his old car to other places where they might sell a drink or two—Moose Lick and Jew Jake's and Salt Lake Sally's—which is why the "Highway" part of his name stuck.

Round was no fool. He knew Doc and Horace wanted him on the road mostly so their place wouldn't look like it was the only entertainment stop in western Montana. And he didn't mind. He drove and drove, when there were offers. And there were many, though he liked The Bar of Justice best. Everyone knew him there and no one minded that he played so much of the new swing music coming out on the radio and on the recordings. Why he caught onto it so early and liked it so much no one could tell. Most of all they liked it that he could play anything, even if he heard the tune only once, even obscure cowboy songs like "Cyclone Blues" or "Drink that Rotgut." Sometimes the cowboys and loggers who tried to sing him one of their favorites would be too drunk to remember the tune, so Round would play some other song that might have been sung to him the night before. No one cared. They liked to watch the big brown hands roam over the keyboard as he moved from a slow piece to a fast one, hardly a change in his expression as his chords filled the room. Big as he was—tall as well as round—he seemed to have no meanness for anyone, seemed content with his music—fast or slow, sad or happy.

Cody Jo liked his playing as soon as she heard it. She liked watching him too, realizing he had some rhythm deep down that didn't need to show on his outside because it was such a natural part of his inside. She was surprised by how quiet one number could be, how rag-timey the next. And she liked it that he knew so many of the new tunes, ones she knew from back east.

"Yep," he'd say when she'd suggest a song. Or he'd just play it, his hands flowing over the keyboard, the fiddles picking up the tune, all of them playing in a way that made everyone want to dance.

Gus Wilson liked the music especially, but he was so undone by seeing Cody Jo he had to calm himself by dancing with Rosie first. Rosie caught him sneaking glances at Cody Jo when they turned or came close, anytime he could actually look without some odd sense of guilt creeping over him.

"You might as well up and ask her," Rosie finally said. "If you don't you're liable to trip and hurt yourself. Go ahead. Beat out those others. There's plenty who want to partake."

Gus followed Rosie numbly as she led him over to Cody Jo, who stood waiting for the next number.

"I believe Gus wants a dance," she said, as Gus stood there. He was feeling that lurch inside him once again, blood lifting into his face. "Gus is a good dancer when he puts a mind to it, which might be a relief after all those clunkers you been herdin' around the floor."

Cody Jo was thankful the cowboy who'd been dancing with her had left, but she was worried about how undone Gus already seemed. Just then one of the tallest men she'd ever seen ducked his head and came into the room, seeming to fill the door as he did. He was clean-shaven, his face browned by sun, his hair a thick mane of white.

"I believe Fenton has come out of the mountains," Rosie said. "You should meet him before he heads out with Jasper or Buck for a drink. He's pretty good on the dance floor too—when his friends or that hooch don't get in the way.

"Well, Fenton," Rosie called. "Out of your mountains at last."

Fenton signaled a hello and came over. "Best meet our new teacher, before you disappear again," Rosie said to him. "She's got some civilization, which is rare around here. Not much at all up in your forest primeval."

"So you're Fenton Pardee," Cody Jo said, shaking Fenton's hand and taking in the height of him. "They didn't tell me you were white on top. But you certainly are. . . . Like your mountains."

Fenton was even more surprised by this confident schoolteacher than she was by the white hair. He'd never seen her before, and here she was acting completely at home with him.

"Cody Jo?" he said, quizzically. "I worked with a man named Cody. Long time ago."

"You mean the one who had the big show and tried to bring all you have out here back to all of us back there?" Cody Jo asked, amused.

"I do," Fenton said. "A big show it was."

"An impossible one, it seems to me. My mother was a Cody. From Virginia. She might have been somehow related to that man, but I think they went in opposite directions."

"I believe he was why I went in the opposite direction myself," Fenton said.

Before he could say anything else, Cody Jo was out on the dance floor with Gus, who'd finally bolstered up enough courage to take her arm.

Knowing he had to say something once they were out there, he launched into telling her about his sawmill, a subject once started not soon exhausted. But his nervousness was soon gone altogether, so wonderful it was to be dancing with Cody Jo. She followed along perfectly, giving Fenton a wave when she went by, once even calling out to ask if they danced in his mountains.

Fenton enjoyed watching all the unattached cowboys circling for their chance with the schoolteacher—or with Angie, who looked particularly pretty and whose dancing with anyone else always nettled Buck. When Jasper Finn, the pack-trip cook, showed up, the two of them enjoyed watching together.

Jasper almost always came to the dances, though more to drink than to dance, which no one had ever seen him do. He'd been a rail-crew cook when Fenton discovered him playing poker one night in The Bar of Justice. He'd been so careful about his cards and so religious about keeping his eyes off the girls, Fenton couldn't help but take a liking to him. His weakness for drink was one Fenton decided he could tolerate, and it wasn't long before Jasper was the regular cook on Fenton's trips—his talents fueled mostly by Fenton's cooking sherry.

They enjoyed watching the dancers now, commenting about how many were waiting their chance, about how surprised one or another would look when Rosie picked them off to do her own dancing, about how formal Buck acted when he danced with Angie—how irritated he became when anyone tried to cut in.

"That schoolteacher does civilize our boys," Jasper said, noting how much smoother each dancer seemed to become when dancing with Cody Jo, how polite each one was when still another cut in.

It was a good dance. Fenton liked the music almost as much as he liked watching the dancers. He'd heard most of the songs Round was playing when Round practiced up on them down at The Bar of Justice. They sounded even better with the fiddles, Brown's left hand keeping the beat—the fiddlers and the dancers picking it up.

But when Jasper suggested they go outside to partake of his bottle, Fenton agreed, knowing it was unseemly to watch the dancing too long, especially when his mind was mostly on Beth. She might not be as handsome and self-possessed a woman as this new schoolteacher, but she was comfortable—and she'd been very much on his mind since he left the mountains.

Because Gus was lost for anything to say when he was dancing with Cody Jo, he'd wound up telling her everything he could think of about his sawmill. In fact, he'd told her so much about the Wilson brothers' operation that Cody Jo decided it was a perfect destination for one of her field trips. She wanted to show the students how much could be done with a little ingenuity anyway, and from Gus's description he and his brothers had used more than a little. They'd rigged ramps and guides and jigs so they could mill logs with a gas-driven engine right there on the edge of the forest, his brothers trimming ponderosa and fir on the spot, the mules of Fenton and Tommy Yellowtail snaking the logs out in teams when the ground was frozen so they wouldn't tear up the earth.

It was December before Cody Jo could organize her students for the trip, which was a perfect time. Gus's brothers were felling the trees out in the woods, Tommy Yellowtail skidding them out with the mules, Gus doing the milling himself after jacking the logs onto the guides.

Gus had shown Cody Jo and her students the way the little mill ran and had walked a few yards up the skid to place the next log coming in when it happened. He'd looked back at Cody Jo, his gaze lingering on her as she watched the mules work. As he turned back to tend to his own, a snag on the jigged log gouged his face so completely and so quickly no one knew it had happened until the blood gushed up. He'd been so entranced by Cody Jo he'd not seen the jagged danger, axed from the ponderosa and still jutting from the log, not realized the log had canted, the snag now face high and a danger far more tangible than his heart-stopping attraction for Cody Jo.

She was there in a moment, tearing off her own jacket to press it to the wound as he still stood, numbed. He was still numb as she forced him to the ground to quench the blood by pressing harder. Tommy was with them now, fashioning a wrap from his big kerchief, seeing how bad the wound was with eyes that knew all too well how bad things could be. "Gotta get him to the docs," he told Cody Jo, somehow signaling his distaste for them as he said it. "In Missoula."

He would take Gus there himself, he told her—knowing how quickly Gus needed to get there. And somehow knowing too how sick Cody Jo was going to be—about what her students had seen, about what she had had to do. About what she had done. There was no way he could say that to her, or explain, even to himself, how deeply he understood.

What he was sure of was that there were no doctors who could fix what was really wrong with Gus. On the long drive to Missoula, Gus was in despair about what he'd put Cody Jo through, the mindlessness that had overtaken him.

"It was like I'd lost my mind, Tommy," Gus said, changing the bloodied kerchief for one of the towels they'd picked up at Murphy's. "Couldn't see my work for how gone was my head. And I had no right. Couldn't see that I had no right. It damn near blinded me. . . . Blind. I guess, that's what I was."

"It happens," was all Tommy could say. "Good you numbed up so quick. You'll get used to it."

"To what? If it heals at all, it'll be a bad heal."

"I meant numbed up. You'll get used to it."

"Numb means feeling nothing, don't it? How the hell do you get used to that?"

"You do," Tommy said.

Gus kept looking at him, pressing the towel to his wound, wondering what made Tommy so sure.

Word got around quickly, and Fenton, who was talking with Bob Ring at the Forest Service office when he heard, drove into Missoula to meet them. Tommy was relieved when Fenton reached the hospital. Talking to doctors was something Fenton knew how to do. Tommy didn't.

"They're going to try a skin deal," Fenton told Tommy late in the day when he'd finished talking with everyone. "A graft. They got ways of doing it now. They say he'll scar bad. But he'll be okay."

"Maybe he will," Tommy said. "Least he can get back to work. That could help."

"Might could," Fenton said. "Never know, do you?"

They left the truck in town for Gus, and Fenton drove Tommy back to the Swan. They didn't even stop at The Bar of Justice, needing to get back in time to feed the mules.

14

Knowing

Caring for mules, patching equipment, making an occasional rest stop with Beth at The Bar of Justice filled Fenton's schedule that winter. He didn't see Cody Jo again until late spring. By then Gus was almost healed. The graft had taken; he was back concentrating on his sawmill once again, doing what had to be done. A few people out in the Swan were sure something in him would never heal, not all the way, but most took his scar in stride. Things happened when you worked in the backcountry, felling trees and traveling over the passes. They figured this was just another.

It was in April, the snow mostly melted away, when Fenton and Cody Jo ran into each other. Fenton, returning with a truckload of gear from Missoula—mostly repaired panniers and tents—was feeling relaxed and comfortable after a night with Beth. He stopped in at Murphy's for coffee just as Cody Jo was leaving with her groceries.

"It's about time you showed up." She stepped back to look at him, flushing a little. "Though I'd rather see you at the recital than have you run me down right here in front of Dan Murphy."

"Recital?" Fenton was startled by her familiarity. For a moment he thought she was talking about some new kind of equipment.

"Of course, 'recital.' The third one—and the last one. Seven-thirty tonight. Some culture will help before you go back into those mountains. Especially when you begin giving that nice Mr. Jasper orders—and bossing all those others around too." She seemed to find some humor in watching him. "You're invited," she concluded. "I'll even count on you."

Then she was gone, leaving Dan Murphy, who'd watched the exchange, amused. "Just close your mouth," Dan said. "You got no choice. She's come to know more about most of us in this valley than we know about ourselves."

The door opened and Cody Jo's head popped back in. "There'll be tickets at the door," she said. Then she was gone again.

"See?" Dan Murphy said. "A real go-getter." He smiled, enjoying the baffled look on Fenton's face. "Truth is she arranged a whole season's pass for Rosie and me. Didn't cost us a nickel. Damn near worth it too."

"She *is* different," Fenton said, getting his coffee and eyeing Murphy to make sure he wasn't being joshed. "But I doubt different enough." He thought about Beth, who in her own way wasn't really different enough either. "Bet it's just some damn lecture about gettin' kids to school on time and readin' books at home. Stuff we know we got no time to hear about—let alone do."

"Could be." Dan mopped at his counter. "But the truth is that woman mostly gets her ideas across from what she does, not what she says. Least as far as I can see. And whatever she does, there's some excitement with it. You should watch when she gets Rosie in a huddle with the mothers. And let's thank the Lord she's down on them cranky teetotalers."

"Thank nature; leave the Lord out," Fenton groused, still rattled by Cody Jo. "Seems to me nature just dealt those old Prohibition girls a bad hand. Not the Lord. Not us. They just ain't very happy. And they don't want us happy at all. The booze thing might just be a handy tool."

"Could be." Dan mopped at his counter. "And could be, if it's nature who's doin' the dealing, she saved her best cards for our schoolteacher. You'll see tonight. If you work up courage enough to go."

"Courage I got. Findin' time to use it is my problem. I got gear to unload."

"If you want unloadin' equipment to stand in the way of enjoyin' all that life, go right ahead. Truth is that school never had it so good. . . . And to have that woman so sensible about this teetotal shit just adds to what she's already done for this damn valley." Murphy sounded so argumentative Fenton had to laugh this time.

"Well, I'm sure glad she's here," Fenton said. "If you say I should be. I like this country around here. Don't want to have to head for Canada to find a little life, or to wet my whistle either."

Murphy wiped more at his counter, relaxing a little as he thought it over. "With her around, might be no need for Canada. People like her might just straighten out them do-gooders. Do what we couldn't."

"You mean teach them old girls to relax and live a little?"

"Teach us too. Could be both sides have been too damned pissed off at each other to do either."

By early evening Fenton found himself heading back for the school-house, despite some weather coming in. A cloudbank was building over the Missions. He was glad he had his gear stored, glad he had some raingear along too. There'd be a wind. Had he been in the mountains, he'd be at work already—tightening up his canvas, cinching down his lines, throwing manties over saddles, anchoring things with rocks.

Cars were already in the lot at the schoolhouse. A fifth grader was at the door with programs. Fenton saw pretty quickly why Cody Jo had been so amused as she'd chided him about culture. There were only four events: a reading of "Invictus," a recitation of "The Cremation of Sam McGee," a piano rendition of "The March of the Wooden Soldiers," and Bump Conner singing "My Buddy," accompanied by violin. Bump's participation explained why all the Connors were there. But many other parents were there too, the men in clean shirts with their hair combed, most of the women in dresses. The Jamisons looked expectant, and Fenton saw why: pretty Sue Jamison was scheduled to recite "Invictus."

Dan Murphy pointed out a seat, a tag on it reading "Reserved for Fenton Pardee." There were plenty of other chairs still empty, but Fenton accepted this one, assuming it was the schoolteacher's idea of a "ticket." He sat and listened to the rustlings going on behind a partition, students getting ready to perform.

The first thunder cracked through so sharply it made people jump. Fenton, who'd been expecting it, put his hat back on and left to get his lantern and his rain gear. When he returned he folded his slicker near the wall and put his lantern beside his chair so he could get at it.

Out of the window he could see lightning streak across the sky, a clap of thunder close behind it—the schoolhouse lights dimming as it rumbled through. He heard the rain start up and was feeling around for his matches when the lights went out, flickered back on, then stayed off. He got his lantern going and found Cody Jo right there in his ring of light. She didn't seem nearly as sure of herself now.

"I baked cookies," she said, her eyes big pools in the lantern-light. "Should I pass them around?"

"Might sog up. Let's get Buck's generator going instead."

Fenton got into his slicker as Buck appeared, wearing his hat but no rain gear in sight.

"Didn't bring any, did you?" Fenton said, snapping his slicker closed. "A damn mule coulda told you it would rain. I do believe they outrank you in the brain department."

"It'll hail in a minute and them balls will just bounce off," Buck said. "I'll hold that lantern. You fire her up."

The only light in the schoolhouse now came from the intermittent lightning—and the glow here and there of a cigarette. Rosie Murphy began to sing a song about "ten thousand goddamned cattle" and a cowboy whose sweetheart leaves for "a son of a bitch from Ioway." The Conners picked right up on it. It was the same song their mother always sang when she put them to sleep. It made everyone feel better and they kept at it, singing the "Little Brown Mule" and "Forty Mormon Women" and "The Dying Cowboy." They were starting in on "The Zebra Dun" when the generator kicked in and they had lights again.

Everyone clapped when Fenton and Buck came in, Buck wet as a duck despite the hail coming down hard now, the noise so constant Cody Jo had to play some chords to get everyone's attention. Rosie held that they should keep on singing but Cody Jo would have none of it, introducing Sue Jamison as the first performer.

A big hail-ball shattered a window, splattering broken glass across the room. People moved their chairs around to avoid the glass as still more hail balls bounced across the floor. Fenton, his slicker still on, backed himself into the opening and nodded to the girl to keep on reciting. Everyone was looking at Fenton and laughing, especially when the hail let up and they could hear Sue say "My head is bloody but unbowed."

After that the hail became so fierce it was hard to hear anything she said. But with Cody Jo's prompting she got through it, sober as an owl until she reached "I am the master of my fate; I am the captain of my soul," and broke into a big smile.

"I sure as hell ain't the captain of my fate." Dan Murphy was in front of Fenton the moment the little round of applause ended. "This hail could break all my damn windows. Buck was already moonstruck when he set the damn things."

"Where is Buck?" Fenton asked. "He's wet through already. He can stand in this window while I go out in the hail and patch things up."

"How you gonna patch anything with them hail stones poundin' at you? All I know is you gotta get Cody Jo home. Rosie and me'll sprint for the store. See if it's still upright."

Buck appeared, Fenton backing him into the window before he could protest. "Stand here till you hear me pounding," Fenton told him. "I'll tack somethin' over the window to keep out the hail."

The hail was so loud Buck couldn't hear Fenton's hammer as Fenton tacked the board over the window, just knew he'd been pushed inside so the board could be flat. When he thought it was secure he started outside to help, but the hail drove him back. He saw Fenton had a geography book open over his head now, but before he could find one himself Fenton was beside him, looking the room over to see if anything else had gone wrong.

The hail seemed to slacken and Fenton found some plywood to hold over people so he and Buck could take them out to their cars, Buck grousing that he felt cheated because he hadn't been able to hear Bump sing.

"I didn't want to sing in the first place," Bump said as the Jamisons gathered to be taken to their car. "Sue is the only one any good. You got to hear her."

"Then I guess you're still unbowed," Fenton said. "Loan your brother your slicker or take over and help me get these people through the hail."

Bump took Buck's place under the plywood and helped ferry the Jamisons to their car, Sue soberly approving him as he did.

By the time they got back the hail had almost stopped, the ground a white mat as they crossed it. People slipped away to see what damage their own homes had suffered, thanking Cody Jo as they left and leaving her to worry about Buck.

"You need dry things," she said, a little shocked by all the water Buck's clothes had absorbed. "And something to eat. I have cookies."

"I'm bruised, mostly," Buck said apologetically. "Them hail balls got to comin' in right smart."

"If you'd thought to bring a slicker, you'd be all right," Fenton said. "At least partly. Hard to tell how the rest of you would do."

"I'll get the cookies," Cody Jo said. "He's wet and tired and you aren't making it any easier for him."

"He don't mind bein' wet," Fenton said. "What he minds is Angie not being here to tell him he's a hero."

"Wish she would," Buck said, rubbing at his back. "Mostly she just tells me where I'm wrong."

"Oh Buck," Cody Jo sympathized. "I bet, down deep, she thinks you're wonderful. Maybe she just doesn't know how to say so."

"Doesn't have a bit of trouble sayin' what she thinks," Buck said. "Which is most of my problem."

"And I'm sayin' let's get the hell out of here," Fenton said. "You're soaked. Bump's wishing he could sing 'My Buddy' for that Jamison girl. And we got a tuckered out schoolteacher here."

They walked out into a white landscape, and Fenton helped Cody Jo into his truck. Buck started his engine and beamed his lights on the generator so Fenton could see to shut it off. Cody Jo watched as Fenton returned, his outsized shadow bigger and bigger until it was gone and he was there beside her in the cab.

He wound down his window, "Better drive slowly," he called out to Buck. "That road'll be slick as elk guts."

He started the engine. "Just an expression: 'elk guts,'" he said, not sure if schoolteachers had any idea of how slick elk guts could be. "All he needs is to slide off the road and bend up his truck. He's discouraged enough by Angie. Not much else on his mind."

They drove in silence, Fenton careful to avoid a slide himself.

"I have cookies," Cody Jo said suddenly, uncovering a plate of them, still a little warm.

"How'd you get these through the hail?" Fenton was impressed. "Not even wet." He bit into one. "And I have a hunger. So interested in that culture you offered I slid right past dinner."

"Oh dear," Cody Jo smiled at him. "Hard to be 'master of your fate' with no dinner!"

"Which is why I take Jasper Finn along to manage my cook tent. The man can get dinner out drunk or sober. If Buck or Spec got to stop what they're doing to think about rustling up a dinner, they're likely to forget what they were doing when the dinner idea came up—or remember it and forget the dinner. . . . Could you make these cookies in the mountains?"

Fenton was always on the lookout for cooks who might serve on his trips. Wrong as such an idea might be for the schoolteacher, he couldn't resist exploring it.

"If you have an oven I could, I think. Which would give you a chance to laze around and play with your mules."

"We got a wood box that heats right up," Fenton said, looking at her. "And keepin' track of mules up in that country is not what I'd call lazin' around."

Fenton focused on the white strip of road ahead and Cody Jo couldn't help looking at him, the moon—free of the clouds now and reflecting off the hail—making clear how serious he'd become.

"It can't be that mysterious. . . . Can it?" She was impressed by how carefully he navigated the patchwork of white and shadow marking the road ahead of them.

"It can," he said, "though it's more like unpredictable. . . . Like Dan and Rosie there."

Ahead, tilted almost on its side in the roadside ditch, was Dan's Ford. Dan was up in the road waving a shovel at them. Rosie's head poked up as she tried to climb out, but the pitch was too steep; she dropped out of sight just as Fenton pulled to a stop.

"See you circled around before settling on that ditch. Like a dog makin' his bed," Fenton said. "Snugged her in tidy too."

"We did go into a little slide," Dan said. "Would have come out of it fine if Rosie didn't make me overcorrect."

"She has a way of gettin' a man to drive into ditches." Fenton pulled Rosie from the Ford as though freeing her from a hatch. "I'll hook onto you with a lash rope; scoot you right out."

Rosie gave him a hug. "Sure glad you got here, Fenton. Dan was fixin' to hit me with that shovel."

Fenton relit his lantern and gave it to Cody Jo, who held it high, embracing Rosie as she did. "Rescuing you caps off the evening," she laughed. "Culture and cookies and then a rescue." She turned to Fenton. "Can you find a way to make this happen in your mountains? Culture for you; a rescue for us; cookies for everyone? Isn't that supposed to happen in the West?" Fenton had his lash rope around the Ford's bumper. He tied a bowline and looped it over the truck-hitch. "Bill Cody tried to sell that," he said. "Make-up stuff. What's real is already up there." He got in his truck and pulled the rope taut, motioning for Dan to start the Ford up to help.

The wheels of his truck skittered sideways before they found a purchase. The Ford came along behind it, almost crossways in the ditch before its front wheels bumped up into the road, its rear end sliding along before it popped up too.

Fenton backed his truck up and undid the rope. "You should take a look," he said to Cody Jo. "A lot to learn up there where that snow never melts. Springs bubble up all year. It's downright educational."

They all agreed that Cody Jo should go on with the Murphys, saving Fenton the drive in to the store then back out again. Cody Jo put the plate of cookies on the seat beside him. "You'll need these," she said, "so you can be 'master of your fate.'"

Then Cody Jo and the Murphys were gone, leaving Fenton to drive home alone through the melting hailstones. He did a few chores, then settled in front of the fire with the plate of cookies, thinking of the schoolteacher and wondering what it was about her that touched him so.

15
High Country

Jasper Finn was a kind of magician, at least in a high country camp. As soon as his kitchen was unpacked, he would get out a meal. He could do it in the dark or in a downpour, even if they coincided. Snow didn't bother him, nor did sleet or hail. But bears were a worry—which is why Fenton's packers always took along a little cooking sherry. Everyone knew Jasper's bear fantasies could get out of proportion when he had whisky, but with a little cooking sherry to keep him fueled, he seemed to balance things out—putting aside his fear of bears and remaining productive and good-natured in the worst of conditions.

It was on a small trip with Buck and Tommy when he was telling one of his stories that he almost severed his thumb with his cleaver. That came as a shock to everyone—and as an awkwardness. It was hard to imagine how the camp would run without Jasper, but it was clear something needed to be done with such a wound. Tommy, who had his own drinking problems, though hardly ever in the mountains, cleaned and bound the wound himself. Then he took Jasper out to be sewn up, as even Tommy knew he must be. That left Buck to muddle along with the food, though Buck's mind was on Angie so steadily he hardly thought about Jasper's sherry, or anything else that might spice the meals up. If the guests—whose generosity with their own whisky had led to Jasper's undoing—hadn't been so inventive in using the kitchen, Tommy and Fenton's reputation might have taken a dive.

But, except for the loss of Jasper's services for a month, things worked out. They wouldn't have, however, if Rosie and Cody Jo hadn't heard about Jasper's accident and filled in for the next trip, doing a little rescue work themselves, which led to some surprising changes for the people in the Swan. And welcome ones.

It all started when Rosie, hearing Fenton was so desperate for a cook he might enlist Buck and Bump, threw up her hands and volunteered— if Cody Jo would help out. Her other stipulation was that Buck come along to wrangle. Dan would need Angie's full support at the store, an impossibility with Buck there—and no Rosie to slow Buck hanging around and looking for an opportunity.

Fenton was thankful, figuring he'd need Buck anyway. It was his biggest trip of the year: three Chicago grain traders he'd taken for elk the year before wanted to show their families a country far above where wheat was grown and harvested and traded. It was a landscape they'd come to cherish, just as they'd come to cherish the straight-speaking packer who led them.

Except for a record-breaking downpour that washed out most of the drainages and almost drowned Goose, their most unflappable horse, it was like other big trips Fenton and Tommy had led. But in more subtle ways it was a trip like no other. Fenton was the first to admit that. And, of course, for Cody Jo it was the beginning of a lifelong adventure, one that overshadowed everything she'd known.

It started the very first day. She was looking up, admiring the line of Fenton's mules as they turned again and then again to climb the switch-backs above, when one of them—curling around a U-shaped turn—kicked loose a boulder. It slid, tipped all the way over, then thudded onto the trail below, landing squarely between Fenton's last two mules. All the mules bolted forward except Sugar, the little Tennessee mule Fenton used as his caboose. She scrambled back with such force she yanked the mule in front of her off the trail and onto the rocks. Fenton tried to stop his string as he watched the mule fight for some footing, but the others crowded forward, stretching the animal farther out onto the rocks: the mules ahead pulling one way; Sugar behind pulling the other.

Tommy Yellowtail, close behind Sugar with his own string, leapt off his pinto to climb onto the rocks himself and cut the breakaway rope, the pigtail, from the struggling mule's packsaddle. Suddenly freed, Sugar lurched backward, falling onto her rump in a cloud of dirt and scree. Paying no attention to Sugar, Tommy let go such a string of language that the struggling mule on the rocks practically leapt up onto the trail above, crowding the mules ahead who lurched forward from the sudden release.

"That pigtail should've broke," Fenton called back to Tommy, as he settled his string down. "Why do they always hold when they shouldn't?"

"Like your people," Tommy said. "Do things when they shouldn't."

"You sayin' my people swim against the current?" Fenton called down to him. "Hell, that's part of our program. But we get money for it. Cody got his by takin' the west east. Those Christers get theirs by passin' the collection plate to the sinners. It all works out. . . . Can our mules slip by that boulder?"

"Might could. If it'll slide a little."

Cody Jo, unable to make out what they were saying, watched Tommy brace his back against the wall of the trail, his boots on the boulder, tendons bulging as he strained to slide the big rock to the side. It moved an inch; no more. Then Fenton was beside him, the two of them using their legs, pushing the boulder, resting, straining again, pushing farther, then again, stopping only when it was perched on the trail's outer edge. Tommy retrieved Sugar to make sure her packs would clear it as Fenton climbed the rocks to Babe, his lead mare, who was standing still as wood, the long string quiet and patient behind her.

Fenton saw Tommy lead Sugar past the boulder, her packs just clearing it as Tommy took her around the switchback to reach Fenton's mules.

"They'll clear," Tommy called up to Fenton. "She's our runt."

"Splice that pigtail back weak." Fenton said. "Gotta break free if she pulls back again."

"A goddamned gnat could break it now," Tommy said, finishing the repair. "Hope she don't turn and head for Texas when it gives."

Then they were moving: seven packed mules behind Fenton, five more behind Tommy, five more trailing Gus. After Gus's string came Buck—lovesick and blue—then the dudes, the men leading their families and relishing the danger, now that it had been resolved.

Bringing up the rear were the cooks. It was all new to Cody Jo, whose eyes were fixed on the pack strings ahead, loads swaying as the mules moved, slowing at the switchbacks, picking up their pace at the right moment, calm, orderly, almost graceful in their attention to the trail, to any boulder they must step around, any protruding rock that might scrape their packs and cause trouble.

The excitement of the dislodged boulder had unnerved Cody Jo, who felt queasy as her gelding moved past it. She was shocked by its size. Had it kept rolling it would have taken tons of earth with it, part of the trail as well. She felt still queasier about having insisted on riding her flat saddle through such country.

"You'd be better off riding one of ours," Fenton had said, tying her rain gear onto his saddle because there was no way to tie it on hers.

"It's a beautiful day," she'd said. "Stick my slicker in some pack."

"Makes it hard to reach," he'd said evenly. "Afternoon storms come up pretty quick."

There were clouds by afternoon, but nothing that looked like rain, which pleased Cody Jo as she helped with dinner. They were camped by a grassy flat at the foot of the pass that crossed the Swan, as spectacular to descend as it had been to climb. They were headed down toward the South Fork now, a stream snaking through their meadow, the animals cropping grass and crossing the creek, their tails swishing, the mules shaking themselves after rolls on the sun-warmed sandy benches.

Tents went up quickly, quietly, Gus and Buck working with no apparent haste but everything coming into place naturally, a little village of canvas growing along the tree line. The big cook tent had gone up first, the sides rolled up to welcome the slanting afternoon light. Cody Jo was impressed by how quickly Rosie got things in order, stocking the woodstove, making cool lemonade, dicing vegetables for a stew as she talked with the guests, pouring lemonade for this one and that.

When things quieted, Rosie took Cody Jo downstream to a big pool. They bathed, Rosie sponging happily, her skin as smooth as a child's where the sun hadn't done its work. Cody Jo braced herself against the shock of cold, then lay nymphlike under the rippling waters, asking Rosie questions, loving the humor in Rosie's answers and the greens of the meadows, the sounds of the waters and animals—and Rosie's laughter.

Fenton was back in the cook-tent when they returned, enjoying lemonade and answering questions himself. He smiled at the sight of them.

"Fresh as a new day," he said. "And after all that dust."

"All in the presentation," Cody Jo said. "Looking crisp is the key."

"You do," Fenton admitted. "Look crisp I mean. I'm commencing to be thankful old Jasper carved up his hand."

He was surprised by how seriously it came out. He'd meant to be funny, at least playful. It had been anything but. He left the cook-tent without realizing he was leaving, quieted by something inside him that seemed to crowd everything else out.

Cody Jo didn't see him again until she was serving up the stew, putting big chunks of bread on each plate as she did.

"I'm a server-upper," she said. "For men with combed hair."

"A guy could comb a long time for this." Fenton held his plate out, blotting away with a sleeve the drops of stream-water still on his forehead.

"You're just getting weak-minded from all that trail work," Cody Jo said, turning to serve Tommy now.

"Looks tasty," Tommy said, looking from Cody Jo to Fenton. Fenton was still watching Cody Jo.

"Praise from the packers!" Cody Jo said. "And not a taste taken."

"Could be your presentation," Fenton said. He was still looking at her. Tommy was still watching him. "It's a nice presentation." He hesitated, about to say more when he was pulled away by one of the men and found himself deep in conversation, other guests gathering around.

The topic, he quickly learned, was Lost Bird Canyon. The year before he'd taken this very man up a little spur trail to its head. It was there the man had shot his elk, not far from the same camp where Tommy and Fenton had met. As he'd gutted and quartered the elk, Fenton had told him about the canyon, the long trailless drainage that flowed eastward to meet the South Fork at White River junction, White River flowing in from under the Continental Divide and shaping the wide hospitable benches over time. White River was known for its wonderful fishing, for the wildlife making those benches their home. It was the party's destination, Fenton planning to take them there on the well-marked trails down the valley where they camped now to meet the South Fork ten miles upriver from the benches.

"Why in the world," the grain trader said to Fenton—the rest of them listening and approving and completely caught up in the idea—"don't we go right down that Lost Bird Canyon to White River? It's shorter. Might take a little longer. But it would be a real adventure."

Fenton didn't need to register the look Tommy was giving him to realize how out of hand things were getting. He'd come up that canyon, somehow, to meet Tommy Yellowtail in the first place, a matter he wished he hadn't told this grain trader as he'd packed the man's elk back to this very camp. He'd not told the man about losing a mare while coming through that canyon, and suspected he should not tell these people either. They wanted an adventure, but a safe adventure. Fenton and Tommy's job was to keep it safe.

"Sounds shorter," Fenton said. "But whatever route I followed has surely disappeared by now, been blocked by deadfall. That stream meanders all over that lower canyon too. Doubt anybody's been through there but me. Lucky I made it at all."

"We're not anybody, Fenton," the man said seriously—believing it, needing Fenton to realize he understood. "We'll help you open the trail. The kids'll have something to write about in school."

"This country ain't for school," Fenton said, looking at them, knowing all too well the troubles they'd face. Which made him more than happy to accept the drink someone offered. One reason Fenton's trips were so popular was his access to the good whisky Dan Murphy and Doc Messler provided, and he needed a taste now. He didn't like the turn this conversation was taking.

The fire was inviting. They settled by it, drinking and talking, Tommy Yellowtail saying little and drinking not at all. He watched Fenton, listened to Fenton tell his stories. And he worried. Cody Jo listened too, not worried at all about what Fenton might agree to do, enjoying his ease in his mountains and with these people who were so different, who counted on him so much.

"Fenton knows just what to do," she told Rosie as they left the fire and sought out their bedrolls. They'd pulled them from their tent to take in the night air and had to move around in them to warm themselves.

"He learned most of it from Tommy," Rosie said, looking up at a star-filled sky. "But it's that Bill Cody who gave him the idea."

"The showman?"

"Yes, that fancy showman. Fenton worked for him. He told me once that Bill Cody might be smarter, but he believed he was wiser."

"Maybe he is." Cody Jo was astonished by how many stars filled the sky. "He and Tommy certainly knew how to handle everything today."

She lay there, thinking about her day—watching the stars until sleep came and took them away.

Before they turned in, Tommy and Fenton went out into the meadow to listen for the horses.

"Thinkin' about Lost Bird Canyon, ain't you?" Tommy said. The bells of the animals sounded faintly out across the meadow as Tommy stopped to pee.

"I am. A little. It's a wonder I ever made it through. Lucky I guess."

"That's right. Lucky. No one even knew I had that camp up there. And you found me, coming from the wrong direction too."

"And glad I was to see you."

"Yes. And we might could go through that canyon again. Just you and me. Not with these people, though. Too green."

"I know that. I got them quieted down."

"Quiet about it don't mean over with it. . . . It's a worry."

Fenton listened as Tommy made his way back to his bedroll. He walked out closer to the stream and took a pee himself, hearing the bells clearly now, feeling better because he did. He was thinking about the way Cody

Jo had watched as they talked around the fire, how complete she'd seemed, even up in this country that was so strange to her.

Rosie and Cody Jo were the first to know about how much Lost Bird Canyon remained on everyone's mind through the night. They'd made coffee for Tommy and Fenton at dawn and sent them after the horses, Cody Jo shivering and complaining as Rosie refueled the stove.

"Hope they find the horses, that's the main thing," Rosie said.

"What do you mean, 'find' them?" Cody Jo asked. Everything in these mountains seemed topsy-turvy to her. "We need them."

"And they need grass. Don't always share our priorities."

"Where would they go?" Cody Jo stopped stirring her flapjack mix. "What would we do?"

"They'll go down the canyon. Or up the canyon. Or up one of those grassy slides. Or maybe they'll go over into the next canyon. And then sometimes they go out."

"Out?"

"Home. Which is why you better get the lumps out of those flapjacks so we can plop them on the griddle. If Fenton and Tommy have to track those devils all over these mountains, they'll need something in their tummies."

The guests had joined them, all of them talking about Lost Bird Canyon, the prospect of it overshadowing everything. Then they heard bells, faint at first and then insistent, coming up the trail with a clatter. Cody Jo went out of the cook-tent to watch, the batter spoon still in her hand as the horses burst into the meadow, mules close behind. Gus was moving among them with a nosebag as the others began haltering them, catching them up.

"It's a pretty sight," Rosie said, beside her now. "But it can be a pretty sad one when them boys come in alone."

"What do we do then?" It was all astonishing to Cody Jo.

"Feed 'em and send 'em back out. Only thing you can do."

The guests were watching too, all of them seeking out this horse or that, pointing out Sugar—everyone's favorite. Sugar bolted and cut wind as if enjoying the attention, sunfishing and kicking out at some phantom before settling, trotting in to bury her nose in Fenton's feedbag.

People began drifting into the cook-tent then, getting coffee, watching the bacon sizzle, talking about the day—about Lost Bird Canyon. It was on everyone's mind.

Cody Jo made eggs to order and Rosie took out plates of food for the men to eat as they saddled. The tents began to come down, the older boys trying to roll them tightly, Buck and Gus rerolling them, showing how to keep the guy ropes inside the canvas, how to put things away so they could be unpacked and ready to go up again.

After saddling, Fenton came in for coffee himself. Cody Jo seemed to be doing everything at once—remaining completely unruffled as she did. Even while helping Rosie finish up the dishes she was chiding the boys, enlisting the help of the girls, laughing with Rosie, making the grain traders feel more like men than they could ever feel in their big offices. Fenton listened happily, not so much because he heard what she said as because of the life in how she said it.

Which was a good thing, because most of what she was saying was keeping the idea of Lost Bird Canyon alive.

"Fenton will know what to do," she told one of the men. "He always knows what to do—up here." She laughed, saying Fenton would find them the "promised land." Then she smiled, looking victoriously at the man. "Which I understand is White River, right across the South Fork from Lost Bird Canyon."

It came to Fenton as a shock: Everyone seemed to be taking it for granted that they would go down Lost Bird Canyon.

"Pretty sounding idea," he said, all of a sudden alert to everything that was being said. "But wrong. No trail at all down that canyon."

Things went so quiet in the cook-tent he knew something had gotten away from him, something he hadn't even known he'd started.

"Why not? You did it," someone said. "You'll be our pathfinder," another added. Then there was a clamor, all of them talking at once.

They held that if he had done it once from the other direction, he could do it again from their direction. If he couldn't find a way, they could always turn back. It was 'uncharted territory.' It was a 'challenge.' It was worth the loss of a few days just to see it. They had Fenton and Tommy to guide them. That was good enough for them.

Rosie and Cody Jo seemed happy to agree with them. "Soon as you boys knock down my stove," Rosie said, "I'm on my way."

Cody Jo added, all sunshine, "Just like you promised," she said to Rosie. "Big country. Big sky. Fenton our hero." She turned to Fenton. "We like you as our hero."

Fenton, rarely at a loss, was stopped. He made a few more objections, all quickly swept aside. His big worry now was how to tell Tommy. Tommy had uncommonly good sense when it came to moving through the mountains. He wouldn't think this made any sense.

But he had uncommonly good sense about Fenton as well.

"No surprise," he said, after Fenton told him. "I seen you gettin' moon-struck over the teacher. Just remember we got to take these city people through too. Bad shit if we have trouble."

"We'll take a look is all. I been wonderin' how I come up through there in the first place."

"You was dumb. Too young to know how dumb. If I hadn't been there you'd still be pokin' around lookin' for a saddle horse. Now you're gonna be dumb again—and you should be smart by now. Know better."

They packed, climbed the low divide that separated them from Lost Bird Canyon and worked their way down its upper reaches by late morning. Fenton looked back, watching Tommy as they passed Tommy's old camp. Tommy, seven mules behind, leaned off his pinto and spit, which didn't fool Fenton. Tommy might be upset with him now, but they both knew it was a good memory—and knew it was a fine camp, for a few people. Just not for this many. Tommy probably thought there wasn't a place in the canyon that would hold them all—a worry hardly lost on Fenton.

Farther down the canyon they pulled up for lunch on a little bench above the rushing stream. Tommy let his mules graze, telling Buck to take over when they started up again. Down the canyon they could see where it leveled and the timber thickened. Tommy wanted to search for a way through. There would be deadfall—bogs too, the stream meandering across the canyon floor, leaving sinkholes and pools and uprooted trees wherever it wandered. That was their big worry.

The rest followed with the mules, arriving at the edge of those woods by midafternoon. Fenton, knowing they'd have to loose-herd the mules through—if there were a way through at all—was breaking up the strings when Tommy appeared, coming from the other side of the stream.

"Like I told you," he said. "Maybe worse. Might not even be a bottom under that shit." Fenton could see Tommy had had a rough time already. The pinto's legs were muddy above his hocks. Mud was splattered on his belly and rump too, and on Tommy himself.

"There's a good meadow a half-mile back," Fenton said. "It'll do for a camp. Take another look. We'll set up and I'll be back. We'll look together. If we can't get through, we can't. "Gotta live with that."

Tommy disappeared back into the woods as Fenton turned every-thing around. He didn't even bother to tie the mules back into their strings, handing a lead line to this person or that, even to Cody Jo, her mule immediately objecting and pulling the rope from her hand. Fenton leaned off Babe and scooped it up himself.

"Hard to hold a mule with no saddle horn," he said cheerfully, not even breaking stride as he let Cody Jo lead them back up the canyon. "Bet that saddle's handy for jumping fences, though—following hounds and catching foxes too. Must be fun to chase the foxes."

"It's . . . it's different," Cody Jo said.

They rode across a big slide, the wildflowers bobbing as they crossed to make camp, the spot almost perfect. Cody Jo, who'd had little to say as Fenton talked, was impressed by how quickly things found a place: a deadfall became a saddle rack, tents were unrolled, lodgepoles trimmed to serve as tent poles, dry wood broken to size and stacked. Fenton and Gus's horses were kept in. The others, mares belled, turned out to graze on the rich grass of the slide.

Fenton was back on Babe, the camp-ax slung under his leg like a rifle when they heard him say what they knew already. "Doesn't look good. But we'll take a look. No one better at that than Tommy."

Then he was gone, Gus falling in behind him, the bucksaw in one hand, Gus looking even more discouraged than usual. As easy-going as Gus usually was, he'd been looking discouraged ever since the snag tore open his face—discouraged and resigned. Fenton didn't even have to look at him to know how he felt about Lost Bird Canyon.

The ground was soft; it was easy to track Tommy's pinto, though they weren't sure they were on the tracks of his first exploration or his second, not until they heard Pinto's whinny. They tied up there and went ahead on foot, finding Tommy high on some deadfall studying the canyon floor.

"Can't see how you got through at all," he called to Fenton. "Looks like trees have clogged up the canyon forever." He worked his way back to them across the jumbled logs.

"But I did get through," Fenton said. "I'd like to know how, even if we can't now. It's a mystery, is what it is. And I *hate* mysteries. Why Paint Boy did himself in has been driving me loco for too damn long."

Tommy, saying nothing, turned away, crossing the creek on some deadfall and disappearing. Fenton wanted to kick himself for bringing up the Cheyenne. Any mention of him made Tommy think of Hope Woman, who was gone forever—if not in body then in spirit. When people put on the Black Robe, Fenton knew, they were gone. No escaping it. The less

Tommy thought about her, the better. Special Hands might give Tommy more pleasure than anything else, but that was the only sweet part of Hope Woman's legacy. The rest was a sadness they just had to endure.

Tommy was calling out to them now, calling from across the canyon where he'd been stopped by a steep bluff of rocky outcroppings and precipitous chutes. When Fenton and Gus reached him he was already heading up one of the chutes, picking his way carefully, holding onto roots, moving gracefully for a man his size. "No bogs up high," he called down. "May be a way to move along up high we can't see from down low."

Fenton and Gus looked at each other, swatting away mosquitoes as they did. "We'll take a look," Fenton said. "Bound to be better up there than down in this wet."

"You lead," Gus said. "I've made enough mistakes this year. But I sure as hell know one thing."

"What's that?" Fenton asked, looking for a safer way up the cliff than Tommy's.

"That you didn't get through this canyon. That's what. Be hard for a mouse to make it, much less packed mules."

But by the time they reached Tommy, Tommy had found a way.

"You come through this way." He was standing on something better than a deer trail, a clear route that tailed off in either direction. "My people must've used it, crossing for buffalo. Didn't move nothing. Just stayed high, along these shelves."

They followed the route, way leading into way, paralleling the stream from high above it as they moved from one grassy ledge to another, sometimes climbing onto still another before dropping again, dropping until they found themselves on a long traverse angling down the grassy benches to the South Fork.

Turning to retrace their steps, it all became clear. The mouth of the traversing game trail was choked with willows. Had Fenton been on horseback, he wouldn't have seen it. But he'd lost his mare that morning, so he'd been walking, crashing around in those willows and somehow stumbling onto the route. Now it was the upper part of the route that worried him. But if he'd gotten to where Tommy found the trail, there had to be a way to continue. This mystery, at least, was unraveling.

But not three hundred yards beyond where they'd found Tommy, the way seemed hopelessly lost again. Not until Gus, in desperation, dropped down a little chute did they find the continuation of the route, this time switching back toward the South Fork before taking still another switchback that eased them into the canyon's very bottom, crossing the stream and the canyon floor along the edge of a boggy meadow to climb the other side, contouring high along the opposite bluff before dropping back down just above their horses.

It was a relief to Fenton. It could be done. There were logs to move, there was that switchback to repair, the soggy valley floor to navigate—but it could be done. He'd done it. They could do it again.

"Can't bring them with us." Tommy said it as though he had a direct line into Fenton's head. It was late, the daylight all but gone as the three of them at last headed back toward camp, the campfire a flickering spark up the canyon. As they neared it, the sound of a bell came from above, one of the mares shaking her head high up on the slide.

"Probably you're right," Fenton finally agreed. "Lots of dicey places to get up those cliffs. Tricky."

"Lots of shitty bogs to cross to get to them dicey places," Tommy said, wanting to be clear. "And that's worse."

"I've been mistrusting my decision-making," Gus said, realizing a decision was about to be made. "You two work it out. Alls I know is that up here Tommy makes good sense and down below Fenton wins us all kindsa drinks tellin' people what happened when we ignored it. It's a toss-up about whether we stay safe now or hear Fenton explain why we wasn't later. After all I been through, I'll side with what's safe."

"That's a long speech for you, Gus Wilson," Fenton admitted. "Let's get us some grub. See what a full stomach tells us."

They were the center of everything when they got to camp; questions came from everyone. Fenton stepped aside, belling Babe, then leading the three horses downstream and pushing them toward the slide to join the others.

He washed up in the stream before coming back, tired from the long day, his head full of things he couldn't define. As he neared the fire he saw that Tommy and Gus were being asked so many questions they couldn't start eating. Cody Jo must have seen how reluctant he was to join in. She met him outside the ring of light with a plate of food from Rosie, a cup of whisky from her.

"I believe you have saved my life," he said, sipping the whisky. "I'm sure not ready to answer all those questions."

"You think we can make it, don't you?" Cody Jo said quietly. "You're just worried that some know-it-all like me will do something foolish."

"Trouble is, you make me believe a know-it-all like you just might know it all. Gotta remind myself you haven't been in these mountains."

"You know them," she said. "And you know us. You must know a way to make it safe. To get us through."

"There's a lot that I don't know too. What scares me is that I still want to try. And not just for you. Tommy, he knows better. Knows not to try. And he's been through more than the lot of us put together."

They looked at the people by the fire, Tommy stoic as he tried to eat, Gus doing the talking now, his scar showing white in the firelight as the questions came and he struggled for answers.

And then they were calling to Fenton, asking Fenton.

"Well," Fenton heard himself saying, "there is a way. Tommy found it." Tommy was looking at him, looking as if he was having trouble hearing what he knew he was going to be hearing—but hearing it anyway.

"We can always turn back," Fenton continued, aware of the quiet that had come over them. "We can work on the route in the morning. If we do get it cleared, we'll be at White River by afternoon."

Again there was silence.

"And what if we don't get it cleared?" The question broke the quiet so suddenly it unsettled Fenton, who looked at Gus and then at Tommy before looking back on the rest of them.

"We lose three days," he said finally. "Maybe more. That's what."

The talk picked up again. But it was sober now, with none of the bluster of the night before. They'd heard from Gus, and from Tommy too, and understood they wouldn't take this chance.

Cody Jo took Fenton's cup and came back with more whisky.

"Are you taking this risk for me?" she asked. "Haven't I caused enough trouble already?"

"Wouldn't call it trouble," Fenton said, taking the cup. "Trouble's not as enjoyable." He took a sip, surprised again by what he was saying. "To tell the truth, I just might be takin' it for me."

16

Sugar

They were at it not long after daybreak, Fenton putting the youngsters to work with shovels to open the route across the shaley bluffs, using the strength of the men to clear deadfall and cut through brush, getting Tommy and Gus to look ahead for trouble, marking the spots that needed attention.

Tommy had told him what he thought of the idea the night before. Fenton tried not to think about that as he used a length of lodgepole to lever logs from the wet ground so the men could push them to the side.

"You're moonstruck. That's the goddamned problem," Tommy had said, his disembodied voice coming to Fenton out of the darkness as Fenton got into his bedroll.

"Don't know what you're talking about," Fenton spoke back to the darkness. "It's just that I came up through this place that same day I found you. Doesn't seem like a bad idea to find how I did it. Why not go down the way I came up?"

"Your mare died down there, don't forget. You had to walk out. You was dumb to try it and lucky to make it and now you're bein' dumb again and hopin' for more luck when what you really want is to romance that schoolteacher. Both Gus and me know you should be smart enough not to try."

"Try which?" Fenton had to smile. "Navigation or romance?"

"Both," Tommy said. Then he repeated what he'd just said, underscoring each point with his vivid language to make it stick.

It was the longest speech Fenton had ever heard from Tommy. He was surprised.

"Jesus, Tommy, I'm not romancing. I just want to get these people through to White River. Let's think how we can, not the reverse. Only thing that bothers me is that soft little meadow. One of our mules might break through. What if it's got no bottom?"

"Might could lose yours for tryin' shit like this. There'll likely be lots more trouble in that canyon than that bog. That's a truth you should study on."

Then the voice was gone, leaving Fenton to lie there in the quiet and listen for the bells. He thought he heard one, a faint ring up high. He sat up, listening closely, making sure. There it was, that clear sweet ring in the night. Silence again, and then a more insistent ringing—one of the mares shaking her head. He was relieved. Hearing it so clearly seemed a good omen. He lay back down and closed his eyes. But his sleep was fitful, filled with edgy dreams.

The lack of rest didn't seem to bother him now as he opened the route, levering up the log from the forest's floor. The others pushed it aside and he moved on, stopping to look out into the minty green of the little meadow camouflaging the bog. The ground on its upper edge seemed firm enough, but it was clear they'd have to lead the saddle horses and free the mules so they could navigate it on their own.

When the way looked passable, he sent Buck and Gus back to camp to bring in the mules, saddle, begin balancing packs. Then he mounted Babe and led Pinto through the newly pioneered route, Tommy following on foot, patching and repairing where the animals hesitated. As they returned along the edge of the green meadow, Babe sank up to her hocks. Pinto, wary of the jumbled deadfall that clogged the forest, edged out a little farther and sank deeper. Tommy watched, expressionless, as Fenton pulled them on through and onto safer ground—both men knowing this was the only way to cross the canyon, both hoping for something solid under that pristine surface.

By noon they had everyone fed and mounted, packs balanced, hitches tied. In an hour they were down the canyon and into the copse of trees, where they separated the mules to let each make his own way.

Fenton noticed the darkening sky as Gus led them up along the first cliffy bluffs, Tommy behind them leading Babe, the mare the mules would follow without fail. Buck and Fenton brought up the rear on foot, their eyes on the route and the mules, ready to move in if there was trouble.

They had little difficulty, dropping down to cross the canyon, the guests dismounting at the meadow to lead their horses through. Fenton watched closely as they crossed the muddy spot, each animal sinking deeper, the sucking sound of a final hoof coming free suggesting there was purchase enough after all. It was a relief when all had passed and were following Gus toward the stream.

Babe and the first mules cleared the mud with no trouble, each nosing at its wet before slogging through, encouraged by the horses ahead. Then trouble came, coming so unexpectedly there was no way to anticipate it, cut it off, get a lead on little Sugar to show her she was safe. She hesitated, just as the others had, but focused on the dry ground above the mud, seeming to forget the width of her packs. She stepped up seeking firmer ground and forced her way along a slanting lodgepole, her weight bending it back as she scraped along, the tension increasing until she faltered and the lodgepole released, springing back and propelling her out into the soft meadow. She went knee-deep in murk, struggled for balance, tipped back onto her haunches, her packs pulling her over so completely she rolled all the way over them and farther out into the meadow. When her feet came under her again, she struggled to stand but found herself chest-deep in brown water and torn turf, her packs holding her fast. She stopped struggling, looked back at the other mules, then broke the deep silence with a long, mournful bray.

Fenton, frozen as he watched the struggle, ignored her and moved quickly to the mules who had been following. He eased the first across the wet, then got the next, then the next. Buck, swearing as he pushed them through, crowded them toward the saddle horses waiting at the stream crossing.

Helpless and alone out in the broken meadow, Sugar could only watch as Buck pushed the last mule along the trail. She brayed. Brayed again, the sound cacophonous, and rising so desperately in the still forest that Fenton sent Buck back to free her from the packs.

"Mount everyone up and move along, Tommy," Fenton said before turning back himself. "I'll try to pry her loose without the packs. . . . Weather's comin' in. Things might get bad."

There was quiet now, everyone suddenly taking in the deep gray of the sky. Gus and Tommy tightened cinches, the men helped their children get mounted again,—saying nothing, knowing nothing needed to be said.

"What about Sugar?" Cody Jo asked. "She's so frightened."

"Sure as hell should be," Fenton said. "May help her fight her way out. That and some grizzly that wanders by."

"Grizzly?" Cody Jo couldn't believe what she thought she'd heard.

"They like it when whatever they want gets bogged," said Tommy, climbing on his pinto. "Like findin' a hot breakfast."

"Better move," Fenton said. "Take Babe, and Buck's horse too. "Sooner everything's out of sight, sooner she'll want to follow. Be bad if we don't free her before this rain. . . . Damn good mule, too."

Cody Jo was looking back even as she rode up the steep chute. She could make out Fenton walking back toward the broken meadow. Then she had to grab her gelding's mane, pull her weight forward on the flat saddle as they scrambled up the bluff and onto the crude route high above the danger, far below them now, the troubles of Sugar out of sight, only her mournful cry still lifting up through the forest.

Cody Jo found a place where she could dismount and did, leading her gelding along the narrow way until they reached the open game trail slanting down to the South Fork. She dropped behind then, shooing the gelding after the others and turning back, letting Gus—riding drag to keep everyone moving—pass by her.

"They'll have to drag Sugar's pack up to some dry," Gus told her. "She's mired awful deep." His scar glinted white as he scanned the sky. "This storm ain't gonna help."

Cody Jo broke into a run, moving back along the narrow traverse swiftly to slide back down the chute, cross the stream, find Fenton.

When she came to the meadow, she found him bending over Buck, his hands on either side of Buck's face. "Glad you're here," he said, hardly looking up. "Buck got his nose moved around. I'm tryin' to get it straight while he's still numb."

"Oh dear." She was shocked by the blood soaking Buck's shirt and splattered across Fenton. "How . . . what should I do?"

"'Bout as straight as it's gonna get. Wash him off in that creek and take a look-see. I'll get the packs. Sugar fought everything so hard she damn near split open his head."

Fenton started out through the mud toward Sugar.

"Bet he's gonna cut the damn ropes," Buck muttered as Cody Jo led him back to the creek. "If I'd known he was willin' to cut rope I might not have got to where that mule's head would make my nose bleed."

He walked out into the deepest part of the stream and sat, splashing water on his face.

"You ever had a bloody nose, Cody Jo? Comes out right quick."

"I'm more worried about your head, Buck. Come here. Let me see."

Buck waded unsteadily toward her. "Angie worries about my head too." He stood knee-deep in the creek as she wiped away clots of blood. "But she ain't as gentle."

"It'll swell," said Fenton suddenly behind her. "But I got Sugar's packs up on dry land. Let's scoot. When we're gone, she might fight her way clear. She plumb quit after she broke Buck's nose."

"Ought not take a bath in your clothes," Tommy's voice called out from above. He slid Pinto down the chute with Goose behind him, the most serviceable horse in Fenton's string. "If you'd waited you coulda got a shower-bath," he said, gesturing up at the black sky.

"Gonna be a gully-washer," Fenton said. "Buck's got his nose spread around, Tommy. Take him back on Pinto and ready them to move. I'll take Goose and fetch Sugar's packs."

"I'll go too. Poor Sugar." Cody Jo was about to cry.

"You stick with Tommy," Fenton said. "They'll need some of your school-teacher cheer when the sky opens up."

Fenton hoisted her up behind Buck, who was swaying dangerously on Pinto.

"Keep him in the saddle," Fenton told her. "He could tip off." Then Fenton was gone, leading Goose back to collect Sugar's packs.

When they reached the traverse, Tommy broke them into a trot, Cody Jo reaching around the floundering Buck, using the saddle horn to keep him upright. The others were already in action when they arrived—breaking out raingear, finding shelter under trees, asking questions. Tommy and Gus pulled Buck from the saddle, sat him on a log, and got him into his slicker.

Cody Jo felt sick. She'd packed hers away that morning. Gus would either give her his or they'd have to go through the packs for hers.

"I'll go back for Fenton," she said suddenly, sure she was going to cry. The rain began coming as she got on her gelding. "He'll need help."

"You can't go alone," Gus said. "Fenton won't have it."

"Leave her go." Tommy handed Babe's lead line to Cody Jo. "We'll need him to cross—quicker the better. River's gonna rise." The trail seemed narrower to Cody Jo as she rode back through the rain—the gelding slipping on the slick shale and scrambling back as Babe pushed from behind. They were sliding down the chute to the stream just as Fenton crossed, all Sugar's gear tied onto Goose.

"Sugar'll have to make it on her own," he said. "Couldn't budge her." He saw Cody Jo was crying and untied his slicker from Babe's saddle, putting it on her as lightning crackled, thunder close behind, the rain coming harder now.

Cody Jo was so shaken she wasn't about to manage the snaps on the slicker. Fenton reached up and closed them for her. "Bet you gave yours to one of the kids," he said, reaching into Babe's saddlebag to pull out a scrunched-up poncho. "I carry an extra just in case." He pulled it on in the downpour, the poncho barely reaching his waist. "We better skedaddle." He had to shout through the pounding rain. "River's gonna rise."

Cody Jo felt helpless as she watched Fenton force Babe back up the slick chute, Goose scrambling and slipping behind them. She clung blindly to her gelding's mane as he fought his way up. Fenton broke them into a trot when they reached the narrow traverse, thunder cracking down with the lightning now. Cody Jo was astonished by Fenton's calm, slowing Babe where the trail might give way, moving more quickly when he could, watching ahead and then looking back—checking everything as they moved through sheets of rain.

Everyone was moving even before they appeared. Tommy and Gus had them mounted, pack mules divided into strings of three as Fenton took the first three toward the river, plunging in immediately. Gus freed the others as they reached the bank, letting each make his own way through the churning rapids. They watched through the downpour as Fenton found a shelf to cross onto a midriver bar. It was only hock-deep there and he used it to quarter upriver to reach a rocky crossing of still swifter rapids leading to the far side of the South Fork. Cody Jo watched with the others as Fenton moved up the bar. He looked hazy and iconic through the sheets of water, moving his mules up against everything the river was bringing down, looking back as he rode, making sure everyone saw the hidden shelf needed to reach the bar, moving upriver on it and crossing the deeper rapids to reach the safety of the White River benches. The view took away what little breath she had as she got ready to plunge into the river herself, fight it as Fenton had, fight it in order to reach the safety of those benches.

It was Goose who caused the trouble, the sturdy grey following the mules across the shelf and onto the bar then up against the river. Only then did Goose realize he was following mules, not the horses he wanted to be with. They remained back on the bank, waiting until the mules proved it was safe. Halfway up the bar, the reality came to Goose. He turned back toward the bank where the horses waited, heedless of the danger that the quiet water running under the bank might hold, heedless of the shelf Fenton had found to get them safely onto the bar he was abandoning. He slid under the quiet waters as though being pulled. First his body, then his packs, finally his head, bubbles rising to show where he'd gone under.

Tommy and Gus were moving quickly along the bank, getting the riders to follow Buck, barely steady himself, as he led them across Fenton's shelf and started them up the bar. Gus followed, the boy who'd ridden Goose clinging to Gus, eyes squeezed shut against the rain, against the horror of watching Goose disappear into the spooky waters, waters, waters so still and deep they showed no life until they broke into ripples and foamed into rapids to cross the shelf Fenton had used to start across the river and reach the bar.

The saddle horses were on the bar now and moving up it when Tommy, trailing the rest, saw what he so wanted to see, Goose's nose coming up first as the deep currents washed him down into the shelf where Tommy waited. Tommy watched the water lift Goose until Goose's packs emerged, the horse blowing water and shaking himself as he struggled for footing. Tommy saw him come up only to fall, the weight of the water-soaked packs too much until a string of Tommy's curses forced him upright. He staggered after the horses now, as frightened by Tommy as he was pulled toward the other horses, all of them making their way up the shallow bar before crossing the deep rapids leading to the benches.

Cody Jo, riding near the end of the long string of horses, couldn't believe it when Goose appeared behind them, ghostly-looking through the downpour, struggling to stay ahead of the swearing Tommy. When they reached the bank, Goose lurched up it, free of the river at last, his packs a terrible burden but his fear of the furious Tommy driving him on. They climbed from the river onto a flat, climbed again onto a wide bench where Fenton was already unrolling a tarp to lift against the wet. Buck, trying to help, became so unsteady he fell, Gus quickly taking over and helping lift a long lodgepole in place, using it as a beam for the heavy tarp.

Cody Jo, sheltered under Fenton's slicker, felt helpless as she watched how quickly a camp emerged from the chaos. Tommy, whose badgering of Goose had stopped the moment they reached the broad shelf, had immediately dropped Goose's water-laden packs and turned to the work at hand, the rain hardly slowing him as he led mule after mule under the high fly, storing gear in this dry place and that as other tents went up and the kitchen fly appeared, Gus bringing pitch axed from a fir to get a fire going the moment the stove was assembled.

Fire was soon relayed from the cook-stove to a campfire, the root of a dead fir sheltering infant flames until the root's pitch took, black smoke lifting from wet wood, the wood drying as snags broken from beneath the sheltering branches of conifers fueled the smoking fire. Gus and Tommy—even Buck—never stopped moving. Nor did Fenton, who gave directions as he moved: getting gear in place, unsaddling, checking animals for sores, getting guests into tents as he and Tommy began freeing their mules.

Buck was covering the saddles with manties when Fenton took over, sending him to Rosie so she could chill his face with cloths.

"It's swole," Buck told Rosie. "Fenton says I won't be no use until I'm unswole."

"Which means icing it." Rosie sat him down and tilted his head up. We'll bring your bedroll in and put you on your back. Chill that blood and it won't swell your face—maybe."

"Will his eyes close?" Cody Jo had a bucket and was ringing out another cloth soaked in the icy-cold waters of White River.

"Mostly," Rosie said. "But that'll give him a chance to think about Angie. We'll cool his face while she warms his heart."

"Wish she'd warm something else," Buck groused. "Fenton says to be patient. Says a girl like Angie don't like to be rushed."

"He's got a point," Cody Jo said. "A girl likes to know what tempts her in the moonlight will look okay over coffee in the morning."

"I seen her at breakfast many times," said Buck. "It don't seem to impress her."

"Maybe because you act like it's moonlight at breakfast." Cody Jo had to smile. "Some girls like to talk *with* you before you go into your moonbeam routine."

"He'll look more like a rainbow trout than a moonbeam," Rosie said. "Won't be much romance in our Buck for a while."

"We'll see," Cody Jo said. "It's surprising what makes a girl choose her man." She handed Rosie another chilled cloth. "Angie might surprise us." She gave Buck a pat and left. Rosie needed still more icy water from White River.

The rain had stopped at last. Both Gus and Tommy were sure it had been the heaviest concentration ever.

"I believe near a foot," Gus said. "Half hour more and we'd of lost Goose along with Sugar. Maybe lost some others, too."

"We ain't lost Sugar yet," Tommy said. "Though it's likely. Alls I know is there's strange shit goin' on. This rain. Sugar. Buck's nose. Could be we got ourselves crosswise with these mountains for comin' down that canyon where we shouldn't."

"Another of your Indian signs?" Gus was astonished by the things Tommy knew—or could predict. He'd always suspected Tommy knew something was wrong with Paint Boy, though Tommy never said a word about it. There were lots of things Tommy never talked about.

Gus and Tommy were rigging lines so people could dry clothes in the morning. Cody Jo watched them work before continuing off to the big rock slanting down into the waters of White River. As she filled her bucket she heard Fenton's voice. "Drink some," he said. "Like ice. A sight better to drink from than bathe in. I'm damn near sorry I did." He had on dry clothes and was sitting high on the slanting rock, his soaked clothes wrapped in the torn poncho. She climbed up the rock and sat with him, ashamed she'd caused so much trouble.

"I had your slicker, all day. It saved me. You saved us. And got soaked for your kindness."

"Figured you gave yours to one of the kids. And I had my poncho."

"No. . . . I didn't. I'd packed mine away—this morning."

"That's rich. No place to tie your slicker so you packed it. And never a complaint. Bet you wanted to throw a tantrum when this rain came."

"I did. And I wanted to tell you you were wonderful. But . . . I couldn't. But you really were. And you were knowing too—bringing us down that canyon."

"Wasn't knowing so much as dumb. Ask Tommy. But we made it. That's the thing. If Sugar was here and Buck's nose wasn't flattened, we'd be all right. We'd be fine."

He stood, looking clean and tall. His hair white as snow under the moon as it broke free of the clouds.

Cody Jo stood as well, looked up at him in the moonlight, touched by the moment and all that Fenton had done to save them. She had no words to say it so she reached out to hug him, ever so briefly, in thanks.

He returned the hug, felt her body against his, her breath on his neck. Felt something he'd never felt running through him.

It wasn't Beth he was holding, it was Cody Jo who was holding him. And suddenly everything changed.

17

The Red Bear

For the second night Fenton hardly slept. But this time there was no worry about getting through Lost Bird Canyon to the White River benches; this time the worry was what to do now that he had done it. He tossed and turned with it, feeling Cody Jo's breath, hearing her sigh, her body almost his. Whether he slept at all, he didn't know. Which is why he didn't know if it was reality or a dream that brought him upright in the night to hear the long mournful cry of a mule. It came again, barely discernable—but clear, lifting across the deep rumble of the South Fork waters, not from farther up the benches where they'd turned out their animals. He listened again, but it came no more. He settled back into his bedroll, that cry mixing somehow with the reality of Cody Jo.

In the morning he told Tommy. Not about Cody Jo, which it seemed to him Tommy understood already, but about that mournful call in the night.

"Sign," Tommy said. "Dreams and such leave signs. Won't know 'til it happens."

"If you have to wait 'til something happens, who's to say what's a sign and what isn't?" Fenton asked. "Your people can be as hard to figure as those Black Robes."

They were walking up the White River drainage to find the horses, the South Fork farther and farther behind them. As was the source of that lonely call, though it haunted Fenton, even as they looked for tracks.

"Because our signs make sense," Tommy said. "They're real. You get to see them."

"Like that Gros Ventre who came back as a grizzly to haunt your people? Wasn't that just some squaw's vision?"

"No vision when horses' guts is ripped out, dogs killed, tipis tore open. Sign was there when they killed the man. Didn't see it 'til he come back for revenge—come as a griz."

Fenton was always taken by how seriously Tommy took the subject of signs.

"Maybe your people shouldn't have killed the Gros Ventre," he said.

"And maybe you shouldn't have come down that canyon," Tommy replied, considering the comparison as they walked.

"Shit, Tommy. 'Maybe' gets to be a big word when you bring it home that way. To tell the truth, the only sign I'm lookin' for now is Babe's. And I don't think we need it. . . . I hear her bell."

They brought them in with no trouble, Fenton leading Babe, the rest happy to follow after their long morning's feed. They kept in what they needed and pushed the others out to graze, Tommy turning and speaking to Fenton as though they'd never stopped considering.

I'll tell you why it's a sign, it's a sign because you couldn't never have heard Sugar in the night. Not across that river. Still sounds like a buffalo run."

"I couldn't hear Sugar 'cause Sugar's underwater. Or half-eaten by your damn grizzly. No way she could survive that storm," Fenton said, trying to ignore what had been gnawing at him all morning. "That's the only reason I couldn't hear her."

"Might be surprised," Tommy said evenly, as though he already knew what was gnawing at Fenton. "Mules is tough, when it counts."

"If it'll make you feel any better, I'll ride back there and take a look-see. Soon as that river goes down so I can cross." Fenton began brushing Babe. Brushing her gave him something to do.

"You been tellin' me that all morning," said Tommy.

"I haven't been saying anything. And you know as well as I do she'll be lunch for the coyotes—if I find anything left at all."

"I don't know," Tommy said, watching Fenton brush. "Neither do you. All I know is that river's gonna drive you crazy—until you cross it."

And the river did drive him crazy. He had Babe saddled for three hours before he could cross, going down to the river to check and returning to badger Buck, who was alternately putting cold cloths on his face and trying to rivet together a broken breeching. Buck's eyes were swollen slits. He had to tilt his head back to look up at Fenton.

"You could go loco before that river drops," Buck said, craning his head up to look at Fenton. "Either sit down or go away. You make me so nervous I can't pound my rivets."

"And I get nervous just watchin' you try. Your face is gettin' purple. Orangish too. Lucky your teeth only got loosened. They'll tighten. What worries me is your nose might not." Fenton was edgy as he talked. "Where's Rosie? She should soak you in more towels."

"Cody Jo and her hiked up White River. Glad they did. Nothin' but jabber all morning."

"What the hell about?" Fenton asked. "Not much to talk about around here, except how your nose is gonna come out."

He wanted to ask more but went to check the river instead, too muddled about Cody Jo and the crossing to know what to ask.

By midafternoon the river had gone down enough to cross. He was tightening Babe's cinch when Cody Jo showed up, leading her gelding. She had Buck's saddle on him, her slicker tied behind the saddle.

"I thought if I used this big heavy saddle and tied my slicker on it you two might take me seriously," she said.

"I always take you seriously," Buck said, trying to smile. He liked being kidded by Cody Jo, though he didn't like her insistence on the cold towels. "Bump might beat up on me if I don't."

"And I might beat up on *you* if you think you're gonna follow me across that river," Fenton told Cody Jo, climbing up on Babe. "This is just a duty ride—to make sure about Sugar. Won't be pretty."

"Who's talking about pretty?" Cody Jo asked, mounting the gelding and settling herself into Buck's saddle. "I've caused enough trouble already. I want to help now. I want you to take me seriously."

There was everything serious in what she said, nothing funny.

"Maybe you'd help most," Fenton said, just as seriously, "if you stayed here and let me get this done. I'm not even sure I can get across the river. And I don't want you to see what I might find if I do."

"And I don't want you to find it alone," she said. "I've made my mistakes. I'm riding this saddle now. I understand some things I had no idea I'd ever be considering, much less understanding."

Cody Jo sat a horse beautifully. Fenton thought he'd never seen anything as winning as she looked at that moment, her back straight, her oneness with her horse complete. He knew the river would be no problem for her, nor would the ride in to the little glade. What he didn't want her to see was what had happened to Sugar—how grim these mountains could become.

Buck, mystified by the conversation and uncomfortable with the long silence, settled things.

"You two better start," he said, his head tilted to take them both in. "You might not get there before it's time to be back here."

That was enough. They dropped to the river and crossed, saying little as Fenton took advantage of how the storm had improved the bar they'd used the day before. The crossing behind them, they broke into a trot, moving fast across the rain-washed forest floor to find the game trail contouring down from the Lost Bird Canyon cliffs.

Cody Jo had to let Fenton help her down the final chute to the canyon floor. The heavy rain had changed everything, the sun muted now by the dripping canopy of trees, the green of them darker and deeper, the mosquitoes thicker. She was taken by how naturally Fenton adjusted to things as they made their way. When he'd seen how little trail was left, he'd taken his gun belt from his saddlebag, buckled it on, and tied the horses there—continuing on foot along the narrowing trail.

The stream crossing was altered as well. Fenton studied the bank before helping her skip across on logs and newly packed debris. He studied the opposite bank even more carefully, scanning it as they made their way to the big fir marking the crossing. At one place he stopped and looked out through the woods. She heard a click as he reached down and did something with the Smith and Wesson.

"Never know," he said. "When you might need an act of mercy."

It came suddenly to Cody Jo how grim things might be. "Could it be that bad?"

"Lots of possibilities up here," Fenton said, helping her along the bank to reach the big tree. "Best not to overlook one."

When they reached the fir he stopped, studying the ground.

"Mule track," He seemed surprised, almost unbelieving.

"Does that mean she's alive?" Cody Jo's voice caught at the thought. "That she's here, somewhere?"

"If whatever scared her from the bog didn't get her, she just might be."

Fenton lifted his voice into the lilting cry he used when he took grain to his animals. "C'mmm-on!" His call sank into a silence before echoing back across the canyon, almost lingering as they listened for anything moving, any rustling out where there was no way to see.

Nothing. The silence washed back to surround them. Again Fenton offered the drawn-out call. Again the echo came back, haunting and sad. The silence returned.

"Well. . . ." Fenton looked around as though assessing what to do. "I've tracked mules before. Soft ground'll help. Wish Tommy was here."

"Would he know a better way?"

"He'd pick up the track, like we will. But then he'd get a notion, follow a hunch, figure where she's going. If she's alive, he'd find her."

"How? What's his magic?" Cody Jo watched as Fenton picked up the track, just as he said he would, and followed it along the edge of the bog and into the woods.

"It is a kind of magic, the way Tommy does it. But I'm not sure he knows he has it. He just uses it."

They followed a labyrinth-like course, circling and back-tracking and ducking under deadfall no mule should be able to manage, the track always getting closer to the South Fork—as though Sugar knew the direction to go, just not how to get there. Finally they were stopped by an impenetrable logjam blocking the mouth of the canyon, the creek now impossible to cross. Fenton was baffled, and he was worried about Cody Jo. She had followed him quietly, astonished by things he would point to. The track—now and then clear even to her—was mostly invisible, grass flattened this way or that, or marked by a bit of hair on a branch, a twig pressed into the forest floor. Once, in a rocky patch edging up toward the bluffs, Fenton knelt, putting his cheek to the ground as he scanned for a hint of grass leaning away, somehow different. Rising, he took them across the traceless flat and into the timber to pick up a sure sign twenty yards farther, following it farther and still farther down the canyon—until there was no farther to go.

"I've worn you out," Fenton said. They rested by some willows and he watched Cody Jo wave away some buzzing near her ear. "At least we know our mule's alive—if getting stopped by all this didn't drive her crazy. Wonder where she's gone. . . . Wonder how Tommy knew."

"Tommy knew? Knew what? That we'd be stopped too? That we wouldn't find Sugar?"

"Knew the water didn't get her. Or the bear. Maybe knew the bear might scare her out of the bog. Knew things I sure didn't."

"Bear? What bear?"

"There were tracks at that stream crossing. Tracks all around that boggy meadow too. But none down here in these woods. Guess our bear was just checking things out. Maybe he had a full tummy."

"Oh." Cody Jo looked back at the way they'd come. "A bear watching us." She wasn't sure whether she should be frightened by a bear spying on them or impressed that Fenton knew it. All she knew was that they were as alone as human beings could be, that she would be lost without the reality of Fenton. She was reaching out to touch him and say so when a bray lifted from the very willows they stood by, the bray anguished and pitiful, startling to them both. They were scanning the brush, looking for the source of that desperate cry when it came again: harsh, almost demanding. . . . Finally they saw her, could make out the little mule through the scrim of leaves, her head still lifted, her mouth wide as she ended her lonely cry, which halted as abruptly as it had begun. Sugar ducked her head, shook it, looked out at them as though ready to give voice again.

"My goodness." Cody Jo had to laugh, her relief breaking through the sudden silence. "You're lonely," she said. "You've missed us."

"She has." Fenton laughed himself, partly in relief but mostly out of pleasure in watching Cody Jo as she pushed aside the willow branches and reached out to stroke the needy mule. Sugar quivered under her hand, stutter-stepped and nosed at her, rubbing her long mule-face against the schoolteacher, needing every bit of that contact she could manage.

Fenton pulled his trouser belt free and threaded it through the ring on Sugar's halter, used it to lead her from the willows and back up the canyon. Darkness was coming in. He was thankful they had no trouble making their way back to the boggy meadow, which they circled to reach the big fir marking the crossing.

Seeing the still dark water disguising the ford, Sugar balked, terrorized by what might be there. Her rump dropped as she fought back, scrambling backward with such force she almost pulled Fenton down.

"Thinks it's mud," Fenton said, realizing how late it was getting. "Doesn't know there's a bottom. I'll scoot back for Babe. She'll cross anything. Sugar'll follow Babe to hell and back." He handed Cody Jo the makeshift lead, crossed the creek and headed up the chute.

Just as quickly, he was back, skipping across the water on logs and debris. "Take this." He unholstered the big pistol. "She's cocked. Be careful. Shoot up in the air if there's trouble. Don't want to hit anything."

He was gone again, gone so quickly that before she could speak he was up the chute and put of sight. "Why shoot then?" she mumbled half-heartedly, putting the pistol on a log so she could rub Sugar's neck.

Sugar seemed more nervous than ever in the dying light, quivering as Cody Jo stroked her, inching back even as she accepted Cody Jo's hands smoothing her neck, rubbing her flank, moving along her soft underbelly where mosquitoes were gathering.

"We'll be all right, Sugar," she said soothingly. "Fenton's gone for Babe. He'll bring your friend. He knows what to do." She put her cheek down on Sugar's withers, smoothing the mule's flanks and watching shafts of late sun slanting through the trees.

The forest was still, the creek the faintest gurgle as it wound down the canyon. Her weight on Sugar seemed to settle the little mule, who quieted as Cody Jo looked out through the jumbled timber, taking in the darkening canyon. A slanting ray of sun caught something bright above her, high on the big fir. She looked up to see that the bark was peeled away, yellow sapwood exposed. It seemed to be oozing more sap even as she looked at it. Above the peeled wound were claw marks, yellow streaks going down to it.

A sickness welled up in her, sweat breaking out on her forehead, chills running along her neck and down her arms. When she looked again, the sap was still lifting from the scar—higher than a horseman could reach–lifting as though protesting the violation.

Sugar seemed transfixed, ears forward, not a flicker of motion as Cody Jo's knees weakened and she slid down Sugar's withers and crouched there, weak and helpless. She thought of the pistol but couldn't focus on where she'd left it, or how to use it, hardly remembering where she was—knowing only that she was not alone, that something was watching, that Sugar knew it too.

Her head went down. The sour taste of vomit, metallic and sour, lifted into her mouth, a queasiness washing through her as she realized she was looking at a track. It was pressed deep into the soft earth, the fresh pad-print—wide as a plate—filled with water as she watched.

How long she crouched there she couldn't know, knowing only that the seeping stopped, as the shadows grew longer. Finally the ache in her folded body began focusing her mind—which was going everywhere, unable to settle anywhere.

She knew she had to stand, if she could make her body do it. Sugar, still as she was, could brace her—if she could straighten up. And she had to; she had no choice. She lifted, sighing as she did, the sigh escaping just before the crashing in the brush scant feet away. There was a blur of red fur as Fenton's voice burst through the woods, rocks tumbling as he slid Babe down the chute.

"There he goes," he shouted. "Big one." Babe splashed across the creek and then Fenton was holding Cody Jo, comforting her. "Never saw one that red," he said, his eyes taking in everything. "That old log's a dandy place to store my pistol." He balanced Cody Jo as she tested her legs. "When that big bear was takin' a peek at you." He retrieved the Smith and Wesson, holstered it, looked up at the scar on the fir. "He left his mark. I never know whether they want to stretch themselves or just tell us they aim high."

"I knew . . . Sugar knew too. Thank God you came."

"Bear's the one to thank. Guess he just wanted to look you over." He smiled as she tested her legs, liking the look of her. Then Sugar was nudging Cody Jo with her nose, pushing to get past, get closer to Babe.

"Let's cross. Get up that chute while there's light," Fenton said. "Sugar wants to go now. I believe that bear scared her into a serious romance with us." He snapped a lead on Sugar, dallied the other end around Babe's saddle horn and skipped across the creek, leading Babe as she splashed through, Sugar happy to follow, happy to leave that canyon.

"Grab her tail if that chute's too steep," Fenton called back. "Won't be the first time she's pulled someone out of trouble."

Cody Jo did, and Sugar pulled her up easily. Relief washed through her when they reached the trail above, moved along it. All she wanted to do was follow this man, his horse, his mule, away from this canyon.

There was still a light when they heard the gelding nicker, the sound soft and comforting as Sugar crowded herself into Babe's rump, needing all the contact she could get after her night alone.

"They do crave company," Fenton said, tightening the cinch on Cody Jo's gelding. "Let's scoot across that river. Sugar'll be in blue heaven when she finds the others up on those benches."

"I think those benches are your blue heaven, Fenton Pardee. I've never seen a man so much at home as you are up here."

"I might aim a little higher," Fenton said, not sure where this was going. "Might aim up where you can see out over this country."

He threaded the end of Babe's latigo through the keeper and turned to help Cody Jo mount, his movements so easy and sure that Cody Jo could think of nothing to do but hold him, put her head against his chest.

"Oh Fenton," she said. "You've aimed high enough already. I think . . ." Fenton thought she might be beginning to cry again. But she wasn't.

"I'm falling in love," she said. She turned away then, found her stirrup, felt Fenton's strength helping her into the saddle. "I think I'm learning how much of you there is to love."

Even if Fenton had found something to say, he wouldn't have known how. He climbed on Babe, took Sugar's lead, and they forded, the light of a lifting moon shimmering over the waters of the Southfork as they splashed across and climbed onto the White River benches.

18

Blue Heaven

The rest of the trip sailed by in a blur. After their one clear day, the weather came back. No big rain, but grey skies and drizzle—the fish rising as though they couldn't find enough to eat.

Tommy Yellowtail didn't seem surprised the night Fenton returned with Sugar, the little mule quivering with anticipation as they pushed her out to join the others high on the White River benches.

"Sign. Like I said," Tommy told Fenton, sitting late by the fire. Fenton looked tired. He was tired, weary from so many questions and still a little dizzy from the way Cody Jo had watched him search for answers. "No way you could hear that mule across the water's noise," Tommy said. "But you heard. Knew she was alive. Probably knew more, too. Never know about that shit."

"I guess you never do," Fenton said, pouring some whisky into his cup. "You want a little of this or are you still in the abstineous condition?"

"I'm abstineous. Don't need that poison up here. I'm hopin' Special Hands figures that out."

"I believe that boy means more to you than the whole damn tribe." Fenton said, still so befuddled by his thoughts about Cody Jo he hardly expected Tommy to hear him.

"He *is* my goddamned tribe," Tommy said, tossing a pitch-heavy log onto the fire and watching the flames lift. "I'm just wonderin' if that sign had anything to do with him. . . . With me. . . . Sure did with you."

"If there was a sign, it was only about that mule." Fenton sipped at his whisky, contemplating it. "Strange enough all by itself."

"If you could see the way you was lookin' at that schoolteacher, you'd know there's more things that sign could mean."

"She is a sight to look at." Fenton shifted his position to get below the sudden heat. "But that stuff is all hooey. What could a mule call in the night mean about a schoolteacher? You probably think it's hooey yourself." Fenton looked across the fire, wanting a response this time.

But Tommy was gone, off to seek his bedroll.

Fenton shrugged it off, remaining there by the fire, sipping his whisky and admiring how fire brought light into the darkest night. He didn't have time to digest what had happened, at least not on that trip. All he knew was that Cody Jo seemed everywhere, day and night, in his mind and in his heartbeat and in everything that went on in their camps. She kept them all cheerful, cheerful in their slickers when they were on the move, cheerful in their tents when not. She invented games and skits and storytelling to keep everyone occupied. And when she wasn't entertaining the others she'd go out with Fenton to check his horses. There was no more talk of what they meant to each other, but all kinds of talk around it, each thing one said weighted with meaning for the other.

"This really is your blue heaven, isn't it?" she asked him one morning. They were stopped above a meadow, watching the horses. The horses hock-deep in grass and still as statues as they waited for some sun. "Whatever blue heaven means for you and Sugar."

"I expect it means a different thing for me than for her. But there's things that might hold, for us both."

"'Hold for you both?' Maybe they should write a song about that. What holds, what's true — for different people, sometimes for all of us."

"Someone will, probably. Just won't be about what holds up here."

"What does? What holds up here?"

"A morning like this. At least for Sugar. Others around, a full belly, the sun breaking through, the peace."

"And for you?"

"Some of the same—but darker. Gets complicated."

"Make it simple." She looked back at the horses, comfortable under the warming sun. "Make it so a schoolteacher can understand."

"Hell, we all know, for certain, when life's this good." Fenton looked above the horses to the mountains lifting beyond, searching for his words. "I guess that's the heaven part. But a guy knows, deep down, it won't last."

"And that's your blue part?"

"I think it is."

"But you keep telling me this country will last."

"After they dig roads across it and punch holes through it, it might wind up too battered by the people who don't know any better to do any good for the people who do." He pulled his eyes away from the high ridges and looked at her. "What makes a guy blue — when he finds himself at home up here—is that the comfort he's come to know won't stay. He can't teach it; he can't pass it on. It'll be gone. Die with him."

"That's not true, Fenton, not what all kinds of different cultures, different churches, even different books tell us. You know that. Knowledge gets passed on."

"Some kinds, maybe. But not the kind a guy gets from this."

"Oh Fenton. It can be passed on too. Think of all the wisdom, the spiritual truths that get passed on. That get taught."

"I do. And I guess I think you should know what any good schoolteacher should," Fenton said, admiring the commitment Cody Jo always brought to whatever ideas she had. "When people run around swearing they have the gospel, have got a lock on some truth—here or off in China—it's about as reliable as a runaway mule. The peace a guy comes to know with this country up here he has by his lonesome. It's his deal with Mother Nature. It ain't transferable."

Cody Jo was a little shocked by the easy acceptance, even comfort, Fenton seemed to take in his loneliness—his oneness with his high country.

"Any good schoolteacher," she said finally, "must ask questions. . . . But we have to believe in people, too. We must."

"You could aim higher," Fenton said, looking back at the ridges lifting above his horses. "There's more. I just don't believe there's any way to fit this high country into your schoolroom."

The sun didn't break through for good until the last day, the sky so blue it almost hurt. Cody Jo, graceful in the saddle as anyone could be, rode just ahead of Fenton and his packers, their strings light-loaded now, so easy to manage they reached the corrals by midafternoon.

Unsaddling and turning the mules out was short work. The gear divided into camp equipment, soon to be packed back in; and the quest's duffle, on its way out. The dudes went through it, claiming their own, and suddenly cameras were everywhere. Each of them wanted a picture of the horse they'd ridden, the mule they'd favored, of Rosie and one packer or another. All of them wanted a snapshot of Cody Jo. And of Fenton.

Finally she broke away and took him aside. "I think I understand now. See what makes you stay up there, find a home up there." She was looking at him intently, as though she wanted somehow to see deep inside him.

"Realize, for me, that it doesn't change a thing. Nothing. How at home you are up there just makes me feel closer to you down here. We'll be just what we were to each other that day we found Sugar. I think we'll have that always. . . . I think you see that too."

Then she was back with the guests, posing with Rosie or Buck or one guest or another. When they called Fenton over to get another picture of the two of them together, Fenton found himself too full of her to speak. When he returned to his work, his mind was still with her, thinking of all the things she hadn't needed to say—and of all the things he couldn't.

The rest of the season swam by. Buck's nose was still crooked but the bruises were fading. Jasper was back to cooking again. The fishing trips turned into hunting trips with hardly a missed stroke. They set up a high camp for hunting, moved it lower as the weather turned—the snow coming early but melting off to give them a few more weeks for Jasper to work his magic. The hunters' range diminished as the days shortened, and they found themselves drawn to the camp more than the game. They liked the comfort of Jasper's humor, his stories, liked best the liquor Dan had sent in to cheer them.

Somehow Dan's liquor seemed even better to them than the liquor they found in their cities, where they drifted between bars, seeing important friends and making important deals. Fenton was sure it wasn't much different, but he knew they relished it more. He thought what drew them most was the comfort of the country and the mountain lore of his packers. He thought Jasper and his packers might seem as much a part of the rugged world around them as the game they sought. And he figured all of it together said something more important than their own world of deals and trades, a world they'd left in order to borrow from this one–this world with a heartbeat as constant as the waters running through it.

They broke camp and made it over the passes just ahead of the big November storm, cleaning gear and pulling shoes and repairing tack until December, when Fenton was at last alone, the log house ample for his needs and stocked for the season by Jasper, who soon left to winter in Missoula.

Not many days later, another storm hit, sealing Fenton in for a week. The storm broke for a few days and Cody Jo appeared—on snowshoes with gingerbread baked for him and carried with care in her pack. Bringing it seemed the only reason for her visit. At first.

"This storm's got another week," Fenton told her, surprised and made a little awkward by her sudden appearance. "You might not get back before it sets in again."

"Then you'll have to feed me," she said. " We'll have gingerbread for desert."

She gave Fenton all the news from the Swan and then helped him with dinner, helped him relax. She seemed to know just what to do and to discover just what was needed.

Later he found music on the radio and got out one of the bottles he'd salvaged from the hunting trips. They sipped, talking quietly now, easily now, the fire a steady blaze against the wind and the drifting snow outside. Cody Jo knew the new dances and when the music was right she got Fenton to try them with her. Fenton loved the way she danced. There was an easy grace in all her movements, as though the music came from within her rather than from the radio.

She helped Fenton surrender to it too, become one with it as they danced. . . . Then she helped Fenton surrender to her, become one with her. All of it so natural that Fenton felt no embarrassment, her body so naturally given that his breath seemed gone, his heart stopped.

When he spilled out of himself too soon, she made no fuss, found a blanket and eased him into sleep right there on the couch. They awoke in the night, the fire low, the blanket no longer enough. They went into the bedroom, and warmed under the big quilt, made love again in the darkness.

Four days later, the skies cleared and Fenton found himself changed in more ways than he could describe. Where she was, he was. What she felt, he felt. They would look at one another saying nothing, then go on as though they'd said everything. It seemed a miracle to him, as though he had walked through a door only she could open, was in a different world because she was with him, heard different music because she heard it too.

His only worry, when he worried at all, was that he might have lost the world he knew, the world he had traveled all those miles after the Bill Cody disaster to find. But he was too dizzy with the reality of her to take that into account. On the fifth day he took her back to do her teaching, the snow melted enough so they could ride. He returned in a daze, almost afraid to think of the wonder of it because he might find it had all been a dream.

But it hadn't been a dream. As winter melted into spring, Fenton found the locus of his life became her schoolhouse; the locus of Cody Jo's, his ranch house. She would come at unexpected times, surprising and delighting him. He would stop at the schoolhouse whenever he could, asking what she needed, liking to watch her at work, helping if he could. The students would grin, delighted by his big presence, the famous packer paying attention to them, to the pretty schoolteacher who in so many ways was showing them how to live.

They were so lost in one another they barely talked about the future, just lived in the now of one another, trusting without a thought of judging. Fenton went to The Bar of Justice and explained his absence to Beth, who said nothing, only smiled her bittersweet smile even as she took pleasure in knowing it was more than the mountains that had kept him away.

Something in her always knew how it would be, though she had no way of expecting a Cody Jo.

When the passes opened, he was across them and working with Tommy once again. But it was different. Tommy wasn't the only one who knew about Cody Jo. Buck knew. Dan and Rosie and Gus—most of the people in the Swan—knew. Though they said nothing. They waited, most of them amused by the thoughtfulness that seemed to have come over the freewheeling packer. Tommy was the only one who worried. He knew too much about the pain that might follow. And Gus understood Tommy's worry, though he'd made his peace—and he'd healed. He would carry the scar always, but he'd also learned. He knew that whatever happened, Fenton could manage. It might not be easy, but he would endure. To Gus, the only resolution for matters of the heart seemed to be to endure.

When Fenton went across the passes, Cody Jo booked a fare on the Great Northern and traveled back to see her aunt at the Chicago University. That aunt understood Cody Jo's past better than anyone. And she had long ago come to terms with the fact that in some ways she accepted Cody Jo better than Cody Jo could accept herself.

On the way, Cody Jo stopped at the Fort Riley hospital to see her father, a gentle man who loved his daughter without reservation. After Cody Jo's mother died, he'd joined up, offering the Army his doctor's skill at setting bones and patching wounds. When the war ended, they'd sent him to Fort Riley, where there were as many horses as there'd been in his Virginia hunt country, which made it easy. He was as accepting of his daughter there as he'd been in Virginia, and she was soothed by his trust—comforted by this man whose love made her whole.

Fenton asked no questions about her need to be away. It wasn't in him to ask someone as even-keeled as Cody Jo why she must do things as she did. Rosie understood, and made sure he wasn't plagued by things he needn't fear. But he became quiet on his trips, reflective. His packers watched and held their peace, but they were pleased to see the change when, just before hunting season, Fenton found her waiting at the corrals, took her in his arms there.

Not much was said. There wasn't time. Fenton had to be back over the pass the next day. But his spirit seemed restored, whatever had made him blue, gone. He enjoyed things again, was amused by the rangers and their rules, the firefighters and their gear, the elk as they bugled and stomped and rolled in the desperation of their rut. Tommy was pleased that Fenton was himself again, was joshing Buck about Buck's ideas for campsites, telling stories to Special Hands, complaining to Jasper about the special foods he needed—the cooking sherry, always the cooking sherry.

After that, when he rode out to make a run for supplies, he'd find a way to stop at the schoolhouse, but their visits were brief and their farewells too many. It wasn't until hunting season ended that they could be together as they wanted to be. And they were, with a happiness Fenton hadn't thought existed outside the mountains. He took comfort in it, though he sensed there was more to come—that Cody Jo had come back from her travels with something she needed to say, to explain. He waited, knowing only that nothing she could tell him would change the fact that she was his life, forever, that somehow he'd been blessed.

Just before Christmas, she told him everything: About her mothers' sudden decline. About taking to books to steer around it, if not books then the horse-showy life of her rolling-hilled Virginia world. About liking school but being surprised that the colleges would seek her out, want her. She was even more surprised, she told him, to find she'd been so wrapped up in books and horses that she'd missed entirely what she'd come to mean to men. Not even realizing that until the summer dances in the soft Virginia nights when the bachelors and young officers, and some of the married men too, made it all too clear. All of them drinking and talking softly on the porches and terraces, making her dizzy with their confessions—with their urgent whiskied courting. Their needs clear from their posture and their promises, from their talk running deep into those summery nights.

She told him about going off to the college in Massachusetts, her mind still spinning from the heady evenings of summer and some tide rising in her she had no way to understand. The girls at the college did understand—knew racy things that Cody Jo didn't. They taught her to smoke and how to do the dances. How to tempt boys into coming on trains and in cars from other colleges, boys with the same needs the men in Virginia had, carrying in them the same tensions about the war, its threats of violence, its promise of romance.

College work was easy, she told him. It was the life that was too fast, her own life too daring, the boys coming to see her on the trains too insistent, too needy, too reckless with drink and crazy vows.

When her mother died, her father brought her back to Virginia. Not so much because he was worried about the letters from the dean as because he needed her, hoped she might slow him from throwing over his practice and devoting himself to patching the torn limbs of the broken boys floating home on the hospital ships. But having her there didn't mean she would be with him there. The men in the hunt country were even more taken by her now—this new kind of college girl who smoked and drank and used her laughter to ward them off even as her dancing drew them closer. Her father saw it—but didn't judge, knowing only that the attention did her no good. He sent her off to his own level-headed family back in Michigan so he could do his duty: join the war effort, devote himself to easing the pain of so many broken by it.

It was what he needed. But Michigan wasn't what Cody Jo needed, a conclusion his own parents quickly reached. As far as they could see, a good mind kept busy was the only thing that might temper such a restless spirit. They sent her back to her college for direction, which was all they could think of to do.

Her mind did cool, she told Fenton, holding him tightly because of what was still to come. It was the rest of her that wouldn't. "Maybe the work came too easily," she said. "Something in me was too sure. Too wild. Something was wrong." She was watching him now, determined to tell all, needing to tell all—collecting herself to say it truly.

"At the end I won these awards. Made these societies. They meant a lot to my father, more to my aunt. Not much to me. It hadn't been that hard. I hadn't been that good. By then my father was at the Fort Riley hospital mending broken bodies and shattered minds—patching bones broken by the remounts, which was the easy part.

"I went to be with him, not knowing what I needed, what I should do. And there it was all over again: the dances, the receptions, riding on the Sunday hunts. The men. I . . . I went for one of them, Fenton. He'd done something brave in the war, gotten a promotion, become a captain. He was good on a horse and on a dance floor—and he wasn't after me like the others. He was apart even when we were together. We'd go to hear the bands in Kansas City, stay there through the nights. I became his . . . his woman." She looked at Fenton, wanting to get it right. "Sometimes I would even sneak into the Bachelor Officers Quarters. I think I was crazy. I must have been crazy."

"You were in love." Fenton's mouth was dry with the reality of her, her courage, her need to tell him all of it. "Tommy was like that over Special Hand's mother. He didn't have a choice. You didn't have a choice. You were caught up. You had to follow your heart."

"It goes deeper. There was someone before him. In college. I think he slept with me on a dare. I didn't even care. I was as wild as that boy was."

"Glad you didn't go and get yourself killed with one of those guys." Fenton held her closer, wanting her to share herself with him forever. "Some of them got no choice but to try somethin' crazy. When they lose, they got no more chances to take. Ever. Glad you got one left for us."

"You want us to take it together, don't you?"

"I do. Hope you won't be as sad as you sound right now."

Then she told him about finding herself pregnant. The agony of knowing it couldn't work. Wouldn't work. The darkness that crept over her. Told him about not telling anyone: not the captain, not even her father. About taking her despair to her father's sister in Chicago, confessing to her alone how she had lived, what she had done, the cost of it, the life beginning inside her she had no way to sustain.

Her aunt, a no-nonsense woman, said nothing at all, just went to a university friend and brought her back to listen to all of it again. The two of them listening and questioning. Talking with her again. Probing the matter deep into the night. And the next morning too, in a kitchen sunny with the sane light of a new morning, the tablecloth fresh and white, their heads clear as they went through what it all meant again. Then again.

"They made me know what I was doing, Fenton." Her voice was low as she considered it. "Made me know what I would lose. They are modern women; they thought of everything. Were ready to talk about anything. . . . But I'd done the talking inside myself already. I had in me things that ran farther and deeper than anything they could know. There was nothing they offered that could touch how dark was my world." If tears were coming, she fought them back, determined to finish it out.

"I was that way when we went to Canada, the friend of my aunt holding me through the night. Holding me afterward when the man told me what had happened—that there would be no new life in me again. Ever."

Fenton wasn't sure he could speak. Crazily his mind was on the captain. It seemed to him that anyone who'd had a chance to hold such a person as Cody Jo and lost it must live in despair forever. Any worry about leaving his mountains to be with her dissolved into his belief in her, in her courage—her acceptance of what she had done.

"And so you came to help these kids," he said finally—glad he could say anything at all and surprised such a thought hadn't come to him before. The need in her that led her to a place like the Swan, a chance to have what she'd lost.

"Maybe," she said," trying to see clearly a possibility she hadn't considered before. "I just knew I needed to get away. Be by myself in a safe place. I never dreamt there would be anything like this country of yours, Fenton. Never dreamt there would be someone like you to show it to me."

"Hell. I think you make it possible for me, to tell the truth." Fenton felt as though he were suspended somehow. He could sense nothing of what was around him, even of where he was. Only what was connecting them. "I think you may take the 'blue' right out of that 'blue heaven' we talk about. I believe I *can* share it all with you, somehow. Never thought a man could . . . until you."

"But not with your child, Fenton." Cody Jo watched him, took him in so completely Fenton thought her tears might come at last. "Not with your children. . . . That tears me apart all over again."

For a moment Fenton just held her, not sure he could say what he wanted to say. "I never expected I could explain what I found up there to anyone, Cody Jo. Even to myself. You can teach a kid to read and write, but what's inside him has to be his own. Grow from something inside. That you can touch what's inside me up there might be enough. Might just cross the blue out."

Fenton felt so completely at one with her, he was surprised to find he was aroused, that he wanted her as much as he needed to share this idea with her. He was awash in how fearless she had been, the strength it had taken to go to her aunt in Chicago rather than back to the captain at Riley. As far as he was concerned, any man lucky enough to know her would cross any country, ford any water, risk whatever counted most for a chance to share his life with Cody Jo.

∽

They were married that spring on the edge of Fenton's big pasture. It was the most important event anyone in the Swan could remember, all of them liking to see the colorful packer so pleased with his world, so taken by Cody Jo. And they were stopped by their schoolteacher's looks, her smile open and warm, and welcoming, her eyes blue as a summer sky, her figure more slender and graceful than any had suspected could be under her schoolteacher clothes.

Cody Jo's father gave a toast, one of such understanding and acceptance—and thanks—it brought a lump into the throats of the lumbermen and cowboys, tears to the eyes of their women. The two professors from the Chicago university watched Fenton, liking his open ways, liking him most of all for how much he saw in Cody Jo—the way he watched her, found comfort in her, even drew strength from her.

Tommy Yellowtail, with Special Hands, was there too. Fenton and Tommy were still close, though Tommy understood the difference Cody Jo had already brought to their lives. Fenton hardly stopped at The Bar of Justice anymore, even for a drink, a matter Tommy also understood.

They still had their time together in the mountains, but more and more of that was consumed by responsibilities—meeting schedules, managing camps, comforting guests. The good talks they'd shared had a way of fading into the past.

Tommy still went to The Bar of Justice, of course, but on this day he watched Fenton moving through the wedding guests with an appreciation that surprised him. He didn't like to admit that at times he wished there were something better for him than The Bar of Justice. But he knew Hope Girl was gone forever.

He had Special Hands, who was better in the woods than most men. And he had the mountains. They might not be the best thing he could have, but they were what he did have.

He knew they would have to do.

19

Hitched

It was a good marriage—though there were some in the Swan who doubted it could be. Their worry was that Fenton would find himself too devoted to his mountains; Cody Jo would be too involved in her causes, which seemed to include every student she'd ever had in her little school.

But it worked. When Fenton came down from the mountains, Cody Jo was there with news and humor and all that life that seemed to spring from every idea she had. When her students appeared on their doorstep, Fenton was there with backcountry wisdom and backcountry stories. . . . And they liked being together, dancing and going to town and talking about Buck and Angie, Tommy and Jasper; particularly Special Hands, who had grown into a gifted tracker and hunter.

Tommy's powers were diminishing. Fenton watched with concern as he began taking on weight, finding more pleasure as the years passed in watching his son than in watching the mountains, gathering his own knowledge from the movement of elk and deer, the secretive ways of the bears. But it was a natural transition, and Fenton tried to take it that way, turning to Special Hands for the mountain wisdom that once came from Tommy.

Cody Jo complained about the lodge Fenton couldn't quite finish, but her complaining was rich with her love of Fenton. She still had food ready for his packers between trips, had a bed for guests before they started on them. In her own way she became as interesting to them as the big packer who showed them the country, the shaping power of mountain water, the shrewd habits of mountain game. They would listen, arrested by her passion as she listed her objections to Prohibition and to Wall Street and to the ruthlessness of big business. She explained how such darkness must be countered by education. They would nod in agreement and soberly accept Fenton's drinks from her as they listened.

Fenton and Cody Jo were never out of liquor—or food, or the bed-rock stuff that made life an adventure rather than a battle. And Cody Jo was never out of reasons people should pitch in and help those who had to battle to stay alive. The depth of her concern for the downtrodden astonished Fenton, and made him love her all the more.

"I do believe we're like a harnessed team," he'd tell her. "So comfort-able being hitched one can pull when the other can't."

"You and your equine metaphors," she'd reply. "What you mean is that you're shocked you don't *mind* being hitched."

"Don't mind at all. And it's no shock." Fenton would make her a drink, charmed by her. "Any guy who's around you for ten minutes could see why. . . . You're sure not the usual schoolteacher."

As the Great Depression brought in its darkness, Cody Jo's sympathies struggled to provide some light. The stock market crash itself didn't bother her: "Greedy men taking a tumble," she told Fenton. But the thought of men out of work, leaving their homes and families to take some wild gamble in hopes of supporting them, did. It tore her apart.

It didn't help that Cody Jo and Fenton's prospects only seemed to grow as the rest of the country's diminished. That was a frustration for her. It seemed that more and more of those with wealth came to their door-step as the soup lines for those with nothing grew longer. Prosperous men seemed to want to buy from Fenton the adventures their lives of comfort and privilege ruled out. And if they didn't come they wrote or called, seeking a time they could—men with money to buy meat making a case for going into the mountains to hunt for still more.

"Just shopping," they'd say comfortably, armed with the best rifles money could buy, and using a line that drove Cody Jo to distraction.

"What are they talking about?" she'd ask. "Can't they see what's happened? People are starving!"

"Hell, I think I know what they mean when they say that," Fenton said one night before a big hunting trip. They were in bed talking over the day's happenings. "They just don't know how to say it, even if they could understand it."

"It hurts, Fenton, to see all that money thrown around. It could be feeding children, feeding families." Cody Jo was always looking for a way to chan-nel the surfeit of those with too much to those who had nothing.

"I guess old Roosevelt's looking for a way to spread it around. Just wish he'd unplug the fancy talk and plug in some practical ideas."

"Which is what these men surely must have: ideas. They manage people. They manage production. They manage money. . . . They do everything. Why can't they manage some kind of help?"

"All I know is that it isn't the meat they come up here to hunt. Not for their stomachs, at least. Not for their family's stomachs either."

"Then why? What are they after?"

"I think they come for the peace of it. The order. Old Mother Nature's been around a long time. She's always looking for a way to balance things out. In that high country you can see the balance."

"Oh Fenton," she had to smile. "Just when I'm ready to hit you over the head you turn into a rustic Romantic."

"Maybe. . . . Whatever rustic Romantic means. I just got a suspicion nature's done a better job with the mountains up there than it's done with the people down here. Might take the old girl more time to balance us up than it did them peaks and valleys. We're trickier. Takes more than water flowing downhill to straighten people out. Until she figures out what it does take, I doubt any of us can do a hell of a lot—not alone."

"But together we can." She lifted her head to look at him, convince him, kissing him, speaking into the hollow of his neck. "Let's get started— together. We'll make a difference. We have to."

"I'll get started. Tomorrow. For the South Fork. I may not be able to explain why it is these dudes want to see my country, but I can show it to them. Some might even come far enough along to see the big picture."

She laughed. "Sometimes I get the big picture too. What you want to do is change the subject around so you can turn off that light and give me one of your fancy goodbyes. . . . Am I right?"

"You are." Fenton doused the light and took her in his arms. "We might could help Mother Nature balance things out right here at home. . . . Helps to have things balanced out—when there's a rocky trail ahead."

They did have a balance, the two of them, one they needed to think about less and less as their summer days shortened into fall. They became a rhythm in one another's lives—and in a lot of other lives too.

Angie had married Buck, feeling so sorry for him when he came out of the mountains with his nose askew she melted.

Spec had become so at one with the mountains he took on a wisdom that more than compensated for his father's failing ways, except when Spec was drinking. When he was drinking, his wisdom would dissolve. A meanness might even take over, sometimes causing Tommy to spiral down into his own despair, one so deep he would begin drinking himself, wanting only for Special Hands to be back in the mountains where he wasn't desperate to fill some emptiness, where he was a natural part of a world he understood.

"Something in town brings it on," Fenton told Tommy, "some weight on him not even those girls down in The Bar of Justice can lighten. Though they help," he had to admit. "They slow him."

"He don't crave that booze in the mountains," Tommy said. "That's all I know."

"He's not the same man in the mountains," Fenton answered. "That's all anybody knows."

And he wasn't, his work in the mountains was always a boon to Fenton, his work with Buck a happy opportunity for them all: Buck all cockeyed ideas that hadn't a chance; Spec all instinct that could be counted on, a wry correction to Buck's loopy ambitions.

Things balanced out for Fenton and Cody Jo in other ways too. Outside the mountains Cody Joe was a steady miracle of efficiency, Dan Murphy and Rosie ready to provide her whatever she needed.

In the mountains, Jasper was able to do with Cody Jo's supplies whatever she suggested, a balancing act in itself. Fenton managed it all, careful to keep Jasper fueled with something high-test enough to keep him going but not so high-test his talent would self-destruct.

Fenton was pretty sure it was the cooking sherry that gave Jasper the courage to crack a black bear across his nose when the bear nuzzled into the cook-tent for a better sniff. And he was thankful it was a black bear that just bolted off with a squeal. A grizzly might have run on through the tent and taken Jasper with him. But it was a signal event, giving all the rangers and packers up and down the South Fork a story to share. And it put a string in Jasper's bow forever, one that surprised him as much as it did Buck—and amused Special Hands even more than Fenton.

Competent a crew as they were, Fenton knew he needed something Tommy had provided that Spec and Buck did not: He needed someone who could sense where the stock had gone in the night rather than someone who stood there cursing and baffled in the dawn like Buck. And he needed someone to take care of the camp rather than slip away from it to learn the ways of mountain game the way Spec did.

And he found just what he needed in Ty Hardin, old Eban Hardin's grandson—more boy than man when Fenton found him, but just what he was looking for.

Jasper took credit for the find, having confounded Ty in a checker game at the Elkhorn—Jasper drinking his beer and telling his stories and making fun of how bandaged up the boy was. But Fenton had met Ty earlier at Horace's feed store. He already had a sense of his worth, despite the cast on the boy's arm and the patch over his eye and Will Hardin's gloomy prognosis. Will was so morose about the doctor's bill for patching up his son that he hardly mentioned Ty's worth when unpatched, which turned out to be considerable—despite all the trouble Ty had caused his father when his horse rolled on him as he rescued a calf. Will figured the calf must have been sickly anyway. That depressed him even more.

Will had never been anything at all like Eban, his own father. He neither understood animals nor wanted to. As far as Will was concerned, the only luck he'd had was Mary Hardin, who was as focused on the good as Will was on the bad. He knew his son had in him much of what had worried him so about his own father, which meant he was never as pleased about the problems Ty solved as he was depressed about what Ty's solutions might cost, in dollars and cents as well as in peace of mind.

Fenton seemed to understand Will's boy as much by instinct as by reason, a matter Tommy made sure Fenton considered before he took Ty Hardin on.

"A lot of them young ones that ride off ready to do good come back all crippled up, more like Will than Eban. What makes you so sure it's Eban's blood that'll take in this boy, not Will's?"

"Because of the animals. He's good with them. Being good with them is an education all by itself. About everything. Horace says everyone in the Bitterroot knows that boy has a way with animals. If that isn't Eban then I'm Will, and I'm a long damn way from Will Hardin."

"Boys change when they age," Tommy said. "Sometimes they head down the wrong trails."

"Your Spec won't change. Not if he stays in the woods. And he wouldn't be Spec if you hadn't let him learn from the animals he finds in these mountains."

"But he sure as shit gets in trouble in Missoula. Where the hell you think he got that?"

"Damned if I know—unless it's you, Tommy. All I know is he'd be free of trouble if he stayed in the woods. You always were. Maybe it's just got so there's not enough woods to go around."

"You think you got enough mules up in those woods to complete the education of that boy? Cody Jo'll have something to say about that."

"Mules we got. Ways to manage them we need. A matter she knows all too well."

And Cody Jo did know. She had logic as well as good instincts, which is why giving a fifteen-year-old boy such a load to carry made her nervous. She was even more nervous about how quickly Will Hardin jumped at the idea of shipping his boy off to Fenton. She knew Mary Hardin well enough to know the decision to send Ty away wasn't one she made. Mary was all mother.

But Fenton took the whole thing in stride. "I believe Will thought it might be a better deal for him if we took over the doctor bills too," he said to Cody Jo after reading Will's postcard. "Looks like he wants Ty to come up here permanent."

It was a plan that Cody Jo would have rejected had she more clearly seen it coming. But she hadn't. And things happened fast, Ty becoming a part of their lives so quickly the reality seemed what should be—not what shouldn't.

Ty had hitched a ride out with two of the Wilson brothers, both still a little drunk from their time at The Bar of Justice. They'd put Ty in the middle of the cab and told him bear stories all the way to Seeley Lake. When they got there, they were sobered up enough to consider turning around and going right back to The Bar of Justice. And they might have, if Gus Wilson hadn't been waiting for them, wanting to cut them off before some crazy idea took root.

Gus saw right away how green this boy they were sending to Fenton was, and something in him must have realized how determined the boy was too. Horace Adams had given Ty a prize Meana saddle to deliver, one that Fenton had wanted but found too dear to buy. Horace had loaned the boy his own coat too, claiming that with things as bad as they were there was no way he'd get into the mountains that season anyway—and no way he'd sell the saddle either, which Fenton might as well use and oil and see if it wouldn't catch someone's fancy.

The care the boy had taken with delivering the saddle had impressed Gus, whose no-nonsense manner dispelled any ideas his brothers might have about turning around and heading back for The Bar of Justice. He introduced himself to Ty, who clearly was relieved to shake the hand of someone who was sober, calling Gus "Mister Wilson" right away and asking how soon they might be getting to "Mister Pardee's."

Gus was amused by the formality. "When you get there you might just wish you hadn't been so anxious," Gus said. He's got new mules to shoe and old gear to repair and once you get into those mountains of his you'll think a day off is just as invented as those bear stories you heard."

"You mean they made up those stories?" the boy asked.

"Partly, I'd guess. Partly not. When you run into your first bear you'll wish it was all invented. Just figure on learning fast—and keep hoping you'll live a long enough life to enjoy some of what you learn."

When they dropped Ty off at the fork to Fenton's place, they told him more about how fast he'd have to learn, pointing out that Fenton was married to a schoolteacher whose goal was to teach Fenton's packers something new every day they were out of the woods.

"Half the time she succeeds," Gus Wilson admitted. "Even with Buck." He took off his hat, looking at Ty and running his hand through his hair. "She's an unusual woman, Ty Hardin. I doubt if there's anyone more so."

He put his hat back on, his scar glinting white in the late sun. "Least not here in the Swan."

20

Postulate

If any formal packing instructions were ever offered Ty Hardin, no one knew. All anyone knew was that Fenton found Ty staring out across a meadow taking in the ridges of the Swan, the Meana saddle hooked over one shoulder and old Eban's kit bag in his other hand. Surprised as Ty was to see Fenton driving the truck, he was not at all surprised that Fenton seemed happier to see the saddle than he was to see Ty. It was a good saddle, and Ty was only a boy.

"Throw your gear in the cab and hop up on them bales," Fenton said, jabbing a thumb at the precariously stacked bales teetering on the bed of his truck. "A little weight up there and they might stay put."

Ty climbed up onto the bales and flattened himself, holding onto a rope cinched from front to back to keep things in place. It seemed loose to Ty, who took up what slack he could with one hand and held onto a bale with the other. On the next curve the stack went over anyway. Ty slid off with the tumbling load, landing on his feet—the rope still in his hand but finding himself inside the loop now. He had to run to keep from being tripped, fending off bales as he did and banging on the door of the cab to get Fenton' attention.

Hearing the noise and seeing bales bounce past, Fenton hit his brakes and saw Ty run past and suddenly go down, a final bale hitting him as he tried to sit up.

Fenton was out of the truck quickly. "'Fraid you might be too skinny to keep my bales steady," he said. He held out a hay hook. "Catch your wind and we'll throw a few back on. I'm not sure Spec and Buck can get shoes on my new mules anyway. . . . Maybe that's why I misremembered that curve."

They loaded, Ty trying to get back his breath as he stacked the bales Fenton kept throwing up to him up on the truck-bed. He was thankful when Fenton decided to call it quits.

"The boys can come get the rest. Let's go see if they made any progress. I doubt those mules know how to pick up their feet."

They found Buck and Special Hands at the corrals. They had a shoeing kit out and had thrown a mule to the ground, hind feet roped to one side of the corral, a foreleg tied to the other. The mule thrashed at the air with his free leg, quieting for a moment before letting out an anguished bray.

It was clear he hadn't gone down easily. Spec held one of the ropes taut as he encouraged Buck, who looked as though he'd shouldered the brunt. His shirt was torn and one of his hands was wrapped in a bloody cloth, which was coming undone as he tried to control the mule's flailing leg.

"See why my driving was irregular?" Fenton muttered. "They're scarin' the lights right out of my mule." He climbed the bars and dropped into the corral, Ty close behind, the two of them moving together to rescue the mule.

Swan people later held it was at that very moment that Ty Hardin began taking over the gentling of Fenton's mules. In fact it took the rest of that day and most of the next, but their take on it was close enough to become gospel. Ty did help them tack shoes onto Loco, which soon became the panicked mule's name, and Ty got shoes on Cottontail the next day. Cottontail was the other mule Fenton had bartered from a dirt farmer driven so far from the Oklahoma land he knew that he wasn't able to prove-up on the Montana land he didn't.

The two green mules were about all the man had left when the bank foreclosed. "I'll take them off your hands," Fenton told him, suppressing the sympathy he felt as he peeled off a few bills. The man's family said nothing as Fenton wished them luck. They were headed for Butte, the man figuring the mines were his last chance. Fenton thought they might be— but considered it a risky chance at best.

"A rough lot for them," Fenton said at dinner after they finally got the shoes on Loco. He still couldn't shake that picture of the man's forlorn family. "What the banks don't take away, the union men want."

"But it's the unions who might save him," Cody Jo said. "Give him a way to have a dinner like this, to sit around a table and have a place for his family." Her heart was so much in what she said, her commitment so complete, a door suddenly opened onto a new world for the boy from the Bitterroot.

And it was a larger world than he'd ever imagined. They talked about Roosevelt and the WPA and the migrant workers, they talked about land use and wages and factories. Buck, his hand fat with bandages after Cody Jo's ministrations, argued that the government should let a man hunt where he wanted, farm where he could, just stay the hell out of his hair. Spec said the government should treat Buck's people as roughly as they treated his, then they could all fight it together. Cody Jo held the government had an obligation to help, to make sure those who had too much didn't trample over those who had nothing. And Fenton pointed out that it was all balance, that loads had to be evened out for everyone, like a well-packed string. "No reason to have one mule carry twice as much as another, unless you gotta favor a sick one or take care of an old one. The thing is that each has gotta carry a load he can handle—that way they can all enjoy some rest at the end of the day. Some good feed. A sandy place to roll."

It was an education for Ty. Finances to him meant cattle prices, and too few cattle to barter with. That was about as far as they got in the Bitterroot. For Cody Jo and Fenton, finances seemed to include everything, leaving Ty as dizzy about their concern for people fleeing the Dust Bowl as he was about their concern for people seeking a drink to ease the pain the Dust Bowl brought. He became even more dizzy watching Cody Jo: the looks of her, the flush in her face as she talked, her laughter, her kindness after she'd urged Ty to tell his story. Most of all, the way she watched him when he found himself blabbering away to answer her questions. He'd felt queasy when he realized that the room had gone silent, that they were all watching him. He stopped in mid-sentence as he realized she was watching too, supporting him, trusting him. And when it came to him that her faith somehow made the others believe in him too, he became even more queasy.

It was Fenton who saved him, suddenly taking them all off in another direction with questions about how to doctor a horse.

Fenton's kindness was one Ty would never forget.

Their acceptance of him made him work all the harder to shoe the cottontail the next morning—do it without throwing her. Cody Jo and Fenton hadn't let anything throw him the night before; he wasn't going to let anything throw him now.

Buck and Spec might have gotten the shoes on Loco by throwing him, but Ty knew Loco was the worse for it. And he had helped them do it, knowing as he did it that it was the wrong way to go. He wanted Cotton-tail to work with them now, not against them. After what Cody Jo and Fenton had done for him, he knew he wanted to work with them.

What he didn't realize, as he soothed Cottontail, was that he wanted to work with them forever.

It was hard to tell if it was what Fenton saw in the boy that led him to give Ty such a flood of responsibility or just necessity. What was clear was that Buck's hand would put him out of commission for almost a month. And there was much to do—some planned, most not. Ty's first two days of packing certainly weren't planned. First they had to take Bob Ring's runaway horses back over the pass, where—Bernard Straight, the new assistant ranger told them, panting with exhaustion—Ring was waiting, his leg broken. Ring's daughter, Wilma, was the only one with Ring now, Straight told them, and Straight was sure Wilma was getting more des-perate by the minute for fear no help could be found. Bernard Straight was desperate himself. He'd tracked Ring's horses all the way out, running when he could, walking when he couldn't. The horses sprinting away each time he drew close.

"Probably chased the damn horses over the pass himself," Fenton muttered to Ty, telling the boy he'd better get some sleep now because there wouldn't be any later.

"What's done is done," Fenton told Bernard. "Can't start back yet. Gotta cross early—on hard snow. You sleep now. I'll figure on how to make do with old Bob's leg. . . . Sure picked an awkward time to break his damn leg."

Whether Fenton slept at all that night, Ty never knew. All he knew was that the next two days were ones he would never forget, though the details always got scrambled.

It was dark when they rode out, Ty seeing that whatever Bernard knew about ranger work didn't carry over to horse work. Bernard was leading Wilma Ring's little mare, Apple, who gave him fits coming up the switch-backs, even breaking free as they came to the cornice at the top. If Ty hadn't grabbed the lead and managed a dally, she might have slid back and gone all the way off the cliff.

"Willie will be pleased," Fenton shouted to him in the half-light of that dawn. "She'd a lot rather see you lead that mare into camp than find it all broke up down below."

Fenton was already on the snowfield, the rest of the horses strung out behind him. He seemed to enjoy watching Ty struggle with little Apple.

Ty was riding a gray mare Etta Adams had been spoiling all winter, and Fenton liked the way Ty was bringing her along. He liked it even better that Ty kept the mare quiet as he led Apple back up the cornice. At the bottom of the pass they crossed a meadow, a stand of timber reaching out into it. They forded a stream, and there was Ring propped against a lodgepole, his leg wrapped tightly in strips of canvas.

"I believe you're not too interested in circulation, Robert." Fenton dismounted and studied the bluish tint in Ring's toes.

"And I believe the guy upstairs wasn't listening," Ring said, looking up at Fenton Pardee, a man he couldn't help liking, though all too often he grew suspicious of Pardee's intentions. "I prayed for his help, and he sent you."

"Don't get picky. I brought somethin' that'll give you a boost, though your Fed bastards might throw a fit." Fenton threw him a bottle of Doc Messler's whisky and began to unwrap the leg. "Might make me more acceptable in that rarefied company you keep. Drink and think about your good lord. I'll take a look at your leg and think about you."

"I believe He did listen," Ring said, after taking a pull on the bottle. "Some better than your usual." He took a second pull just as a thin girl with the bluest eyes Ty had ever seen came from the creek, a bucket of water tilting her to one side.

"I wrapped it too tightly, didn't I?" she said to Fenton. "I wanted to keep it still."

"You did that, Willie. Now if we can get old Bob to drink a little more, I'll try to set it right."

Crying, Wilma helped a grim-faced Ty hold her father—sweating and swearing and drinking more—while she watched Fenton do what he could to set the leg, fashioning a splint with wood and a thick saddle pad. They let the exhausted Ring rest when they finished, turning to help Bernard strike the camp and pack the horses.

By late afternoon they were ready. Fenton led the string onto the trail, Ty following on Smoky—the grey mare that had given Etta Adams such fits—leading Ring's horse as the ranger pitched and tossed in the saddle. Wilma followed on Apple, weeping as Ring alternated between shouted profanities and raucous Pentecostal hymns. Bernard, somber as a funeral director, brought up the rear.

Ty managed Smoky carefully, the young mare finally understanding her task and striking a steady pace as she climbed, crossed on the tracks they'd packed into the snow, and started back down the switchbacks. Ty moved her slowly on the downhill, careful not to unseat the tilting Ring and worried about his leg, protruding grotesquely off to the side.

It was a day, and a wound, that Ring would carry always, his gait ever-more checked by an awkward hitch. It left its mark on Fenton too—not one he sought, but an advantage he didn't shy from using. The Forest Service people were beholden to him for saving Ring, which gave him leverage with the many rangers and game wardens and government officials whose say-so became the law of the South Fork. It was an advantage Fenton welcomed—and used with care—through the years.

But in fact it was Ty's life that was most changed by that day and night, and by the next day and night as well—days that would become the opening chapter in a life few other mountain lives could match.

Though Cody Jo was waiting at the corrals to take Ring and Wilma to the hospital, and Bernard was off to make his report, the work for Fenton and Ty was just beginning. They had to take tents and still more provisions back over the north pass to catch up with Spec and Jasper, now a day ahead of them with the party they were preparing to take in when Bernard sought their help. It was Buck's fault that the tents had arrived a day late, but it was Spec's fault that among the five animals left to be packed were Loco and Cottontail, who had never been packed at all.

Packing Loco turned out to be an adventure that was told and retold for years to come. Fenton had wanted to show Ty some hitches, but had to devote so much attention to getting the hysterical mule to accept the packs that instruction was impossible. Not until Loco went over backward and stunned himself were they able to get near the mule with the packs. Fenton later called it nature's blessing, Loco being so groggy when he got back on his feet he had to concentrate entirely on staying upright, which was the only thing that made packing possible.

Cottontail was not such a trial, but the delay Loco caused meant they had to cross the pass in the dark and ride through the night. And they had to hurry through that night as well. A storm was coming in and all Spec and Jasper had as cover for the guests was a kitchen fly, no help at all in a serious storm.

That they had to hurry may have been the reason Loco pulled back and dragged Cottontail into a creekbed, but Fenton thought it most likely that Loco had finally come out of his trance and become suspicious of the clatter Cottontail's feet made on a little bridge. Mules objected to what they didn't understand, and hooves on planks made a spooky sound for Oklahoma mules, especially on a night so dark even Montana mules had trouble staying on the trail.

Whatever the cause, it all played a part in the packing education of Ty, who not only had to crawl down into the creekbed to free Cottontail, but quickly found himself on his own—abandoned by Fenton, who took the mules bearing the tents and went ahead to shelter the guests before the skies opened.

No one in the Swan could explain how a skinny boy—with a single day's packing under his belt and two green mules to pack—could put a pack string back together in such inky blackness. Even more inexplicable was that he could find his way to Fenton's White River camp, a feat that caused them to chew the story over again and again.

There was the lightning, someone would always point out, but another would counter that lightning startled a man so much it wasn't useful. They thought it probably did make a difference that Ty had Turkey, the only packhorse in Fenton's string of mules, and Sugar, the little mule who gravitated toward the White River camp as no other. Turkey had such a nose for grain he had a way of seeking out Fenton's camps wherever they might be. And Sugar, having been abandoned in Lost Bird Canyon all those years ago, always made the White River camp her top priority. But those things didn't begin to explain how the boy could do what he did do: wrestle Cottontail's water-soaked packs out of the streambed, balance them out on a mule as green as Cottontail, and then ride through darkness and rain into an ominous dawn to find a camp he'd never seen—in a country he'd never known.

Somehow Fenton had dared to have faith in him. And somehow the boy dared to have faith in Turkey and Sugar, setting them free in the rainy dawn and following them through wet meadows and dripping timber to cross the South Fork and climb the mud-slicked White River benches to reach Fenton's camp. It was almost as though some fate had planned it that way.

Fenton, warm and dry under the canvas they'd set up moments before the skies opened, hardly spilled a drop of coffee as he watched the boy come over the last lip and into the clearing, quietly observing to Jasper that they might have found themselves a packer at last.

How Fenton was so sure Ty could find him was as hard to explain as why Fenton and Ty were so comfortable with one another from the outset. But somehow everyone in the Swan knew—from that very first trip of that very first summer. Something about the two of them together seemed natural and acceptable, at least to the people of the Swan.

Fenton had indeed found his packer, though that wasn't the only thing uncovered that rainy morning. Special Hands, gifted hunter that he was, hated to pack. He found it tedious one moment and deadly dangerous the next. Realizing what Ty had been able to do told him one thing, but more important was that the boy cared so seriously for his animals. Spec watched Ty fight off weariness to tend to them and realized the boy not only had stamina and good sense, he had a bond with his pack animals much like the one Spec had with the elk and deer and bear roaming through his woods.

Which is why their working together became more than a convenience, became a kinship that rough life in rough mountains could nourish as nothing else. Ty wanted to learn everything Spec knew about the ways of the animals they hunted and the forest that sheltered them. And Spec wanted to honor Ty for all the things he did to free Spec to learn from the woods and the cirques—from the animals who made this country their home, helped Ty make it a home as well.

It didn't take long for Fenton to see what Ty and Spec meant to one another. What he didn't see was what Ty was coming to mean to him— that the same completeness Tommy Yellowtail realized through watching Special Hands, Fenton was beginning to realize through Ty.

He wouldn't see that until the fall when Ty managed to pull Fenton's big hunting camp out—alone—through the teeth of a blizzard that would have done in most men. Fenton didn't even realize what a feat it had been until he felt the sudden relief wash through him when Ty appeared. Alive.

But Jasper suspected Fenton and Ty had a bond that would hold from that first rainy day when Ty rode into the White River camp. There was something in the way Fenton sipped his coffee and watched, something in the satisfaction he took in Ty's focus—bedraggled as the boy was—on his animals.

To Jasper it was as though neither had any other choice: Fenton to cherish what he'd found in Ty, Ty to know what must be done for Fenton.

21
Novice

That first year Ty was so busy learning he had no idea that he was teaching, in his own way. Even Spec learned from him, liking the way the boy could use weather and terrain—even the shifting winds—to predict the nighttime drift of the animals.

Jasper and Buck learned too, liking it that the innocence of this boy made it possible for him to accept their humor about that innocence. He'd even join them in their laughter, his tolerance of their rough ways softening them, letting them accept one another more easily—because he was there.

Fenton even found he was learning. He'd watch the boy climb above the timber to spot the horses in some meadow. Watch him enjoy their simple comfort, still as wood as they warmed under the first sun on a breathless morning. He'd see Ty caught up in the way the light moved down the canyon walls, melting the silvered meadows into a sparkling green and bringing alive the peaks beyond. He wasn't sure he could explain what he learned, just knew the boy somehow made him whole. He guessed he liked watching Ty discover things he hardly understood himself, though he knew they were there, deep inside him somewhere. He even guessed he knew they were there better than Tommy or even Special Hands knew they were in them. What was in them was there too completely for any need to understand it.

Cody Jo might have learned more from Ty than any of them. That truth came in a rush when Ty survived the blizzard. Fenton had brought him into the kitchen. "Here he is, Cody Jo," he'd said. "Worn some, but he's ours."

She'd felt her heart still when she saw him. He'd been in the mountains for most of that year since he'd come to them. She was stopped by how changed he was. He'd grown of course, but there'd been something else.

She read it in his eyes, his steadiness, his acceptance of her, of himself. It stopped her for only a moment, but it was a moment that colored everything about him from that day on. And from that day on, Ty *was* theirs. Fenton shared with him everything he could about packing and the mountains and the people he would be taking into them, various as those people might be. And Cody Jo was surprised by how much of her life she shared with the boy. Something in Ty was as easy and accepting of the music she loved as of the rhythms inside her, the ebb and the flow of her. It was an acceptance that years alone could never teach. She knew there was no way she could teach it either, good a teacher as she was. What Ty had in him had to come from somewhere all its own.

She would talk with Fenton about it, searching for a way to sort it out.

"How did he get this way?" she asked, capturing Fenton in that intimacy they shared before sleep. "You see it too. How did it happen?"

"Maybe from his work," Fenton said. "Though I give him so damn much to do it's hard to figure how anything else has time to happen."

"Maybe it's *where* you give him the work," Cody Jo said. "That country may mean more to him than my music means to me."

"Hard to think it could mean that much," Fenton said, feigning surprise and enjoying the thought of Cody Jo and music. He held her still closer, her body cleaving to his as he considered the ways she could move to this new music.

Music seemed to be washing through all of them in those days. Suddenly big bands were thrilling the whole country, coming to them on records and over the radios and at the big dances. People drove for miles to hear those sounds, and a new kind of dancing came in not far behind. Round Brown played more and more of it at The Bar of Justice, the girls getting better and better at moving in and out of the new rhythms. Cowboys and loggers would drive from all over just to watch, try the new steps out—sometimes not even going upstairs, so caught up were they in the new dancing.

Music always had been a part of life in Montana—in the mountains, on the windswept high plains, and along the lonely roadways linking little towns—the men using the music to fend off their loneliness, the women as a reminder of how much the men needed them. Or maybe to cushion their sadness when the need slid away. Most of the songs were somehow about sadness: loneliness, separation, loss. But they were lovely in their sadness —often lovely *because* of the sadness. It was a music that reached out to everyone everywhere, and Cody Jo seemed to know more about why better than anybody—certainly anybody in the Swan.

Somehow Cody Jo understood the deep jazz traditions of Chicago, knew why the white bandsmen came to the South Side to hear the black ones, loving the beat of that South Side music, learning from it, drinking with the black bandsmen, sometimes sitting in with them, always wanting to be a part of them. The white bandsmen even taking that music east to change the sweet music of New York before bringing it back, reformed, fashioning a still better music out of Chicago's hard-driven Jazz and Dixieland and Blues, out of all the styles that came up the Mississippi and laced their way into the music of Chicago. All of it blending into the new rhythms that made so many people want to dance.

Cody Jo seemed to contain that music in her very being, the new music rising up in her so naturally that others hardly knew how much she knew— about music or about life. They just watched, watched as any many lucky enough to dance with her became one with those easy movements of hers. The movements becoming so much a part of everything she did they no longer needed to think about why, just accepted it, loving her as much for the way she danced as for the way she lived—as much as for what she did herself as for what she did for them. Fenton, of course, did think about it, liking to think about Cody Jo, liking to let her magic claim him just as completely as it claimed her.

She would go to Chicago to listen and to get records and bring them back to play on her phonograph, getting Fenton to dance with her, teaching Angie and Buck, sometimes Dan and Rosie too. Sometimes she would get Ty to dance as well, when she could get him to forget himself enough to give the music a chance. When that happened he would surprise them both with how completely the music took him in—made him a part of it too.

What Ty brought home to Fenton was how some people just had things in them and others didn't. He guessed some had them in them at one time but wouldn't have them forever, supposing Tommy Yellowtail was like that. He knew Tommy had the mountains in him as sure as snow melt when they first met, something Tommy couldn't have put into words. But Fenton saw it right away, just as he saw that Tommy began losing what the mountains meant to him when Hope Woman left him for the Black Robes. The leaving might have been slow and painful, but it had been real. Now maybe things were balancing out—Tommy somehow passing along what had been inside him to Special Hands. Fenton thought that might even be enough, that Tommy might see it as some kind of tribal legacy, a gift that the earth had bestowed on him to be passed on to someone worthy like Special Hands.

Fenton wasn't sure he had all this just right, just as he wasn't sure what real crime the Black Robes committed when they visited their darkness on Tommy's people. Maybe the Black Robes had no choice, set in their ways as they were. Maybe they were so driven by their own beliefs choice was impossible.

What he was sure of was how much Tommy had given him. How lucky he was that Tommy once had been so complete in his own gift that he could let Fenton taste of it too.

The music Cody Jo had in her, Fenton reckoned, was different. It had no chance of fading the way Tommy's gift had. It was in her forever, she no more able to leave it than it able to leave her. What the mountains, their glens and forests and streams, once were to Tommy and now were to Special Hands, music would forever be to Cody Jo.

Now, inside this tall, soft-spoken boy from the Bitterroot, the music Cody Jo loved and the country Tommy and Special Hands were part of seemed to join as one. A man less interested in what made people what they were might have resented it all coming so easily to Ty—if such a man could see those gifts at all. But to Fenton, whose life was mostly helping other people see better, it was something to celebrate, a gift Ty could use to show people their own trails, help them touch things they might not even know were there without Ty to help them.

Fenton's one worry was that Ty wouldn't have the balance that Fenton's love for Cody Jo had given him. He had a lot of faith in that balance. He'd had it ever since that night she'd told him everything.

"I doubt he'll ever have a 'you' in his life," Fenton told Cody Jo. He was sitting with a drink watching her get ready to do something inventive with the dough she'd kneaded and rolled and flattened there on the kitchen table.

"Maybe that's a good thing," Cody Jo said, pushing aside some stray hair with a floury hand the better to see what she was about. "There were times I was afraid I might be getting between you and those mountains you fade into when the snows melt."

"With you I never had to wait for the snow to melt," Fenton said. "You made it all right right here, winter or not. You even made the mountains better when I did get into them. You never took anything away. You added things on."

"Then why worry about Ty? He's going to have as much of those mountains in him as you—maybe more." Cody Jo had a crooked kind of smile, one that sometimes said more than her words, wonderful as her words could be. Now with a dusting of white on her forehead, that crooked smile, the hair that had fallen back, Fenton found himself moved so deeply it was hard to talk.

"There's somethin' about him," Fenton said, his voice husky, "that tells me he might not find a 'you' in his life, someone to make his mountains greener." He sipped his whisky and watched her become quiet, accepting absolutely the seriousness of her place in his world.

"But there's your blue heaven," she said in the stillness, watching him closely. "Won't he find it too? You said it was about as good as a man could make it—up in that world."

There was no smile on her face now, just a connection to him so complete Fenton thought time might have stopped.

"I worry," he said, cupping her face and brushing at the splotch of flour on her forehead, saying with his gentleness more than words could, "that he might have too much of the blue. We gotta do all we can to make sure there's some heaven, somehow, for Ty."

22

Ordained

Ty's first two seasons went by so fast there was no way to tally up how much he'd learned. But by the third season he was considered Fenton's best packer. Fenton didn't say it, not that year, but he saw it, just as he'd predicted he would when he first told Cody Jo he'd hired Eban Hardin's grandson. Jasper saw it too, in his far-seeing but blurry way, and he welcomed it. He liked feeding the boy, telling him stories about wide-eyed dudes and rampaging bears and runaway horses, always amused by how soberly Ty considered his stories.

Buck was actually relieved by Ty's ascendancy. He didn't like having too much responsibility anyway, his mind always more on Angie—and sometimes on Jeanie down at The Bar of Justice—than it was on the trails he traveled or the fords he crossed or on what made his horses slip away in the night.

Spec was the most approving of all. He liked it that the boy knew how to avoid all the troubles that seemed to plague Buck. Ty brought his mules into camp ahead of time, hardly ever having to adjust a pack or doctor a sore or tack a shoe back on because he hadn't fit it right in the first place. He was quiet with the animals, able to find them quickly even on the frostiest mornings. And he could push them back into camp without a lot of confusion, catch them up with no fuss. Most of all, Spec liked it that Ty truly valued the special things that Spec knew, realizing that Ty valued them in ways beyond the reach of Jasper and Buck.

Most important to Spec, though, was that Ty's focus on their camps gave Spec the freedom to concentrate on all that went on outside them, all the life moving through the high valleys that tilted down to the South Fork. He could take as much time as he wanted to study the goats playing on the cliffs, to watch an elk bugle as he went in search of his cow, to spy on a black bear tearing open a log before scooting off to avoid a grizzly moving in to claim the spoils.

But even more touched by the boy—by watching him find his way in this world Fenton had opened for him—were Cody Jo and Fenton himself.

"I think he must be our objective correlative," Cody Jo said, taking Fenton's arm as they stood around one of Jasper's campfires. They were standing apart from the others, watching Ty calm Jasper, who had become so wild-eyed by the bear story he was telling he was frightening himself.

Two or three times a season Cody Jo would join them on one of the trips, which pleased them all—and delighted Jasper because Cody Jo had a way of getting everyone involved in the cooking, giving Jasper a chance to socialize and tell stories. It was one of those brisk Montana nights that drew everyone close to the fire and deep into Jasper's tale of a Gros Ventre warrior finally killed at this very spot, who returned each year as a grizzly to tear up the tents and kill the horses of anyone camping nearby. Ty, seeing how anxious the guests were becoming over Jasper's story, had managed to point out that it was an old Blackfoot legend, hardly stealing away Jasper's drama as he did.

"And what *I* believe," Fenton said to Cody Jo, "is that you're gettin' all tangled up in that teacher talk again." He was as pleased as she by Ty's correction, appreciating how gently Ty had done it. "Now just what the hell is 'objective correlative' supposed to mean."

"Oh Fenton." Cody Jo smiled her crooked smile and held his arm. They watched as Ty poked up the fire before stepping back and settling himself almost out of sight behind the ring of faces, all of them transported by the heightened flames and warmed as much by Ty's gentle correction as by the fire.

"What I mean," Cody Jo said, "is that I think we see the world a little better, each of us, because of Ty. He helps us come together—about things we might not even know are in us."

"Could be," Fenton said, taken by how lightly she kept her arm linked through his. Sometimes the lightness of her touch became so intimate, even sensual, that he'd feel his legs going weak.

"He's sure made it better for all of us," he said, holding onto the moment. "For Spec—Jasper too. Watch. Soon as Buck comes in with the resupply it'll be Ty he wants to tell his story to. Ty he seeks out."

"It's more than that, Fenton. We come together through him. He . . . he helps us touch."

And they did come together through Ty, though neither could say exactly how.

Conversations about Ty seemed to lead them into conversations about everything. Cody Jo told Fenton about her mother's sickness bringing her father to her in ways few daughters could know, making her his friend as well as his daughter. "Might have given me too much confidence," she added wryly. "But it's there, it happened. I am what I am because of it."

Fenton told her about the train wreck that sent him west forever, about Bill Cody weeping there by the wreckage, the chaos, the bone protruding from the body of Old Pap. The old buffalo hunter barely sober enough to know what he'd had to do—killing what he might have counted on more than anything else in all his gaudy world. He told Cody Jo more about that night than he'd ever told anyone, told her about the tears he'd shed himself over the horses and the mules and the buffalo he had to shoot, had no choice but to shoot. She lay against him and felt his anguish, felt him search for words to describe the confusion, the blood, the pain.

They even talked about Paint Boy and Hope Woman, what the boy hanging there did to Hope, to Tommy too. What the Cheyenne father's quest for another life had done to all of them.

"Thing is I kind of knew the boy loved that old artist, needed some kind of different father or something," Fenton said. "And I knew that old artist loved the boy. Wouldn't have been any big deal to Paint Boy. No big thing to the Salish either. They always took their berdaches right into their families. It was that old Black Robe who said the boy wasn't worthy. Wasn't worthy of their Black Robe church. That's what killed the boy, if you ask me."

"That old priest probably had his own problems," Cody Jo said, once again going right to the heart of the matter as though everyone else could see into murky water as easily as she. "The artist surely knew he had to hide his love, but the boy couldn't have known," she explained. "Even if he had known he should hide it, how would he know how?"

"What problems could that old Black Robe have had?" Fenton wanted to know. "All he wanted was for everyone to be scared of what scared him. That goddamned church."

"What scared him wasn't so much the church as what the church put inside him to scare away what else was there. What he needed himself and couldn't let out, probably couldn't even see. Just knew he was terrified, had to keep it hidden."

"You're tellin' me that old boy might have been berdache himself?" Fenton seemed incredulous. "Fierce as he looked?"

"I'm just saying he might have been scared, scared of what was in him. They don't have what we have, Fenton, what I feel when you make love to me. They're not allowed."

"I sure like whatever it is we feel," Fenton kissed her hair, loving the way her body cupped into his, loving her voice against his chest. The reality of her body telling him more than her words could.

"I love that too. But I mean something . . . bigger."

"You mean that we have each other—completely," Fenton said. "Isn't that it?"

Cody Jo tilted her head up, kissing Fenton's neck, the hollow above his collarbone. "Yes," she said. "I think having each other so completely *is* what I mean."

And they did have each other, mostly through the boy now and in all sorts of ways the boy's parents couldn't have known. They found a place for Ty in Missoula at Horace and Etta's so he could go to school there. Cody Jo would come into town and talk with him about books. She befriended Alice Wright, Ty's English teacher—talking with her about what they were reading, about things that mattered—before joining Fenton and the others to watch Ty in the football games.

Ty was good at football. Cutting off his horses in the woods proved good training for cutting off runners on the field. He seemed the only one who could do that when John Lamedeer, the gifted Indian runner from Butte, came into town, all the tough miners' kids clearing the way for him.

Bull Trout had become the school's football coach after his own playing days. He'd moved on to become the principal but he remembered Fenton well, white as Fenton's hair had become. Trout was the one who saw to it that Ty showed up on the football field, sure that tossing around Fenton's heavy packs and wrangling Fenton's swift horses would make the boy useful on the field. . . . And he was right.

It amused Fenton to see Trout again, have him steering Ty into the right classes while making sure there was time for football. And it amused Trout to see Fenton's concern for the gangly boy. Sometimes they'd sit together at the games, Trout observing that Ty ran well for someone so seldom afoot, Fenton saying that running on a flat field took little skill compared to cutting off runaway mules on rocky mountain trails.

In their way they even talked about the education Ty was getting, neither of them focusing in on a truth they both knew but had no easy way to talk about: enlightening as Miss Wright's English classes were, demanding as Ty's math problems were, most of his education was coming from a life far from the orderly classrooms Trout oversaw.

Fenton doubted Trout knew how rough that education could be, but he suspected Trout might approve of it even if he did, hard a way as it was to learn. There was a lot of serious truth in high country, and a lot in the rough-and-tumble life Ty encountered when he wasn't in it too. Spec had taken Ty to The Bar of Justice after that first season. He'd paid for everything, celebrating how well Ty had done in the mountains and also thanking him for being such a good student of the things Spec loved. But it wasn't a good night after all. Spec got so drunk Ty had to cart him off to Indian Town himself, but only after Spec had engineered Ty's own fumbling initiation with Jeanie, the goodhearted and hard-working girl Buck favored.

Round Brown had watched as Jeanie approached Ty, flirted with him and danced with him and won him over. He'd even played "Love for Sale," the song banned on the radio. No one was yet sure of the words, but that didn't matter. The way Round played it, it became bittersweet anyway. At least Round thought so. He thought it was about right for Ty and Jeanie.

Fenton heard about Ty's night later, even talked with Cody Jo about it—later. Cody Jo was an unusual schoolteacher in all sorts of ways, the most unusual being that she accepted The Bar of Justice so easily. She even seemed to understand the part it had played in Fenton's life, accepting that too, just as she accepted the civilizing role it might play in the lives of the lonely young cowboys and loggers taking refuge there. A few nights at The Bar of Justice, she thought, might help them with their own women later.

In some ways she thought it probably helped their women too, taking the edgy desperation out of the need young men have for a woman. She shared that idea one night with Rosie and Angie. Rosie thought she had a point, but Angie's head shook in disbelief. Though she usually listened to Cody Jo, she figured Cody Jo was much too modern on this one. Angie had no way to digest such an idea, particularly if Buck might be included.

Philosophical or not, Cody Jo was troubled that Ty had to start out with Jeanie in such a way. A part of her even wished a girl like Wilma Ring could have played the role Jeanie did.

Fenton had to disagree. "Might have mixed them both up," he told her. They were lying in their own bed considering the idea. "Ty not knowin' if he should do what everything in him was burstin' to do. Willie wantin' to help but half scared of tryin'—and confused about how to."

"You may be right," Cody Jo said, thinking about it and drawing herself closer to Fenton's big frame. "I just wish there were an easier way for him to learn."

"He'll learn. Young guys gotta blow their cork a few times before they can slow down and taste what's in the bottle."

Cody Jo lifted her head, smiling at him, kissing him—letting him know it was all right to taste what was in hers.

Ty made visits to The Bar of Justice after that, but usually he stayed downstairs to hear Round Brown play and to dance a little—to watch Jasper play poker. Only now and then did he go upstairs where Buck and Spec had such good times. The first time hadn't been all that pleasant anyway, accommodating as Jeanie had been. And when he did go upstairs it was mostly after he'd had too much to drink, everything concluding so quickly he hardly remembered what had concluded.

Ty figured he just didn't have that hell-for-leather need that made Buck and Spec so different when they were in town. When they were, they seemed to leave the mountains far behind. With Ty it was different. He always carried a little high country in him—something the rest of them appreciated. . . . And learned they could use. When they had a responsibility to fulfill and ran into a rough patch, Ty would be there with the money or the pickup or the good sense to get it done—or to get them out of whatever jam they'd gotten into.

That was something Fenton and Bull Trout *could* talk about: Trout seeing things in the boy that he'd seen in few others over the years. Fenton coming to count on Ty even more than he would have a son. Which is one of the reasons why Trout and Fenton were so amused when Buck got thrown out of his own house when all he'd done was break a quarantine to crawl into bed with Angie, his own wife. And all of it the upshot of Ty being so responsible.

Thomas Haslam, the young doctor who'd fallen in love with Alice Wright, had diagnosed Buck's kids with scarlet fever, a discovery made while Buck was off mule trading with Fenton. When Buck got back with the mules, the quarantine was on and Buck was out—denied his own house for the duration.

"It's a shit deal," he groused to Fenton. "Angie inside so I can't get at her. Me in the woodshed so I can't get at no one else. Angie wants me right there, to make sure, don't you know."

"Be careful, Buck," Fenton said. "That wall's pretty thin. She'll want to hear you say 'night-night' each night."

"She does. Which is why it's a shit deal," Buck said morosely. "A quarantine can be a long-assed thing."

Whether it was because Angie was so close he couldn't sneak off to The Bar of Justice or because she wasn't close enough for him to crawl into bed with her, Fenton wasn't sure. All he knew was that it didn't take Buck long to figure out that Angie was fine as long as she got a knock back when she knocked good night—and that there was no sure way for her to figure out who was knocking back, even who was saying "good night." All of which led Buck to convince Ty to sleep on the cot and do the knocking, freeing Buck to go hear Round Brown play, and play a little himself—with Jeanie.

Ty took it philosophically. Buck was happy when Angie was happy. And Angie was happiest when she knew where Buck was. It was a system that worked to no one's harm, at least until the Butte football game when Buck won all the bets he'd made and found himself with unexpected money.

The quarantine wasn't quite over, but Buck didn't care. He was so pleased with his winnings and so excited by how Ty had contained John Lamedeer he convinced Ty to stand in for him anyway. And Ty was too tired to protest. He just hoped he'd wake up when Angie knocked.

As it turned out, though, it was Buck's interest in Angie, not Ty's lack of attention, that caused all the trouble.

Buck was headed for The Bar of Justice, a sack of beer over his shoulder, when an image of Angie came over him so powerfully he turned right around and went back to knock on her window and tell her how he felt—all of which he told an astonished Doctor Haslam after he'd broken the quarantine.

"It was standin' outside that window in my good shirt that made me nervous, Doc," he explained. "With the beer. Angie has a way of askin' the damndest questions. So I just threw that beer in and went right on in after it. We was together so quick it cut off her questions, don't you see."

"But why knock on the wall once you were inside?" Thomas Haslam was often startled by the reasoning of Fenton's packers, practical as they could be in the woods. "There was no need to say goodnight anymore."

"Hell, I figured she couldn't worry about me sneakin' off if I was right there in her arms. And I was pretty pleased with the setup I had." Buck thought about that for a minute. "She has a way of doubtin' me about that."

"About what?"

"Thinkin' ahead, don't you know. I never been as good at it as Fenton. Or even Ty."

Thomas Haslam saw the point Buck was trying to make, crazy as it was. "Well," he said to Buck, "at least you don't seem to have contracted scarlet fever.

Fenton even endorsed Buck's position when Haslam told him about it, strange as it seemed to the doctor. "You gotta look at it from Buck's point of view, Doc," Fenton said. "She was mad as hell when she learned it had been Ty knockin' and sayin' 'night night,' but she wasn't mad at Ty. After a week she wasn't even mad at Buck."

"She was mad enough to hit him with that sack of bottles," Doc Haslam pointed out, realizing there was some of Buck's logic in Fenton as well. "Broke some too."

"But Buck got to prove he could outsmart her—and have some fun doin' it. That impressed her. Buck'll go a long mile to impress Angie," Fenton concluded, pleased with the story himself. "That's the main thing."

Most of the men in the Swan got some fun out of the story too, and most of the time Buck didn't mind laughing along with them. Fenton and Bull Trout talked about that at the gathering Horace and Etta Adams gave after Ty's graduation, Trout sad that Ty wouldn't be playing football for them anymore.

Everyone who was important to Ty was there–except Will. Ty wasn't even sure his father knew he'd graduated, which hardly bothered him. Cody Jo was there, talking with Alice Wright, Thomas Haslam close by and as attentive to Alice as a man could be. Angie was there too, pleased with how nice Buck looked as he talked with Jasper and Spec, who were concentrating on spicing up the punch bowl. There were others there too—many gathered around Tommy Yellowtail, who'd gotten so heavy he had to sit and let people come to him.

"Do you think Ty's gotten over being the reason Angie and Buck had that fight?" Trout asked Fenton. "It made him pretty low. Being as responsible as Ty is can play hell with a boy's moral sensibility."

"He's been ragged so much about it I think he's immune now. And it gave him a good chance to chew things over with the doc when the doc checked on the damage. . . . Sure was an exciting way to terminate a quarantine."

"Didn't terminate how our doc feels about Alice," Trout said. They looked across the room, both of them amused by the attention the doctor was giving Ty's English teacher.

"He'll be crawlin' under her blanket before long," Fenton said. "Don't believe he could stand a long engagement."

"They'll be good for us, Fenton. Literate. Fair-minded. He's even been down to check over some of Messler's girls."

It was the first time Bull Trout had spoken openly about The Bar of Justice. Fenton warmed to him even more.

"He has," Fenton agreed. "And he's done them good. But there's not much he can do for our boys if we get into this war. . . . And Cody Jo says we'll be in it soon, says we'll have to stop them before they cross the channel and kill all the Brits."

"We will," Trout said. "She's right. And what they'll want is boys like Ty. They'll make him into a fine young officer so he can get himself killed doing what's right."

"I'd rather we kept him right here," Fenton said. "He'd be better off knockin' on Angie's wall to do what's right. Can't we get him one of those deferments?"

"We could." Trout seemed resigned. "With the Forest Service. But you know Ty. He wouldn't take it."

"I do. And he won't. . . . Which really is a shit deal."

They were right on all counts, a truth that didn't materialize for six months, though the two of them talked about it a second time at the event that happened first: the marriage of Alice Wright and Thomas Haslam.

The marriage hardly surprised them. What did surprise them was where Alice Wright wanted to take her doctor on their honeymoon.

"Will you trust me?" she'd asked Thomas Haslam a few nights before the wedding. "We've got to do it. It's . . . almost as important as . . . this." She kissed his neck, her breath warm, her lips wet. "We can tell them at the wedding. It'll be . . . our surprise."

The doctor—dizzy with his need for Alice Wright and wanting her beyond his understanding—had no way to say no.

"Wherever you want," he promised, "we'll go. All I want is time with you." He held her to him, her body seeming to burn him everywhere. "Europe might be going up in smoke. But we'll go there if you want. I just wish we could start practicing up tonight."

"Not yet," she said, with an understanding that tore at his heart even as it drove him half-crazy. "But just wait. I'll give you everything you want. I'll give you more." She kissed him still again. "You'll see."

What the groan lifting from him signified, she couldn't tell. All she knew was that she had to say it, had to explain.

"I want Ty to take us," she said, wide-eyed at the drama of it, "into Fenton's mountains."

23

Apostle

"That's the craziest idea I ever heard of. Your school may be for everyone, but that high country's different."

It was Fenton speaking as he and Bull Trout sipped punch once again, this time celebrating the marriage of Alice Wright to Thomas Haslam—and marveling at the couple's honeymoon plans. And this time both were actually hoping Buck, or someone, had fired up the punch the way Buck had at Ty's graduation. Trout had opened the school gym for the event, which needed the space. Even Fenton was surprised by the number of people, and by their variety too: earnest colleagues of Alice's, bandaged patients of Thomas's, crew-cut coaches and shaggy-haired packers, and all sorts of friends from the offices and stores and watering holes of Missoula. There were even some loggers and cowboys in from the Swan, and a smattering of Spec's cousins down from Ronan.

Different as they were, all were taken by the news of where the Haslams would spend their honeymoon. Some laughed, some shook their heads, a few were so astonished they became convinced the straight-talking doctor and his bookish schoolteacher must have some kind of mountain research in mind. By their reckoning, that was the only thing that could keep the doctor from retreating to a big bed and getting acquainted with Miss Wright the way everyone knew he'd wanted to from the first.

Bull Trout was the only one who seemed more philosophical than surprised. "Well, it figures," he told Fenton. "She's not like my other teachers, you know—good as she is at pretending. Whatever gave her this idea is bound to be part of something bigger."

"Could be," Fenton said. He was relieved someone had seasoned the punch a little, making him more philosophical himself. "Cody Jo says she gets pretty wrapped up in those books of hers."

"You should see her talking away at your boy about those novels she loves. It is the damnedest thing." Trout touched his glass to Fenton's. "Here's to my Alice and her doc up there with Ty—in your mountains."

"Hope she pays attention to the doc," Fenton said. "Sure don't want the doc gettin' lonely while she tells Ty why somethin' happened to one guy because of some other—and in which one of her books."

Ty Hardin and Alice Wright did have an odd relationship, even by Bull Trout's standards, and Trout had seen all kinds of friendships between faculty members and students. At first he'd been surprised to see the intense young teacher spending so much time with the gangly boy from the Swan. There was a quietness about Ty that Trout thought would discourage most teachers. But none of it seemed to discourage Alice Wright. Ty might talk little, but he listened with a focus that seemed to encourage her, leading her to a complex weaving together of the themes of the books he read, especially those of the new writers Cody Jo had suggested: Dreiser and Dos Passos, Hemingway and Fitzgerald, the Steinbeck novel that stirred everyone up so.

Ty took it all in, not so interested in the intentions of the authors as he was in the people in their stories: why one might get blue when another didn't, what one couldn't see that drove another crazy. Alice Wright even got him reading short stories in the *Saturday Evening Post* and *Colliers*. He liked them with increased interest after she had him read Hemingway's stories. He liked how short they were, the shock of them, liked learning as much from what wasn't said as from what was. He was surprised that Alice Wright liked them for the same reasons, his surprise deepening her interest in what went on in his mind, what must go on up in the mountains. What happened to Ty and Fenton and the others when they disappeared behind the high ranges.

As it turned out, the one least surprised by the honeymoon plan was Cody Jo. She seemed to know immediately why Ty would want to take his teacher to the White River benches, the meadows tilting down toward the Southfork, show her the special places Fenton knew—vistas where you were simply stopped by nature's gifts: the cirque off the north pass, its cliffs spilling huge slabs to shatter above emerald lakes scooped by glaciers; the bluff high above the South Fork, the meadows and timbered flats left in the river's wake as it curled and looped its way along the valley floor; the high benches that stepped their way up toward the China Wall; the Wall itself, where riders could ease up to its broad crest and look down dizzying

cliffs into a different country, this one tilting toward the Missouri—
and beyond that to the Mississippi, the wide gut of the country draining
its way east and south into the sea. And on the way to that high wall—
where you could see back across all the country behind—a place where
water actually bursts from the face of a cliff to start its run west, its force
so pent up by nature's secret ways that it explodes out across the canyon
below, its mist giving life to the willows and the ferns and the timber below.

"Call it Needle Falls," Fenton told Cody Jo one night as they sat before
his fire in the big guest lodge recalling the power of that water. "Water
focused there makes a new world down below, a green world."

"Maybe," Cody Jo said, caught up by something in Fenton's face, "if
you gather a force like that, it can't help but make a new world." She was
taken by how moved Fenton was remembering that explosion of water.

"Like the train wreck, it was. To me. All that life penned up in those
cattle cars—then the crash. Horses so broke up we had to kill them.
Buffalo too. Sure burst open a new world. For me at least. Still makes
me sick—thinkin' about it. The hell we'd made."

And then he told her, as he'd never told anyone, of his breaking away
from the Michigan farm his Bible-driven parents barely kept alive, his
parents counting always on some divine providence to save them, praying
for some divine providence to save them. How he got the attention of the
roustabouts in Bill Cody's show, his size and ease with animals giving
them reason to take him on, teach him to pack and balance and run their
packhorses without everything flying off; how to dress the animals' sores
and wounds too, oil the tack and school the animals to do their work. He
learned everything, he told her, from the rough hands Bill Cody brought
out of the West with the rough animals they hauled around the country,
all of them rubbing shoulders and sharing drinks with the morose Indians
Cody hired to whoop and holler and play dead for his show. Even the quiet
Cheyenne did it, the man who'd taught him most about packing, the
man who'd wanted to learn the most from Cody.

"I always doubted Bill Cody liked doing all that stuff," he told her.
"His men sure had doubts." Fenton explained it all to her there in front of
his big fire. "He was glad to take in the money. And he was tickled by the
big tales that Buntline man made up. But he stayed mostly drunk to keep
up with it, to do the phony stuff. He never took a liking to the phony stuff."

"Surely he liked all that fame and money," Cody Jo protested.

"Made him important—made them others kowtow to him. But he got
no comfort from it. I doubt he ever found peace, makin' up the West and
sellin' it all over the world like storybooks. It was a damn far cry from what

the West is. And he knew it. I don't think he was really happy until he was back here and up in the mountains. Up where a guy doesn't have to canter around wavin' his hat for a tent full of greenhorns."

"Don't men like that? Strutting and waving their hats? Galloping around must be even better. And wasn't he good at it? People spent lots of money to watch him."

"I think somethin' about it made him blue. Maybe blue because he *was* so damn good at it. I believe what he really liked was to be in his camp up on the Shoshone—above Pahaska. I packed him in there some. Him and the big shots he took hunting. By then he had to stay mostly drunk for those guys too. They didn't want him so much warmin' around his own fire as they wanted him wavin' his damn hat around theirs."

"But something was good up there too. Isn't up there where you learned about these fires you like? Realized how much magic can be in them?"

"Maybe. I think I saw what people really wanted by watching them settle down around Cody's fires. There was plenty of drinking of course, but things would get quiet. Guys could tell a story and make you think. A tall one or a true one. Looking into those flames makes you think. A lot. About every damn thing."

Cody Jo pulled her knees up to her chest, watching the fire herself. "There's something primeval in it, isn't there? Looking into flames."

"Sure. We probably always took comfort in a fire, after we got a grip on fire in the first place. The warmth, the way it fights off the dark. The spooky things we don't understand. Maybe that's what Cody went back to that mountain camp for. Some escape from all the horseshit that kept him gallopin' around and wavin' his hat. Not much comfort in wavin' a big hat in a big tent."

"Goodness. Packer philosophy in full bloom." Cody Jo pulled her knees still closer, looking away from the fire to watch Fenton, amused and interested all at once. "All of the sudden your underground pressure seems to be focusing on high country fires." She made herself snug under his arm as they looked back into the fire. .

"It is a comfort," Fenton said, after a while—pulling her still closer to watch the flames. "Brings us together. And with all that's goin' on in Europe, we're gonna need some comfort."

"Ty will. Spec will too, though they won't let you know it," Cody Jo said. "We'll just have to keep our fires going until they get back."

Cody Jo was sure of what she was talking about, much as Fenton wished she weren't. The bombs were already dropping in London. She had accepted it—the war was coming. Everything in Fenton wanted to deny it.

Cody Jo knew Fenton's best packer would be in it—because he'd be sure it was the right thing to do. She knew Fenton's best hunter would be in as well—because there was no way he could ignore a chance to do what he did better than anyone: track and find and kill.

Cody Jo and Fenton both might be a little blue as they watched the flames and considered what was ahead, but they were blue for different reasons: Fenton because he didn't want to face the inevitable; Cody Jo because she so clearly saw what was inevitable—that Spec and Ty would find themselves somehow the losers, not the victors, by going away to fight this war everyone knew must be won.

"What I want to say," Fenton sounded tired, as though it were almost too hard for him to say what he had to say, "is that what happens when that train came from the other direction isn't so different from what happens when all that water is forced to shoot out up there at Needle Falls. It just happens. I had to kill the animals I had to kill, but I was too numb to make sense of it. I just did it. Only later did it come to me that we'd been on the wrong track. That tryin' to take the West east was to kill it. Hell, I had to find a way to live in this country before it came to me how I'd been killin' off the truth of it right along."

"But Spec and Ty won't lose the truth of it." Cody Jo knew what Fenton was thinking. "They've grown up in it. They have it already."

"That's the thing." Fenton was the one who sounded resigned now. "They might not know what they have. Might not know what to hold on to."

"But they'll know. People talk about the West. Love the idea of the West. Books about it. Paintings of it. It does something to them. Does something for them."

"They like make-up. And all Bill Cody was doin' was helping them make up more by advertising what wasn't true in the first place. I believe that's why he was so blue. Why he stayed so drunk."

"Oh Fenton. You're blue too. You may have been numb, but surely it tore you apart, shooting those animals." "

"At least it drove me out of there—like the water bustin' out of a cliff. It got me to these mountains. And got me you, too." Fenton watched the fire, quiet now, just watched, as though there were some answer deep in the flames.

"I doubt I could make it without you now," he said at last. "I think I see my mountains better—because of you."

~

Spec had gotten into trouble at The Bar of Justice. A big-faced government man had called him a reservation breed and tried to muscle away Loretta, the new girl Spec favored. Spec opened the man's scalp with a bottle. He would have cut him up with it too, if the big bouncer hadn't convinced two others to help him throw Spec out. It had taken three of them to do it, but Spec knew who he wanted. He waited outside until morning when the bouncer was leaving, then almost killed him with a two-by-four.

"Would have done it too," the judge told Fenton and Bull Trout, "if that Round Brown hadn't come outside to pull him away."

"Lucky thing Brown's so strong," Fenton said. "Not easy to calm Spec when he's roused."

Special Hands had done such damage the judge saw no choice but to send him to Deerlodge. That same judge made sure that after Spec's release, The Bar of Justice would no longer be in his day's circle, though of course The Bar of Justice couldn't be mentioned, not in the court records. He got around that by designating Fenton as parole officer—knowing Tommy Yellowtail would make it stick.

"And there's the military to think about," the judge told Fenton as they poured a drink in Trout's office. The judge wasn't sure he should be as direct with this big packer as Bull Trout told him to be, but he went as far as he could. "Whether we wind up in that mess over there or not, it wouldn't be a bad place for your Indian. Make his anger useful. Help him understand consequences. He might make a damn good soldier."

"He will be a damn good soldier," Fenton said. "But only at the worst of it. I've been practicin' him up for better things."

"He might know better what's better after he's seen what's worst." The judge replied, appreciating the seriousness of this big packer.

"There's his record," Fenton said. "They might not even take him."

"I'll see they do. That much I can do—for the two of you."

It all made Fenton even more depressed. Mostly because he knew the judge had a point. The war might bother him, but it seemed to do just the opposite for Spec. It seemed to Fenton that Spec and Ty were at a place in their lives where being part of the land they knew was more important, for everyone, than protecting land they didn't from being overrun by someone still farther away just because that someone had the tanks and guns to take it.

What he couldn't get out of his mind was what he'd found, not what someone else was losing. Deep down he had to admit that such bad things were happening in Europe somebody had to do something. It was impossible to live with Cody Jo and ignore that. He just wished it weren't Spec and Ty who had to do the doing.

It wasn't even the draft that was the worry: Bob Ring had offered them Forest Service deferments. The worry was what Cody Jo put her finger on in the first place: Spec would sign up because something in him needed a fight; Ty because something in him said he must. It didn't trouble Fenton that both of them would be disappointed by how little difference they would make. What troubled him was what they could lose—what they might never find again.

He'd had a hard enough time finding it himself, though he would have been hard-pressed to describe what he'd found. He guessed it was the clarity of the mountains, their quiet power, that moved him, a quality many men could recognize but only a few could live with. He was afraid Ty and Spec didn't know that they had in them naturally what had taken him half his life to find. Not understanding what they'd lost could make recovering it almost as difficult as it had been for him to find it.

It was a worry he couldn't shake.

It turned out Fenton was right in more ways than he wanted to be. Spec joined the Marines in November, going off without fanfare, telling Ty he'd chosen the Marines because "they go at things more direct," before swinging by to tell Tommy the same thing. Ty told him to be careful, but Tommy said nothing, just looked at him as if he might be deranged. Fenton heard about Tommy's reaction and thought maybe, just for a moment, the old Tommy had returned, was seeing as clearly as he what Special Hands was leaving. But there was no way to know what went on in Tommy's head now. He hardly talked anymore, not even with Fenton. Fenton thought maybe Ty knew what Tommy thought, but if Ty did, Fenton suspected he wouldn't say; he would be too preoccupied with what he had to do himself.

Two weeks later he did it: went in to Missoula to see the Army recruiters. They signed him up, giving him orders to ship out the next Monday.

Fenton, still smarting from how suddenly Special Hands had slipped away, decided on a going-away dinner at the Elkhorn. There was a good band playing and he reserved a big table. They could all stay in town and on Sunday he'd have a chance to talk with Ty—as he should have with Spec. He didn't know if he could explain to Ty why he worried so about them, but he wanted to try. Explaining things sometimes helped him understand them better himself.

Everyone knew about the dinner. Cody Jo got Etta and Horace, and Angie and Buck too, to come. Jasper showed up for a drink, getting so rattled by the surroundings he went off to one of the quiet bars he liked. Bob Ring was at another table with Wilma and Bernard Straight. Bernard was always after Ring to help him climb the Forest Service promotion ladder, but on this night Bernard seemed to have eyes only for Wilma.

"I can see why he's so focused," Fenton said, watching them. "Willie's about the best lookin' thing in town, next to Cody Jo."

"She does look pretty," Ty said, sipping another beer. "And we got all this beer. We should ask them over to help drink it."

A waitress put still more bottles on the table. "That man talkin' to the bandleader sent more over," she said. "Guess you're joinin' up."

"Doc and Alice are buyin' you some too," Fenton said. "They'd be here but they're at the San Francisco conference. Get back tomorrow."

Ty passed some bottles along to Buck and Angie. "I believe they had a nice honeymoon," he said to Fenton, thinking about their trip. "Though the doc seemed less interested in the country than he was in Miss Wright."

"It might be that he was more interested in Alice's valleys and peaks than the country's," Fenton said, tickled that Ty couldn't think about Alice Wright as anything but his English teacher. "The same way Mr. Sobersides over there is interested in our Willie."

Bernard led Willie out onto the dance floor, Wilma looking over at Ty as they began dancing. She waved at him over Bernard's shoulder.

"When they pick up that beat, Ty, we'll dance too." Cody Jo smiled, as she watched Wilma begin moving to the music. "Won't be much dancing for you in the Army."

"Won't be a lot of things in that damn Army," Fenton said, not much amused now. He caught the eye of a woman in a shiny dress circulating around and taking pictures. As Fenton left to talk with her, Round Brown appeared.

"Heard Spec up and joined," Brown said to Ty. "Now you gonna do that too."

"Round!" Ty was happy to see him. "Highway Round Brown. Have you met Cody Jo?"

"A few times, with Mr. Pardee—and at her schoolhouse dances. It's good to see you." He nodded to Cody Jo politely. When Round Brown was playing the piano, he seemed transported, lifted on the wings of his music. But in conversation he was grave and measured—respectful and imposing at once.

"Of course we've met," Cody Jo said. "And I love to hear you play. Will you play tonight?"

"They asked me to sit in," Brown said. "Some of them know Chicago music."

"Did you send over this beer?" Ty was still surprised by all the attention he was getting.

"Might have," Brown smiled.

"Good," Cody Jo said. "We'll drink your beer and dance to your music."

"This boy can dance," Brown said, smiling a little. "I've watched him. Shame to waste that rhythm in the Army."

"Or to waste it here." Angie, who seemed to jump around to good music even when she was sitting in a chair, could sit no longer. She took Ty's hand and led him onto the dance floor. They were playing "Sing Sing Sing."

"Does that man know as much about Buck's dancing as he does about yours?" Angie asked as Ty picked up the rhythm and swung her out and away.

Ty didn't bother to answer. The music was too good.

At the table he'd felt a little light-headed from all the beer, but that all went away the minute he started dancing. Round Brown had taken over the piano and was playing "Blueberry Hill," his eyes closed as he sang the lyrics, the beat of his piano steady and sure.

"This one is for you and Cody Jo," Angie said, slipping away to get Buck as Cody Jo came out onto the dance floor.

"Your friend Brown is wonderful to hear," Cody Jo said to Ty, moving into Ty's arms and moving to the music. And then it seemed to Ty there was nothing but air in his arms—real as Cody Jo was. She seemed to know every move he was going to make even before he thought to make it. It was as though they were one. And at one with Brown's music too.

"I wish it could be this good for us when you're in the service, Ty," she said. "But it won't be. For any of us. I hope you're strong enough. I hope we're strong enough."

Bob Ring brought Wilma and Bernard over to their table and Fenton offered them some beer, insisting that Wilma have a last dance with Ty.

"He'll be defending our country, Willie," he said. "Better take advantage before they march him off."

"Have you had too much to drink?" Wilma asked Ty, her eyes startlingly blue as they walked out onto the floor. Then she was in Ty's arms and she knew he hadn't—or maybe only enough to make the moment sweeter. Brown was playing "Indian Summer," playing it with such tenderness, and Wilma dancing so wonderfully, that Ty thought he could tell her anything.

"You don't look like you did when we were pulling your father out across that snow," Ty said as they waited for the next song.

"I guess I don't," Wilma said. "Though I'm just as scared. That war over there. You joining up here. It scares me as much."

Then Brown was bringing the band back to them, playing with one finger the first notes of "Stars Fell on Alabama." Ty knew the words, breathed them into Willie's ear as they began moving to the music.

When the band took a break, they went back to the table. Fenton was talking to the woman wearing the shiny dress and carrying the big camera. Soon she was lining everyone up for a picture. Fenton even called out for Round Brown to join them, but Brown would have none of it. "Don't want any pictures of me floatin' 'round," he said.

But he watched as they gathered for the picture. Buck mugging for the camera, Cody Jo serious and looking directly at it, Bernard looking at Wilma, Ty looking bemused and a little confused by the whole thing.

Brown, who was watching it all, looked at Fenton. Fenton seemed weary and resigned. . . . He was looking at Ty.

24

On This Rock

Cody Jo waited until Etta and Horace got back from church. As soon as they got home, she cranked the phonograph and played the song. She'd been thinking about it all morning as Fenton fretted, scribbling notes about next year's pack trips. He wouldn't have Spec or Ty to help him, which meant he'd be back in the saddle most of the time. But what he had to do didn't bother him nearly as much as what they would no longer be able to do. That gnawed at him.

"'My Blue Heaven,'" Cody Jo said to Etta, putting the needle on the track. "Gene Austin. Entirely different from the way Brown played it."

The night before, Etta had watched Cody Jo dance with both Fenton and Ty to Round Brown's deep rhythms. Etta thought Cody Jo became even more a part of the music as soon as Brown began to play. Etta was always taken by how naturally Cody Jo moved to music. How she became ever more a part of it when Brown played was a mystery to Etta. . . . Cody Jo was always a mystery to Etta—as fascinating as she was unpredictable.

"It seemed to me," Etta said tentatively, "that everything became different from the moment Mr. Brown sat down to play." She was bold enough to say that only because it had been so clearly true, at least to Etta. And she knew Cody Jo would pay attention. As unexpected as the things Cody Jo said were, as surprising as the connections she made, she was never dismissive or mean. She didn't rule out the ideas of others, she simply swept them in with her own—which is just what she did now.

"It *was* different. Different right away. I think those musicians knew him from somewhere. Bet he played down on the South Side."

"The South Side?" Etta asked, not quite sure of what "the South Side" meant.

"Chicago. That's where the black bands play. Where the white players learn. It's a big thing when one gets to sit in."

"A white player?"

"Yes. And last night it was a big thing to have Brown sit in with them."

"It wasn't the South Side where they knew him," Fenton said, putting away the notebook he'd been scribbling in and in his Fenton-like way injecting something entirely unexpected into the conversation. "It was Cleveland. He played for a band in Cleveland. Jimmie Lunceford's band."

Fenton and Cody Jo were walking now. The Clark Fork's twists and turns had leveled the ground there in Missoula, and with the late fall air crisp and cool it was good walking. They were talking about the life Round Brown brought to his music, the power Brown had not only in height and size but in some natural beat, some sureness in rhythm and pace—even in mood.

"How did you know that?" Cody Jo asked. "About Jimmie Lunceford's band?" She'd long ago ceased being surprised by the things Fenton knew— but was always interested in how he came to know them. "I think those white bands learned all kinds of things from Jimmie Lunceford."

"Guess Round Brown did too," Fenton said. "Brown was their piano man."

"How did you learn that?"

"I learned it when Round was drinking one night. It's good to pay attention when a man gets some drink in him. You learn things. He was foolin' around with that bluesy music. Slow. Sad. . . . I asked him about it."

"And he talked? That's a surprise. No one's more reserved."

"That night he wasn't. He was sad. He was kind of weary too. 'These blues,' he said to me, 'mostly they come from liquor . . . and women.' Then he told me about his. A fight he had with a man over a woman. Lunceford tellin' him to get out of town. "Head west,' Lunceford told him. 'West.'"

"Then I'm right. Chicago. He played there, not New York. Chicago's West."

"Not far enough for Brown," Fenton said. "He told me he needed to disappear into the West."

"But why? He has so much to offer. He has this gift. Think what his music meant to all of us last night."

"He killed that man," Fenton said quietly, looking away from Cody Jo, looking out across the Clark Fork as though seeking some answers. "Seems like his gift had to disappear with him."

"Oh my God," Cody Jo said. "What a thing to live with."

They walked for a while, Cody Jo digesting it, Fenton watching her and the river and the hills lifting above them.

Finally, he said, "Maybe the West is full of people like that. Some hunting for something; some hiding from something. Be thankful it's big enough to take care of us."

When they got back it was almost noon. People had called. Horace had turned on the radio.

"Pacific Fleet destroyed," an announcer was saying. He seemed nervous and out of breath as he tried to make sense of the dispatches coming in. "Bombed in Pearl Harbor. In Hawaii."

Ty was already there. Angie and Buck showed up too, all of them stopped by the news as they huddled around the radio. They were glued there all afternoon, hardly talking. The reports grew bleaker as evening fell and the news of the destruction became more precise, the announcers more sure of themselves as the shock subsided and outrage took over.

Despite the devastation at Pearl Harbor, all Cody Jo could think of in the big guest bed at the Adamses' house was the blue heaven Fenton had tried to tell her about high in the Swan.

"Yours," she said, "isn't anything like the Blue Heaven in Austin's song, is it?"

"I don't know." Fenton thought about it. "That song aims at comfort too. Peace. It just aims lower. More local."

"There's nothing peaceful about it when Brown plays it."

"But he comes closer to the way I see it, Brown does."

"How?" Cody Jo sat up and looked at him. "How does Brown come closer? Isn't it just that he's more like you?"

"He's not like me. He has his music he can play." The way Fenton said it was full of admiration. "But that doesn't mean he tries to sugarcoat anything. He sure sees the dark side. Brown does. Accepts it. . . . Maybe that's like me."

"You take some kind of comfort in that, don't you? In your loneliness. You kind of like it. Isn't that like Brown's music?"

"Maybe. He surely takes comfort in the blues. Makes them pretty so they'll go down easier. And I take comfort in high country. The peace of it."

"If it gives you peace, why are you so sad?" Cody Jo pulled herself closer, wanting to reach out to him in all those ways his high country did.

"Because I'm afraid Ty's gonna lose track of it." Fenton turned out the light and held her. "Spec too. They have it in their bones now." He pulled her still closer in the darkness. "Being dragged out of it this way might just drive it outta them forever."

~

Ty seemed distracted at the train station, the recruiting officer calling out the names, a sergeant checking them off. He hadn't slept a wink during the night. Everything he thought he knew about the world had suddenly changed—the war coming across the wrong ocean, from a place he'd hardly heard of.

Once again he was carrying old Eban Hardin's kit bag. Once again he had in it the few things he might need—socks and underwear, sandwiches Etta had made for him that morning. He guessed he was as prepared as he could be, though he was still unnerved by Etta's tears when he left the house, by Horace's inability to say anything during their somber handshake—Horace serious and awkward, unwilling to let go of his hand.

Cody Jo and Fenton had brought Ty to the station, Cody Jo looking less sure of herself than he'd ever seen her look, Fenton looking up the tracks and down the tracks, doing everything he could to keep from looking at Ty at all.

"It's hard to know where they'll send us, after the training," Ty said to Cody Jo. "But I'll write." He was made uneasy by all the things he saw in her face. "You write too. Tell me how Fenton's doing without Spec and me. He might miss us hanging around and causing him trouble."

Alice Wright showed up with a small package, precisely gift-wrapped. "I got it for you on our trip," she told Ty. "A music box. When you open the drawer you'll hear 'Red River Valley.' It's to make you remember."

Ty put it in his kit bag and heard the sergeant calling for them to board.

Cody Jo was crying as she hugged him. He was surprised to see Alice Wright was crying too.

Ignoring his long-standing distaste for trains, Fenton climbed on with Ty. He looked around the car, saying nothing. Not until the train began to move did he give Ty the slightest hug. It was awkward—both for its brevity and its seriousness.

"Don't let 'em make you do somethin' crazy," Fenton said, his voice suddenly husky. "Don't go gettin' yourself killed."

He swung himself off, jogging along with the train for a few steps before slowing, offering Ty a last wave before turning back toward Cody Jo.

He knew he mustn't show it, but a sadness in him was running deep. It seemed bottomless as he moved toward her and realized what it was: Ty was going to die. Or Spec. Some faith he'd earned for himself in this world was leaving him forever. It was a hard reality deep inside him. He was sure his world would never be the same.

It hurt him in ways beyond his understanding.

Acknowledgments

Once again deep thanks to the many rangers, packers, and trail-crew members who have shared my fires over the years. They bring crucial life to the stories I tell. Without their knowledge and humor—and resilience too—I would have little to say.

For helping get *Blue Heaven* onto the page, I owe much to the talented people of the University of Oklahoma Press, particularly the keen eye of Jay Fultz, the generous organization of Alice Stanton, and the steady encouragement of Chuck Rankin.

Many thanks also go to those who kept my writing going throughout this undertaking: Danny Torjusen on one coast; Ann Roach (and Joe and Todd too) on the other. I thank Steve Pyne and Karen Wieder for their literary wisdom, Darcy Maiers for his tales of reservation life, and John Hessler for too many things to list here. His judgment, fairness, and generosity were key to the completion of the novel.

And finally there is Barbara Saxon to honor. Her patience; her occasional outrage; her humor and understanding brought light to my days from the fumbling beginning of this project to its completion—*Blue Heaven* becoming a concept she understands as no one else can.